# JULIA'S WAY

*Richly detailed historical fiction
set in 1920s London.*

Middle-class Julia Longfield looks forward to marrying Chester Morrison whom, her father assures her, is an excellent match. But when Mr Longfield dies suddenly, leaving them in poverty, Julia is jilted by her fiancé and it falls to her to look after her family. Then she meets Simon Layzell, owner of a fabric shop, and they decide to go into business. Determined to fight for her family, Julia seizes this opportunity for a new future.

# JULIA'S WAY

## Elizabeth Lord

**Severn House Large Print**
London & New York

This first large print edition published 2011
in Great Britain and the USA by
SEVERN HOUSE PUBLISHERS LTD of
9-15 High Street, Sutton, Surrey, SM1 1DF.
First world regular print edition published 2009 by
Severn House Publishers Ltd., London and New York.

British Library Cataloguing in Publication Data

Lord, Elizabeth, 1928-
  Julia's way.
  1. Businessmen--Fiction. 2. East End (London, England)--
  Social life and customs--20th century--Fiction. 3. Large
  type books.
  I. Title
  823.9'14-dc22

ISBN-13: 978-0-7278-7924-0

Severn House Publishers support The Forest Stewardship Council
[FSC], the leading international forest certification organisation. All
our titles that are printed on Greenpeace-approved FSC-certified paper
carry the FSC logo.

MIX
Paper from
responsible sources
FSC
www.fsc.org    FSC® C018575

Printed and bound in Great Britain by the
MPG Books Group, Bodmin, Cornwall.

# One

Mrs Granby looked up from making fairy cakes for afternoon tea for the wife of her employer to regard their pretty twenty-one-year-old daughter.

'Is there something wrong, Miss Julia? You don't seem your usual happy self, not since you've been in my kitchen.'

Julia Longfield's sweet features gave a half smile as she toyed with two small jelly moulds in front of her where she sat at the food preparation table. 'Of course I'm happy, Cook,' she murmured.

'So you ought to be with your fiancé and his family coming to dinner and you two about to announce your engagement an' all,' Martha Granby went on. 'I say that's wonderful, yet you don't look all that excited.'

'I am excited,' Julia said, but to Martha it didn't sound convincing.

She gave a humph and resumed beating together the eggs, butter and sugar for the light little cakes Mrs Longfield so enjoyed with her four o'clock tea, now almost a ritual in the twelve years Martha had worked here.

Her brows knitted beneath the line of her kitchen cap. 'You do realize how lucky you are,

Miss Julia, a young man like Chester Morrison to love you? With this country still in such a mess since the war finished, you don't have any idea how fortunate the two of you are with both yer dads well off.'

Three and a half years since the end of the war, and things were still bad; a million out of work, maimed ex-servicemen begging on the streets. Pitiful it was to see some of them trudging along in the gutter playing an instrument for a few coins to feed a hungry family; pitiful and outrageous considering their sacrifice.

'Marrying into money too, his father with that printing works, yet to me you don't look like what a young girl in love should look like, my dear.'

After so many years of listening to Julia's childish troubles and, as she grew older, her more adult problems, and giving advice, Martha Granby considered herself on sufficiently familiar terms with her employers' daughter to address her as 'my dear'.

'I mean it,' she went on, 'a fine handsome young man like that with a good family background. Anyone with half an eye can see how much he loves you. The question is, do *you* love *him*?'

'Of course I do,' came the reply but to Martha it still didn't seem to carry the special ecstatic sound of a girl in love.

She put aside the mixing bowl. As cook/housekeeper to the comfortably off Longfield family in their fine house in Sewardstone Road, overlooking Victoria Park, she'd known Julia

6

since she was a little girl of nine who would creep downstairs to confide in her. The child's parents had seemed too occupied with their own lives to listen to their daughter's childish upsets.

Later, at private school, Julia had come home during term breaks to tell Martha all her news, little things about her friends at school, her worries and her joys. Martha felt she knew more about the girl than her own parents did.

Nothing of what she was told went any further, not to their housemaid Mary, certainly not to Annie the present scullery hand and especially not to Fred, Mr Charles Longfield's gardener-cum-handyman and lately chauffeur, who drove him daily to and from his import/export business near London Docks. Fred would have ample opportunity to pass on words overheard about his employer's eldest daughter.

Julia was the only one who ever came down here to the kitchen. Her two younger sisters and one younger brother never did. As a child it had been the little things; the slights, small hurts and rebellious thoughts that, too angrily revealed to her parents, would have had her being sent to bed.

On leaving college her confidences had taken on a more adult nature, often of some young man of whom her parents would have disapproved, or not being allowed to go out alone with friends to a party or dance. Even her taste for the new, fashionable, less figure-hugging dresses with their calf-length skirts was being frowned on by her mother. Victoria Longfield, with her old-fashioned ideas, maintained that

7

nicely brought up young ladies should not be wearing such outrageous garments. She herself still wore the ankle-length skirts and high-necked blouses of 1912 rather than the fashions of 1922 and kept her hair dragged back in an outdated bun that made her look far older than her forty-odd years.

When Julia had wanted her own lovely long chestnut hair cut fashionably short, one would have thought from her mother's horrified gasps that she was intending to smash a holy relic. When her daughter had finally rebelled and taken a pair of scissors to her hair, the woman had almost swooned and Julia's father had gone into a rage. However, not even God could instantly restore what had been chopped off.

Martha had kept her smiles strictly under lock and key. 'Good for you, my girl!' she'd muttered that night in her little room off the kitchen.

This afternoon she regarded Julia severely. 'You're twenty-one and have a mind of your own now. The important thing is, if you're not sure you love Mr Morrison, and to me you don't sound all that sure, you shouldn't go marrying just for money or to please your families. You could regret it.'

Julia lifted her gaze. 'But I do love him. I feel happy when we are together. We laugh a lot and hardly ever stop talking and it's lovely to have him kiss me. He's so very handsome and tall. I love his fair hair and his blue eyes and I know I'd be devastated if anything were to happen between us. But I've never been in love before so I'm still not sure if that is love or not.'

8

So that was the trouble. The girl had been too sheltered, for all she was lively and had an outgoing nature, even if she was in some ways a bit stubborn. Martha felt herself relax as the excited flow of words calmed a little.

'All I know is that he'll be a perfect husband to me. He's kind and mild-tempered and generous. His parents approve of the match and so do Mummy and Daddy. They like him very much and I do too. And we do love each other.'

Martha yearned to enquire if Julia had ever ached for him, for his touch, for him to make love to her, but shrank from plying such a direct question. Yet she needed to say something.

'I might be getting on a bit, dear, but I hope I keep up with modern times. It just seems to me that if a girl isn't sure about, as you said, what love is, especially with the man her family expects her to be getting engaged to, she ought to speak up before it's too late, or at least wait a little longer.'

She paused a moment to judge the effect of her words, but when Julia seemed suddenly very intent on toying with the jelly moulds, she dared just a little more.

'In this day and age no girl has to do what her parents tell her when it comes to marriage; something that, good or bad, is going to have to last the rest of her life. And if it feels wrong at the start...'

'It doesn't!' Julia cut in sharply, looking up at her questioner to hold her gaze until Martha was forced to look away.

'All I want to make clear, Julia, is just for you

9

to think carefully about it, about love. That's all I have to say on the matter.'

And with these words, containing more than a tinge of warning, Martha Granby turned her attention firmly back to sifting flour ready to add to the fairy cake mixture.

In her bedroom Julia should have been dressing for dinner. Instead, still in her underclothes, she stood at the window staring pensively out across the Park, her eyebrows drawn in vague indecision.

The way Mrs Granby had alluded to her marrying for money worried her. Did she truly love Chester or was she bowing yet again to her father's will, knowing that he saw his business as benefiting from his daughter's marriage to the son of a family whose business was larger than his own?

He had inherited his own father's prosperous import/export concern, and at the time had invested well. Everything had been rosy until four years of war had robbed him of much of his trade.

What profit there had once been dealing in spices and silks from India as well as fine Porcelain, ivory artefacts and other similar commodities from abroad had been done for, enemy submarines attacking shipping throughout those four years of utter stagnation. While men fought in trenches, with very little ground ever gained on either side, Britain needed food not spices.

The armistice had seen Germany brought to its knees, with Britain not far behind. While some wardrobe to select a fawn evening dress. For a moment she gazed at it then put it back and chose the pale green silk instead.

'Come on, Julia, hurry up!' came Stephanie's exasperated cry.

'You go on,' Julia said evenly. 'I'll follow in a moment or two.'

'You're still only half dressed. I know you want to look just right for tonight but Mummy will go into one of her sulks again if we aren't at table in time for Chester's parents to arrive. Virginia's already downstairs.'

'I shan't be long!' Feeling strangely rebellious, Julia held up the silky green to regard the length of the material. Mother would be rankled anyway by its modern calf-length hemline.

'If this new fashion continues,' she said almost every time she took note of the recent raising of skirts from ankle length to what she saw as a thoroughly risqué and unladylike style, 'young ladies who should know better will be revealing their knees before long. It's quite vulgar!'

To buy the dress Julia had taken a taxi on her own to Harrods in the West End two days ago. She'd fallen in love with the beautiful water-green silk dress, gold embroidered and sleeveless, with a scoop neck and low waist. The hemline, high enough to reveal the slope of her calf, would shock her mother. But she wanted to shock and continue to shock after all that friction caused by having cut her hair.

Stephanie was eyeing the garment enviously. 'If I was older I'd choose to wear what I like too. I hate having Mummy still insisting on buying

13

my clothes for me. You've got your own allowance and can do what you like.'

Julia laughed. 'You'll be eighteen in a few months' time. Then you'll have your own allowance to do what you like with.'

Stephanie huffed petulantly, watching her sister slip on the evening gown over her lightweight underwear, prinking the material smooth about her waist. With her small breasts she had no need of the strong, unsightly brassieres Mummy insisted she wore.

Easing her shapely legs into white silk stockings, Julia stepped into green court shoes with pointed toes and decorated with a gold tab, then went to the dressing-table mirror to run a comb through her short, chestnut hair. Free of the weight of long tresses, its natural waves sprang back into place.

Stephanie watched with envy. 'The moment I turn eighteen I'm going to have mine cut too.' She pouted. 'I can't wait!'

'You've several months to go yet. Even then Mummy won't be too pleased.' Julia smiled, recalling the furore at having cut her own hair short.

'We'll see about that!' Stephanie retorted. Julia continued to smile.

'Even at twenty-one whatever I do still causes trouble.' The smile left her lips as she remembered telling her father she would do as she pleased after having so drastically taken the scissors to her hair. His reply had been harsh.

'While under my roof, young lady, you will *not* do as you please! You live in this house by

14

the grace of myself and can be shown the door any time if you decide not to abide by the rules I lay down.'

'I'm sorry,' she'd replied, not at all sorry. 'It's cut now and there's little I can do about that.'

'Nor is there much I can do now about the dreadful mutilation of your hair,' he'd ranted. 'But my displeasure remains. Until that deplorable mess you call attractive grows back to something nearer to a woman's crowning glory, I find it painful to even look at you.'

As head of the family in the old tradition, his word was absolute, even to his choice of where they lived.

Her mother would dearly have preferred the more affluent West London but his business was situated near the docks and the Pool of London between Tower Bridge and London Bridge to which ships from all over the world steamed up the Thames to load and unload. 'I do not intend wasting my time travelling there from the West End every day,' he'd apparently said when many years ago her mother had pleaded to move. 'Here is far more convenient.'

So here they lived. Even so, the houses bordering Victoria Park were like bright islands in a dreary sea where business people like her father, with their fine homes and well-tended gardens, lived in splendid isolation from the traditional poverty of London's East End.

Julia's smile was back by the time she and Stephanie made their way down to dinner. To-night her engagement to Chester – the little ceremony of slipping the engagement ring on to her finger – would take precedence over everything else. Thinking of this, a twinge of excitement gripped her. Maybe tonight her father's lips might soften to a smile as the ring, a band of five diamonds, was placed.

In the large dining room the table looked beautiful. Her mother, still overseeing the final touches, was agitated as usual, easily sent into a panic if even the smallest thing was not quite right.

Victoria had been twenty-two, desperately unsure of the world, and Charles Longfield thirty-three when they married. Now at forty-three she was as unsure of the world as ever while he, in his mid fifties, was only too well acquainted with its glorious ups and its harsh downs.

'Haven't they arrived yet?' Julia asked, seeing everything ready.

Her mother put nervous hands to her lips. 'No, and they mustn't, not too soon. Everything is going wrong. Your father isn't yet home. I cannot imagine what he must be thinking. He should have telephoned me if he was going to be delayed. It's very remiss of him.'

Words poured from her lips in a torrent. 'He has still to dress for dinner. After all my well-laid plans, this will prove an absolute disaster. I so wanted it to succeed on such an important occasion.'

'Don't worry, Mother,' Julia consoled, keeping her distance. To go any nearer would mean having to give her mother a comforting embrace and risk her dissolving into tears. That must not happen just before dinner.

'They'll understand,' she reassured her mother. 'Chester's father is in business too.'

From the hall came the tinkle of the telephone. Victoria leaped as if struck. 'It must be your father. How could he...'

'Let Mary answer it,' Julia interrupted. 'She'll take the message.'

She saw her mother relax though her hands remained clasped tightly together beneath her chin. The phone terrified her. She went into an instant panic if it rang, looking for Mary or Mrs Granby to take the call for her.

The dining room door opened slowly, just a fraction. Mary's face appeared round it. 'Madam, it's a person wanting to speak to you.'

The girl's expression sent Victoria into a flurry. 'Not the master? I can't speak to anyone at present. We are awaiting our guests. Julia, my dear, go and tell whoever it is that we are about to sit down to dinner.'

The telephone sat on a small table in the hall, its earphone lying on end beside it where Mary had left it. Picking it up, Julia put it to her ear and, bending towards the telephone's mouth-piece at the top of the long black stem, said tentatively, 'Hullo?'

'Mrs Charles Longfield?' enquired a female voice at the other end.

'I'm Miss Longfield, her eldest daughter. Who is this?'

'I do really need to speak to Mrs Longfield, personally.' The voice sounded annoyingly efficient, not at all apologetic.

17

Julia felt irritation mounting. 'My mother is unused to telephones. You may tell me what you want and if it's important I will tell her.'

'I'm sorry,' the voice replied obstinately. 'But it is necessary I speak to her.'

'I'm sorry too, whoever you are. Goodbye!'

She was about to replace the earpiece when the voice almost shouted down the wire, 'Please, Miss Longfield. It is about your father!'

Julia felt her heart give a little jump. 'What about my father?'

'This is the London Hospital. My name is Cunningham. Would you please bring your mother to the telephone, stay by her side and make sure she is sitting down. I am afraid I have some bad news.'

'What bad news?' Julia heard her voice rising. 'What's happened?'

Her mother, having overheard this last part of the conversation, was already coming from the dining room almost at a run, her face wrought with fear.

Julia turned back to the phone. 'You'll have to tell me,' she said. 'My mother is in no fit state to hear any bad news.'

At the words 'bad news', her mother gave a little squeak of panic, but the person at the other end of the phone was still talking.

'Very well, my dear.' The voice had softened. 'I regret to tell you that your father suffered a heart attack and was immediately brought in to the hospital but unfortunately he died about fifteen minutes ago. There was nothing we could do for him. I am so very sorry.'

18

For a moment Julia couldn't speak. Then she heard herself say, 'Thank you' in a small, stunned voice as she slowly replaced the mouthpiece on the stem's forked metal bracket.

# Two

Turning to her mother, she realized her own devastated expression had caused Victoria's gaunt cheeks to pale.

'What is it?' The words came as a gasp but already her mother was fearing the worst.

'It was the hospital,' Julia whispered, hearing her own voice quivering with delayed shock. 'They said...'

She trailed off, unable to shape the words, but her mother was ahead of her. 'It's your father! What has happened?'

It was like a spectral cry, shrill yet faint. 'There's been an accident. Is he hurt? How bad? Oh, my dear God! And we have Chester and his parents arriving at any moment. What are we going to do about dinner? Will they be sending him home? What will our guests think?'

Inconsistent, illogical, the words tumbled from her lips. Stephanie, drawn from the dining room by the torrent of emotion, ran to catch her as she began to sag.

To Julia the hall seemed suddenly full of people. Mary was still hovering uncertainly in case she was wanted; Mrs Granby, having heard the cries, had hurried up from the kitchen to see what the trouble was; young Virginia was now

20

standing by helplessly, as well as herself, Stephanie and their mother.

'Take Mummy into the parlour,' Julia ordered, half in panic at the sight of them all while she tried to come to grips with her own shock of grief. 'It's all right, Mary, Mrs Granby, we've had some bad news, that's all.'

Choking on the stupid words, incapable of going into any further explanation, she hurried after Stephanie and Virginia as they helped their mother into the parlour, closing the door behind them.

Mrs Granby, back in her kitchen, heard her mistress's screams tear through the house, on and on until she thought they would never stop. She listened as, finally, they subsided into heart-rending weeping; deep, hollow sobs that reached right down to the kitchen and tore at the cook's breast. The master had been in an accident was all she'd gathered. Any other woman would have mustered up some control but not Mrs Longfield. But how bad was the master?

Not knowing what to think, she gazed at the food on the preparation table and on the hob waiting to be conveyed upstairs as soon as the dinner guests had seated themselves. She thought regretfully of the lovely meal over which she had taken such a long time: anchovy eggs for starters; mock turtle soup keeping warm on the kitchen range; a main course of duck breasts in plum sauce, very light with potato croquettes, green beans, carrots and cauliflower; for dessert, strawberry gateaux with cream, all made by her own hand. No one would eat any of it now with Mr Longfield in hospital. She found herself praying that he wasn't too badly hurt.

Biting at her lower lip for that poor creature upstairs, she made up her mind that anything that could be saved would have to be put back in the larder. If not eaten, and she didn't think it would be now, she, Mary and Fred would make use of it for their supper.

She thought suddenly of Fred. He would have been chauffeuring Mr Longfield home from his office. If it was a motor car accident, had he too been hurt? No one had mentioned him, being too distressed about the master. As the driver he could have been killed, but no one had even said what had happened.

Please, she prayed silently, let them be all right.

Already filled with this new anxiety, for she and Fred had always got on well together, each in their separate jobs, Martha shuddered and tried to turn her mind to other things.

She had hardly begun to clear the preparation table when the front doorbell sounded. She closed her eyes in a gesture of despair. What a time for young Chester Morrison and his parents to arrive. Poor Julia, her special dinner utterly spoiled.

No doubt they'd be going to the hospital together. Thinking this she removed the soup from the kitchen range and put it to keep warm in the oven. The family would need a little nourishment to sustain them when they returned. Maybe the master would be with them, not badly hurt after all, and Fred as well, she hoped. Maybe Chester and his family would return with them. Dinner might be on after all. A cook had to be prepared for all eventualities.

Mary almost yanked the front door open to her employer's guests. For a brief second she stared. Then with a rush of incomprehensible words, she shut the door in their faces in panic, not knowing what to do, leaving them standing, mouths agape, while she ran to the parlour door.

'Madam, the people are 'ere.'

Julia looked towards the girl, confused for a moment, seeing her through a mist of tears. 'What?'

'The people at the door – what do I tell them?'

Sense dawned on Julia. 'Oh, God! Chester! Mary, go away! I'll take care of it.'

'Go where miss?'

'Just...' Julia broke off, leaping up from where she'd been kneeling, arms about her mother as she rocked the weeping form as if she were a baby. 'Just go down to the kitchen and tell Cook what's happened.'

'You mean to the master?'

'Mary, please just leave!'

The girl withdrew as if yanked from behind.

Her back erect, Julia followed, leaving her sisters with their mother. She went out to the hall, hastily brushing away tears in a bid to regain her composure, needing to appear in control of herself, even if she felt quite the opposite.

A little of her father's reluctance to bare his soul to the world came to the fore as she took a deep breath and opened the front door to their guests, even managing a tight, polite smile.

Chester and his parents stood there with expressions of affronted bewilderment at Mary's odd behaviour.

'Julia?' Chester began. 'What on earth...Your maid just shut the door on us. We were left...'

'Please forgive us,' Julia managed but her voice trembled despite her resolve to keep a firm grip on herself. 'We've had some terrible news. You had all best come in and I'll explain. We've just been told ... just this minute been told...'

Her words died in her throat as she stepped back to let them in. Tears glistened in her eyes. Seeing Chester, her body suddenly seemed to lose all strength and she began to shake all over. The next minute he was holding her in his arms.

'What is it, darling? Whatever's the matter?'

Following their son into the hall, Chester's parents looked lost with no maid to take their outdoor clothes. Realizing that something was very wrong, his father removed his own hat, coat and scarf, before turning to his wife to help her out of her fur coat, and then draping the whole lot in a bundle over his arm, leaving his wife still wearing her gloves and deep-brimmed velour hat. Chester, still in trilby and coat, held on to Julia who felt as if all strength had gone.

His troubled gaze was trained on her tearful face. 'Darling, what's wrong? What's happened?'

She seemed to hear his voice from a long way off. She let herself fall against him, as if the strength she'd been holding on to for her mother's sake had deserted her.

24

She told them about the hospital's phone call. 'They said it was a heart attack, sudden,' she managed to explain as he held her. 'They said they couldn't save him. We've been too distraught to find out more.'

She felt him gently kiss her brow. 'We must get in touch with them again,' he said quietly.

Never had she felt such need of him as she did now. As they all gathered in the parlour, with his parents appearing somewhat ill at ease, he instantly took charge of everything, leaving her to sit quietly nursing her grief while her mother continued to sob in the arms of her two younger, weeping daughters.

Prior to his arrival she had been expected to pull herself together for the sake of her mother, who seemed incapable of doing anything other than weep. Now she had someone to take over and the relief was indescribable. For the first time, through all her grief, she realized just how much she loved him.

After Chester had gone out to the hall to phone the hospital, they had all sat in silence except for the sobbing of the bereaved woman. It had seemed an eternity until he returned. Suddenly looking so much older than his twenty-four years, he looked directly at Julia.

'Are you all right?' he asked and as she nodded, he continued in a steady tone, 'I shall go with you and your mother and your sisters to the hospital. I've telephoned for a taxicab. I think it best my parents return home in the car.' He glanced towards them and his father nodded almost as if with relief.

'Our chauffeur is in the kitchen,' Chester went on, talking directly to Julia. 'Your cook has given him a cup of tea. He'll go out to make sure the car's ready. The engine should still be warm and start straight away.'

He surveyed each of the grieving women. 'If you are ready, we should get started,' he said gently.

As everyone made to leave, Julia said, 'I'm so sorry about all this,' as if something quite trivial had spoiled the evening.

'Please don't be, my dear.' Mr Morrison's smile was no doubt meant to give comfort as he took her offered hand. 'I should be the one to apologize for intruding at such a sad time. If there is anything we can do, anything at all...'

Julia shook her head. 'Thank you, Mr Morrison, there's nothing. But it is kind of you to ask. I do appreciate it.'

'Not at all, my dear girl, and you'll inform us when the funeral...'

She gave him no time to finish. 'Yes, of course.'

'Chester will be with you at the hospital.'

'Yes,' she replied automatically, leaving an uneasy pause into which his voice burst like a small explosion.

'Well, we'll be off. I pray God give you fortitude, my dear, and comfort you all.'

'Thank you,' she whispered, trying not to break down as his wife came to kiss her cheek. Mrs Morrison's efforts to offer them her condolences served only to incite a fresh bout of weeping from the bereaved woman and she

26

moved away as if relieved to have that job over and done with.

Suddenly Julia wanted to be rid of them. All she wanted now was to have Chester to herself. Had it not been for him she wasn't sure what she would have done, how she would have coped.

As she and Chester conducted her future in-laws to the front door, Julia wondered how her family was going to fare with her father no longer there to look out for them. But as the Morrisons' car moved off while Chester stood with his arm tightly and protectively about her waist, to show that he was here for her and would always be here for her, all she knew was that she wanted so desperately to be married; to be safe, to be loved and looked after and not be left to cope alone with her family in their loss. She knew her love for Chester was indeed complete and perfect.

# Three

The cloudless sky seemed to mock the sombre black of those gathered at the graveside. Chester's comforting hand was tightly clasped around hers. His parents were on the far side but he'd made it a point to be with her and her family. Her mother was weeping copiously, stifled sobs issuing from beneath a black veil. Her sisters wept too and her brother James, sixteen and home from public school for the funeral, had his head lowered, but Julia thought only of Chester standing here beside her, comforting her.

At the funeral service, with sunlight streaming through the stained-glass windows of St John's Church to fall directly on to the coffin, she had listened to the vicar recounting the events of the deceased's marvellous life. Yet his words hadn't moved her at all while her mother had almost wilted with grief so that she had had to support her by the arm to prevent her giving way completely.

As for herself she could find no tears for her father. He'd had no real affection for any of his children, except maybe for James. He had been their father in name only as far as she was concerned; she'd never really known him as any-

28

thing other than a distant, unsmiling figure, more often at his club than at home. Even when he had dined out with business associates he had gone alone. Her mother was uneasy with business people and preferred to spend her time looking after the home or attending her local ladies' friendship meetings. Even there she had always been nervous of making new friends, and the one or two she did have were more like acquaintances.

Timid, frightened of the outside world, ever wary of saying something wrong and finding herself disliked, she even feared to chastise her own children lest they turned against her. She had preferred to leave that sort of thing to their father, who would exact stern and steady correction. To Julia such occasions had seemed to be the only time he ever made contact with them.

As they had grown older their parents had been keen to keep up with those of their own standing and so the girls had attended a boarding school for young ladies, and their father had remained a stranger. Young Virginia knew him least of all, having only just recently left school. James too, nearly seventeen and still studying, would be leaving school next month to go on to university.

Who would manage their father's business now he was gone? Most certainly their mother couldn't. It occurred to Julia that as the eldest child it could be left to her to do whatever was necessary to sort things out and she thanked God she now had Chester to help her. He might even have to manage the business until James was old

29

enough to take over.

All these thoughts went through her mind as she listened to the drone of the vicar's voice: '...earth to earth, ashes to ashes, dust to dust, in sure and certain hope of the resurrection to eternal life...'

Quite suddenly she realized the vacant hole her father would leave in her life, despite having hardly known him when he was alive. In her mind she could see him arriving home in the evenings to hand his hat, coat and umbrella or cane to Mary, never addressing the girl, hardly looking at her.

The umbrella and cane, no longer in use now, stood in the umbrella stand in the hall. Her father's coat hung above them, his dark trilby on its hook, all looking so lonely now.

Mother had lovingly placed them there after returning home from the hospital that night. Julia wished she'd allow them to be stored away. She would often find her mother standing gazing at them, fingering them gently, tenderly brushing the fabric with her palms, running a finger and thumb down every fold of the cloth.

Nor would she allow his study to be disturbed. She seemed to have become possessed with the idea of keeping his memory alive. Having read that Queen Victoria had behaved in much the same way when her beloved Prince Albert had died, Julia shuddered. Perhaps her mother was going funny in the head.

Julia found herself thinking that somehow she was going to have to reason with her mother and make her see that life had to go on and they must now face a different future and be strong. She must use her own strength to help her mother to become strong as well. Otherwise how would they be able to keep things going?

The thought pulled Julia up sharply. It was easy for her to keep going. She had her circle of friends and she had Chester. Soon they would be married, have a family, a lovely home, a bright and promising future, and never want for money. What did her mother have? The woman had lost her mainstay in life. Her children had their friends and would eventually go off and get married, leaving her a middle-aged woman with nothing to look forward to but a lonely old age, enlivened only when her grandchildren were brought to see her.

Julia couldn't envisage her mother ever marrying again. She was a person who did not make friends with other women easily; it seemed even less likely that she would ever meet another man to marry. It was true that this new decade since the end of the war, with its forward-looking attitudes, had dispensed with many of the old Victorian standards, but she couldn't see her mother keeping up with the times.

Julia stared down into the grave where the coffin now lay. As they buried her dead father, she hoped her mother would not descend into a living burial and hide herself away from the busy world.

The vicar was intoning the final words of the ritual: '...the love of God and the fellowship of the Holy Ghost be with us all evermore. Amen.'

Julia came to herself with a jolt. People were

31

beginning to move away slowly and quietly, as if leaving too hurriedly would be almost irreverent. Someone had come up to her mother and was embracing her, immediately prompting an outburst of tears. Stephanie and Virginia had also gathered tearfully around her. Julia stood back and waited. It was all she could bring herself to do.

Chester's arm came about her waist. 'Are you all right, darling?' he asked gently as she looked up into his handsome face. She forced a smile.

'Yes,' she replied, love springing up at the sound of his voice. 'But I'll be so glad to get back into the car.'

'Of course,' he said and began guiding her away from the deserted graveside. 'But first you ought to go over to comfort your mother. She looks utterly drained, it's to be expected.'

'I'll do that in the car,' she replied. A strange sense of panic was building inside her; a desperate desire to be away from the place. 'I'll need you to be with me, darling.'

'I can't, my love,' he reminded her. 'I'll have to be with my parents in theirs.'

'I forgot.' She wilted a little, glancing across at the two black, box-shaped limousines that had crawled to the cemetery behind the horse-drawn hearse, now departed. Her mother, wishing to keep to the old style for her husband's sake, had insisted on the hearse and its black-plumed horses with their padded hooves. 'But I would much sooner be with you, Chester,' she added sadly.

He bent and gave her a swift but loving kiss.

32

'You will be when we reach your home. We'll have a quick glass of wine and a brief bite to eat, make our condolences then perhaps go off somewhere quiet and be together. I still haven't given you your ring, my love. I couldn't before, under the circumstances.'

He hesitated out of respect to her feelings, and then began again: 'Well, it's done now, and I think it time we got on with matters that concern us. I mean setting a date for our wedding.'

An hour later, having made dutiful conversation with the few mourners who had gone back to the house, and attempted to console her mother without getting too caught up in the tears of grief that each embrace prompted, Julia and Chester sat holding hands on a bench by Victoria Park Lake while strollers sauntered by, enjoying the afternoon sunshine.

The day of mourning seemed far away as Chester extracted from a little blue velvet box the lovely engagement ring with its band of five huge white diamonds and gently eased it on to the third finger of her left hand.

His words, 'Marry me, darling, be my wife,' set her blood tingling, her heart racing with joy.

'Yes,' she breathed, 'with all my heart.'

'I love you very much, my dearest,' he told her quietly.

'And I love you too, so very much,' she whispered as he kissed her, a long lingering kiss that had passers-by smiling. But she didn't notice or care.

Victoria Longfield had never felt so alone –

abandoned, almost.

'We're engaged!' Julia had come home to announce, flashing her ring for her mother to see, Chester standing behind her, smiling. And on such a day! Victoria couldn't help herself; she burst out, 'Your father was buried only this very morning,' before fresh tears welled up and overflowed.

Her other three children, sitting beside her on the sofa where they had been comforting her since the departure of mourners from the house, had gasped but Victoria had had more to say through distraught gulping.

'Doesn't that matter to you? How could you both be so cruel? Could it not have waited at least a few more weeks? Are you so indifferent to my poor feelings, Julia, and to the loss of your dear father?'

Julia's eyes, glowing with joy a moment before, had grown bleak.

'I know, Mummy. Believe me, I'm grief-stricken too, but how could I refuse Chester's proposal? It means everything to me. It doesn't alter how much I miss Father or how you must feel.'

'But to tell me now, while I'm pulled down with grief.'

'I'm sorry. And I know how you are grieving but please, Mummy, be happy for me.'

She broke off, realizing how insensitive her words must sound, how they must have pierced her mother's heart. Immediately mortified, she knelt before her while Chester stood awkwardly by.

'It was going to happen some time soon, Mummy,' she tried to placate.

'Why today of all days? Was your engagement so urgent that you couldn't delay it a few months?'

But a few months would not have made any difference. The blow of losing her daughter to marriage would have been just as hard to bear later. Julia knew her mother, almost knew her next words would be the same come next month, next year: 'I have been left all alone. Your dear father has been taken from me, now you're leaving me...'

'You've still got Virginia and Stephanie,' Julia reminded her. 'And James.'

'James!' she heard the desolation in her mother's tone. 'He'll be at university – and much he cares for me, his mother. Like his father...'

Victoria broke off suddenly. She hadn't meant to say that. The pent-up frustration of years of hiding the loneliness she had so often felt, her hurt at finding herself put aside, her need for his companionship ignored by her husband, had burst out in those three last words.

Immediately she tried to make amends with some sort of explanation.

'This whole family survived the terrible flu epidemic two years ago when so many loved ones died. I would tell myself I should be grateful for that during those times I felt forsaken; all those evenings when your father left me here on my own while he entertained his business colleagues. Now I have lost him altogether and

35

that is a judgement on me for being so self-pitying. Not that I ever complained to your father's face. And now you are saying that you too will soon be leaving me – that too feels like a judgement on me.'

Her words must have raised some small prick of conscience for Julia had thrown herself into her mother's arms. 'I didn't know, Mummy. But it's going to be all right, honestly it is. I shall make sure I'm always here for you.'

Futile words! Victoria had caught a glimpse of Chester standing a little apart from them, his features tight, and had instantly read his expression: 'As my wife she'll be there for me, not here for your every whim.'

Turning her eyes away from him, she had found a little courage to vow that from now on she would never lower herself to ask for Julia's help if her daughter didn't offer it of her own accord; never again would she do anything to earn another look like the one Julia's future husband had just given her.

With her small family beside her, Victoria sat opposite Mr Grantham, her deceased husband's solicitor, at the dining room table.

A letter from him earlier had mentioned an urgent matter that he needed to discuss concerning her late husband's estate. For some reason it had instilled in her a feeling of apprehension which wasn't soothed by the man's grim expression now as he shuffled through the papers he'd extracted from his leather briefcase.

After what seemed an age, he looked up, his

36

gaze resting momentarily on Julia. She was the only one here sitting bolt upright, her head held high, while her mother and two sisters still drooped in grief. But it was right that he address the widow of his deceased client.

'My dear Mrs Longfield,' he began. He had acted on behalf of her late husband's business from the time Charles had inherited it from his father, Edgar James Longfield, for whom he'd also acted in that man's later years. He himself had then been a very young solicitor. Yet in all those years he had set eyes on Victoria Longfield on only one occasion; exactly when, he couldn't recall.

'My wife is a very retiring person,' had been Longfield's excuse in response to Grantham's invitation to dine with him and his wife soon after the man had inherited from his late father. 'I shall be pleased to accept, Grantham, but my wife feels she must decline.'

He had never offered again; business had been done either in Longfield's office or his own, at his club or in a restaurant.

Sitting opposite the thin, gaunt-faced widow, who seemed ready to break down at any moment, he felt uneasy at the news he was about to impart to this small gathering.

Julia frowned at the pause that followed Mr Grantham's opening words. His expression was solemn and he leaned towards her, his forearms resting on the table, as if to soften the blow of what he was about to say.

'My dear Mrs Longfield,' he said again, his tone lowering, 'before we begin I must tell you

37

that what I have to say could be somewhat unsettling news. I am not quite sure if you are aware, Mrs Longfield, but regrettably your late husband never got round to making a will despite my warnings of the peril of not doing so.'

Julia reached out and took her mother's arm as she slowly realized what this news might mean, her hand going to her lips in dismay. She spoke for her mother. 'He was a businessman. He must have made a will of some sort. Maybe it was years ago when he and my mother first married?'

The solicitor looked faintly irritated by her interference. 'I assure you, my dear Miss Longfield, no will has ever been made.' He turned his attention back to her mother. 'I urged your husband to do so many times over the years but he always said that everything would automatically go to you as his wife and after your demise to your children. He refused to take my advice that such a course would mean delay. I regret to say it but your late husband was a man who preferred to keep his affairs to himself despite my being his solicitor. I'm sure he resented my intrusion. I regret that he tended to mistrust professional people intensely.'

That mistrust extended to his family, thought Julia. She knew all too well how immovable her father could be, keeping his affairs as close to his chest as a poker player, the smallest slight harboured for years, and ever suspicious of the motives of others, even those of his own family. Cold was a word that came to mind; unapproachable, he had made few friends. Why her mother had married him was beyond her, but Mummy had little spirit of her own and had probably needed the security and guidance of a husband.

'It is to be understood', Grantham continued, 'Mr Longfield once had to dismiss his accountant for dishonesty and from then on he did his own bookkeeping, despite my advice to engage another, more reliable, honest person.'

'He never said a word of it to us,' Julia burst out but was ignored as he continued to address her mother.

'I have to say he would have been better served taking my advice. He was no bookkeeper. A good accountant would have cautioned him against gambling on the stock market. A weakness, I am sad to relate, that finally led him into disastrous debt.'

'What do you mean by disastrous debt?' Julia demanded and when he seemed about to ignore her yet again, she raised her voice. 'Mr Grantham, I need to ask, what disastrous debt?'

The man looked at her, holding her gaze. 'I regret to have to tell you your father was declared bankrupt the day before his death.'

He switched his gaze to the widow as she gasped like one stabbed. 'I'm sorry, Mrs Longfield, your husband borrowed extensively from his bank to cover his losses on the stock market. He allowed himself to be ill advised in his dealings and was exceedingly unlucky or foolhardy. Finally the banks refused to advance any more credit. He then went to others for money.'

Grantham paused then went on. 'I am sorry if

this sounds brutal but it has to be said. The business, all his assets, even this house will be going to pay his creditors. Forgive me but it may be that the worry may even have contributed to his fatal heart attack.'

There followed a hovering silence, leaving Julia stunned. While he'd been talking, her mother's body had slowly wilted so that she had to put her arms about her to support her, with Stephanie on her other side doing the same.

'Please,' Julia entreated, 'I think my mother has heard enough.'

'I am sorry, my dear.' There was just a hint of apology in his tone. 'In any other circumstances I would enquire if you'd prefer me to return at some later date, but your late father's creditors are already clamouring for their money. This business has to be settled so that we may salvage something from this regrettable mess. Mrs Longfield, do you have money of your own?'

'I don't know.' Her voice emerged, weak and shaky. 'I'm not sure.'

'Your husband gave you an allowance, I take it, my dear. You must have savings of some sort.'

'I...' the voice faltered then strengthened just a little. 'It was only a very small one. I left it to him to manage everything.'

'How did you pay the household bills, staff wages, that sort of thing?'

'I left it to my husband. He knows – knew – more about money than I.'

'And clothing?' The man sounded incredulous.

'I have a clothing allowance – for myself and

40

my two younger daughters. Julia is twenty-one, she has her own allowance. All else he would...' Her words began to fail her in a welter of uncertainty. Julia held on to her.

'My mother is distraught, Mr Grantham. My father always saw to it that she had ample money for her needs.' She found herself defending her father as well as her mother. 'He never stinted us, Mr Grantham. My mother was content with the arrangement. She trusted him and he saw to it that we were kept in more than sufficient comfort.'

As she spoke, Julia felt her hackles rise that while her allowance had been more than adequate, her mother had always been content to rely on her husband for her family's needs, maybe by mutual agreement made years ago.

'So as far as you know there is very little to fall back on but your allowance?' the solicitor queried.

Julia pulled her thoughts together. 'It seems so,' she said sharply, suddenly visualizing what the future held for them if there wasn't enough to live on.

'What about your family?' Grantham turned to her mother. 'Could they not help?'

Victoria lifted her head to regard him with a hopeless look. 'My family?' she repeated in a faint tone before lapsing into silence. 'I have no family.'

Her family had been far less wealthy than Charles's. Her father had managed a small hardware store. There had been two younger brothers who had carried it on after the death of their father in 1909. Both had been killed in the Great War. The shop, by then somewhat run down, was sold and her mother had managed on the proceeds with a little help from Victoria until she died. There were no close relatives, Victoria's two sisters-in-law having drifted away after being widowed, one to remarry, the other to return to Yorkshire.

'I've no surviving family to speak of,' she repeated.

'Then your husband's family?' reminded Grantham. 'Could you not appeal to them for help?'

Victoria shook her head. 'I don't think they...' She broke off. This persistent questioning, almost interrogation, was beginning to cause her more distress than she felt already.

Charles's father had died many years ago leaving the import business to him and his brother but the two had fallen out over their legacy and never again spoke to each other. His brother now lived in Canada. She had no idea where. As for the rest of the family, they had always considered Charles had married beneath him and had little time for her. Now she was widowed what reason had they to involve themselves in what now promised to become a severe financial crisis?

'He had a brother,' she said feebly, not wanting to discuss the family. 'But he went to Canada years ago. I don't know which part of Canada.'

'We might probably be able to trace him for you.'

'What good would that do?' Julia cut in, in defence of her mother's obvious growing dis-
42

comfort. 'He and my father quarrelled. They never spoke to each other again. My father maintained the argument was his brother's fault and so do I. We don't need to go cap in hand to him or any of them.'

Whether or not her mother agreed didn't matter. She wasn't going to let her be degraded any further by that family, if there were any of them left.

'So you've no one at all to call upon?' Grantham queried.

'Apparently not,' Julia returned haughtily.

'If your uncle is still alive we'll endeavour to contact him. What is his name?'

Julia looked towards her mother, hearing her respond in a faint tone, 'Albert,' the last consonant fading as the poor woman almost choked on it.

'Albert Longfield.' Grantham rolled it over on his tongue as he stood up to gather his papers and return them to his briefcase. 'We will do our best, Mrs Longfield. One never knows what may come of it. There is always hope. But you must not be left destitute. If it comes to it, until something is settled, you might consider appealing to one of the many charities.'

Never! Julia heard the word in her head, as the man stood up, his business concluded for the present.

# Four

It took only seconds from Grantham's leaving for Julia's bitter reaction to his parting suggestion to vanish. Seek aid from charitable organizations? No, certainly not. Her family would be fine. She'd see to that if it killed her!

Stephanie was helping their mother from the dining room. Victoria seemed to have no strength left in her body. Julia and Virginia followed them into the parlour where Stephanie eased her mother into an armchair as if she were an invalid. But Julia's heart was growing lighter by the minute.

Still bent over their mother's flagging body, Stephanie looked up at her sister as she came in. 'What are we going to do?'

'It's going to be all right,' Julia said, breaking off as there came a gentle rap on the parlour door. 'Who is it?'

Mrs Granby put her head round the door. 'Now your visitor's gone, I daresay you might need me to make some more tea.' She could see from their devastated expressions that whatever news the solicitor had brought, it hadn't been what they had been expecting. 'I'll have Mary bring it up.'

'Thank you, Mrs Granby,' Julia said. But

hardly had the woman closed the door when Stephanie turned on her.

'Julia! What do you mean it's going to be all right? How can it be all right? We haven't a bean. A few bits of savings, that won't get us far.'

Leaving her mother she began to pace up and down the room, tossing her long hair in frustration. 'We've lost the house, everything we own, and I don't think it covers everything Father owed anyway. Not only do we have no money but we have to pay back what he still owes all those creditors!'

'Maybe we might have to go out to work,' Julia shot at her angrily. Stephanie looked as if she had been hit between the eyes.

'Go out to work? None of us has ever been expected to work! And what's Mother to do when we're not here? How can it be *all right*?'

Julia forced herself to remain calm. 'Chester and I will be married soon,' she said. 'And I shall make sure that none of my family will want for anything. He has money. His family are wealthy. He is a partner in his father's business. He'll understand my need to see my family settled.'

She looked at them all one by one. Stephanie had stopped pacing. Young as she was, Virginia was alert. Even their mother had sat up a little straighter, a gleam of hope in her eyes after the despair that had been there before.

'Can you see him denying my own mother a little comfort?' Julia went on. 'He might even agree to settle Father's debts.'

Her mother looked suddenly hopeful. 'Julia, do you think so? It would be such a relief. The very thought of being thrown out of our home has made me feel quite ill.'

Julia smiled at her in pity. 'We mustn't let ourselves be carried away,' she warned. 'I know he'll be only too ready to help but I can't ask too much of him until we're married.'

'But that could be ages!' cried Stephanie crossly. 'By that time the house will be gone and we'll be homeless. How can you get our hopes up only to tell us it could be all for nothing?'

It was Julia's turn to be cross. 'I've made a suggestion, the best I can think of under the circumstances. All I'm saying is that even if we can't save this house, he might be able to arrange to find us another and keep a roof over our heads.'

'It won't be the same,' Victoria bleated faintly, sagging a little.

'It's better than nothing!' Julia couldn't help sounding snappy. 'If it helps I'll speak to him tonight.'

'And what if he feels we are using him?' Her mother's voice was fast becoming a whine. 'What if he feels he cannot help? It's as if we are going cap in hand begging for charity.'

'No, Mummy, it isn't!' Julia began to feel annoyed. 'I shall soon be his wife. Of course he must help.'

'Or feel bound to.'

'That's silly, Mummy,' she countered but her mother wasn't listening, sinking back into despair.

46

'Oh, the humiliation, having to beg for charity after all we had when your father was here.'

Julia found herself in danger of losing her temper completely. 'Please, Mummy, have a bit of confidence in me. I'll speak to Chester tonight. He won't let us down, I know he won't. He's bound to find somewhere suitable for us.'

Not waiting for a reaction, she hurried from the room, already sorry to have lost her temper with her mother.

'Damn, damn, and bloody damn!' She let fly out of their hearing, the worst she could think of. 'Hopeless, the whole damned lot of them!'

Grabbing the telephone from the hall stand, she dialled the operator, giving Chester's telephone number. All the time even worse swear words filled her head, words occasionally overheard from workmen she sometimes passed in the street, words she'd never normally have dreamed of uttering.

'Hullo?' The sound of Chester's voice immediately brought a flood of relief. He would set things right. Even so, having to repeat what the solicitor had said wasn't easy, having to bare her soul even to him.

By the time she had finished speaking her voice was breaking as her family's predicament hit her and she acknowledged that she was indeed asking for charity.

Chester listened to her from beginning to end in silence. Now she waited. She waited so long for him to speak that finally she felt she had to prompt him. 'Chester? Darling, are you still there?'

'Yes, I'm still here.' His voice sounded low, almost distant.

'We don't know what to do,' she said, hating having to prompt him. 'My mother's in a terrible state.'

There was another long silence. She was about to say his name once again when he spoke, a little sharply it seemed to her. 'I'll be there in the car in about half an hour. We can eat somewhere and talk this over.'

'I'll be ready,' she said in a small voice.

'Right!'

That was all he said – no 'I love you, darling' or even 'Don't worry, darling, it'll be all right'; none of the endearments she had expected from him. But then, her news must have shaken him as much as it had her.

In a fever of trepidation she got ready. To her relief he arrived within the half hour. With his arm through hers he led her to the car, helped her in and tucked the car blanket about her knees. He drove in silence and she thought it better not to break into whatever thoughts were in his head.

Julia sat in her room in the dark, the slow thump of her heart deep and heavy inside her breast, almost making her feel sick.

That evening in the tiny restaurant neither of them had been in the mood for eating. Chester had made no comment at all when she had gone over her family's troubles once again. He had merely nodded at intervals as if mulling it all over in his mind.

She had concluded that perhaps he needed time to think before coming to a decision on what to do without embarrassing her. She recalled feeling content with that, loving him for it.

Going home in his car he had been silent and so had she, increasingly sure that he must have been made to feel awkward by all she had told him. When he had taken her to her door he had declined to come inside and was quite evasive when she asked why. 'I need to think,' was all he had said.

She understood, except that his goodnight kiss hadn't been as ardent as usual; a peck, nothing more, saying not to worry. But it had worried her; she was bewildered as to why he hadn't been quicker with a solution to their problems.

'I'm looking forward to Saturday,' she had said to combat the small rush of depression. He always took her dancing where the big bands played and had taught her to tango. They regularly attended fabulous parties, went to all the big cinemas or listened to concerts and light opera. This Saturday they were going to see *The Beggar's Opera* at the Lyric Theatre, Hammersmith. It had been so well reviewed that, to celebrate their engagement, he'd chosen the most expensive seats. It was going to be wonderful.

But he had suddenly frowned. 'I'm not sure about Saturday, darling,' he'd replied. 'I should have told you over dinner, but your plight was more important. My father and I might be attending a business meeting. It could go on until late and give us no time to get there. I'm sorry I forgot about it, but we had other things on our minds. I'll see if I can get the tickets changed to another evening. I'll call you tomorrow, darling.'

Then he was getting back into his car, with no ardent embrace. He'd driven away much faster than he normally did, without the usual several hand waves, in fact without even a backward glance.

She had truly assumed that he'd had his mind on what was best to do for her in her predicament and, thus preoccupied, had forgotten their usual fond ritual. Neither had she connected his inability to take her out this Saturday with anything untoward. But slowly suspicion was growing that there might be more to his odd attitude that evening than she had imagined.

He had called her the following day, apologizing for having had to cancel the theatre tickets, but still with no mention of what conclusion he'd come to about her family's predicament, nor was she going to embarrass herself by asking him outright.

'I shall see you on Sunday as usual?' she'd asked. On Sundays they often took a stroll in Victoria Park if the weather was fine; if not, they might go for a spin in his car. Her question had brought a small hesitation. Finally he had said yes, probably. She could detect no trace of affection in his voice; it was almost as if he were speaking to a casual friend rather than to his fiancé.

Sunday was a fine, sunny day. They had walked in the park, she holding his arm. She'd made

50

herself as pretty for him as she could, wearing a calf-length summer dress in a pale blue, pattern-ed voile with Magyar sleeves and a slightly lowered waistline that was the new season's fashion, a parasol to match and a cream, broad-brimmed hat pulled low over her eyes until her short hair could hardly be seen. Pointed court shoes made the whole ensemble perfect. He hadn't even remarked on how nice she looked. He had kissed her on meeting, but the kiss had been cold, his lips hard.

'I'm sorry about Saturday,' he said. 'I know you were looking forward to the theatre, but it couldn't be helped.' It sounded as if he hardly cared whether it could have been helped or not.

'How did your business meeting go?' she asked.

The non-committal shrug prompted instant concern. What if his father's business was going the way of her father's?

The country still hadn't truly recovered since the Armistice. Of course, some businesses had done well out of it, making the most of their chances, but others were struggling. Perhaps it was worry that was making him so vague.

She'd seen the long dole queues of ex-service-men patiently waiting for jobs that weren't there, women widowed by war trying to exist on a pittance, with little help from the Government, their fatherless children thin and grubby and clothed in rags. They hung around street corners in the poorer parts of the East End while the well off swept by in their fine cars, just as her father might have done and Chester's father no doubt still did. She knew she was probably equally guilty by walking past with her face averted, not knowing quite why except that she didn't want to be drawn into their misery. But if Chester couldn't come to her aid, she could become one of them, searching vainly for a job. The thought brought a shudder.

'Is anything wrong? In your father's business, I mean?' she asked anxiously. If it had fallen into trouble, how could she expect to rely on him to help her family?

'Not exactly,' he replied evasively, not meeting her eyes but staring into the distance as they walked. He began to chew at his lip as if unsure of what next to say. 'Well, to be honest,' he continued at last in a low, uncertain tone, 'things do seem to have temporarily run into a few difficulties lately. Nothing very much to worry about, mind you, but it needs to be thought about.'

He fell silent for a while but as she squeezed the arm she was clinging to, he abruptly stopped walking, pulling her up sharply beside him. This time he looked at her closely.

'The thing is,' he'd said slowly, 'both our fathers' affairs seemed to be doing very well and they thought that once you and I were married, between them they could surmount these difficult times by amalgamating. We could have become one large company.'

'Your father wasn't exactly going broke,' she said miserably. 'Mine was. And we didn't know. We had no idea.'

'And nor did my father. Your father said

nothing to him about that and he was shocked and upset to say the least when he discovered how things were. He feels he has been duped.' Chester's tone sounded as if he was accusing her as well as her father of underhandedness.

'Duped!' she had echoed, pulling away from him in shock. 'Is that what you think too?'

'It's what my father thinks.'

She stood glaring up at him. 'But what do *you* think?'

When he hadn't replied, she'd rushed on, 'And our marriage – did that come into your father's scheme of things, our families being nicely united in this *business arrangement*?'

'Of course not,' he began, but she wasn't listening.

'And you've never actually loved me.'

'Julia, I do love you!'

'And you still want us to get married.'

It was a statement but in that second she'd detected the tiniest of hesitations. She had stepped away from him, turned and run, leaving him standing there. He hadn't come after her, and that had told her all she needed to know. He should have raced after her, caught her in his arms, covered her face with kisses and sworn undying love, but he had done none of those things.

Now, several days later, she sat on the edge of her bed. It wasn't yet daylight. She'd hardly slept last night, knowing what was to happen today. In her hand she held a short letter from him. It had arrived yesterday with the last post of the day. She had no need to read the words again; they were seared on her brain:

53

I love you. I want to marry you, but my family are against it, and I can't upset them at this time. We've a few business problems and I have to help my father get ourselves out of it. It's just a small hiccup but I can't think of us at the moment. Just be patient, darling. When the business is back on its feet, which it will be in a few weeks' time, I'll come and see you and we can pick up where we left off. In the meantime I still love you. Chester.

Sitting there with her eyes closed, she slowly crumpled the letter into a tight ball for the sixth or seventh time and let it drop on to the carpet.

A few weeks' time would be too late. Yesterday, her mother had clutched a different letter, from their solicitor, telling them that today they would be moving out of this house, never to live here again.

She opened her eyes and saw that it was dawn, daylight showing through the half-drawn damask curtains.

She got up from the bed, went to the window and pulled them fully back. The sun was just beginning to peep above the trees and lawns of Victoria Park. She suddenly realized this would be the very last time she would ever see the view from this window of that glorious rosy blush flooding across the broad vista of the Park.

Julia Victoria Longfield closed her eyes against the tears that sprang suddenly, tugged the curtains together again and turned away from the window.

# Five

Julia gazed around her father's small warehouse. She had never set foot in here before yet in a strange way felt she would miss it once it was gone.

By rights she shouldn't even be here. It had been locked, no doubt against any unlawful entry, but by rummaging in her father's old bureau at home early this morning, well before the rest of the family were up, she had found a set of keys. She had some idea that coming here might help her recover from Chester's vile letter, and give her something else to think about.

Having got Fred their chauffeur to drive her, she now found herself wondering what she had expected to do once she was here. She felt rather like an intruder with no purpose but to nose around. It all felt so furtive, so underhanded, just like her mother's behaviour when she had gathered her children about her to caution them against saying anything to anyone about their present situation.

'You mustn't even tell your friends,' she'd warned. 'I want no one to know and start talking about us and shun us as if we were pariahs.'

'But they're our friends, Mummy,' Virginia had said, aghast. "We can't just gather up our

55

things and creep away. They'll wonder. And when they find out, my friends will never speak to me again. It feels like telling a lie.'

But for once in her life her mother had been adamant. 'I want no one to know of our downfall and that is that! We're leaving tomorrow morning. And when any of you see your friends after that, you will just say that we moved because I could not stand to live here now your father is gone, that there are too many memories here. Do you all understand?'

They'd all been stunned. 'Well, I for one am not going to abide by that!' Stephanie had said when they'd gathered in the evening out of their mother's hearing. 'I'm not prepared to lose my friends over this.'

'Nor am I,' Virginia had said indignantly while young James had looked downcast and said, 'I've already lost mine, dragged out of school and not permitted ever to go back because we haven't got enough money any longer.'

It had been too late anyway last night to tell anyone and Stephanie hadn't had the courage to go out with her friends that evening and face them as if nothing was wrong. But she was rebellious all the same. 'I'm still going to write to each of them when we get to this place you've found for us, Julia.'

'But it still does feel as if we're lying, even for a short while.' Virginia had pouted and Julia had quite agreed with her.

But wasn't she lying now, standing here in this empty warehouse, having crept out of her house before anyone was awake? She had merely

56

warned Mrs Granby not to say anything while giving the woman no reason for her request.

She gazed around the empty space. The whole area had a strange, unnerving quietness about it at this hour. Julia shivered.

'It looks larger than I imagined,' she whispered to Fred who had left the car round the back where it wouldn't be noticed.

'That's 'cos it's more or less empty, miss,' he answered dejectedly. He had reason to be in low spirits. Tomorrow the car was to be taken as part of her father's assets in order to pay off some of his debts, leaving Fred out of a job. She had not even thought to ask if he had another to go to, she was so full of misery herself.

Their maid Mary had already gone and was now working in a shop. Julia didn't know which shop and didn't much care. Mrs Granby had refused point-blank to leave, declaring she'd stay without pay until the family had to vacate the property. Mr Grantham the solicitor had kindly written to them enclosing a list of what he considered might be respectable lodgings.

'You cannot take a chance with your accommodation, dear ladies,' ran the words. 'Mr Longfield would not have wanted to know that his family were living somewhere unsuitable.'

A pity he didn't think of that before he gambled everything away, Julia thought bitterly as she read out the list to her mother who'd been sent into a welter of weeping by it.

Mr Grantham had no doubt kept his thoughts to himself regarding the underhanded way her father had mortgaged the house to pay off his debts. But they hadn't been paid off, had they? He'd used the money instead to continue gambling on the stock market, always in the hope, she guessed, of hitting the jackpot – much as a punter at a race meeting might behave, always believing the next bet would be the one to see him right. Her father had been no better than that gambler, yet had cut such a figure of haughty respectability, looking down his nose at others, even his own wife. Now he was dead and all his assets, including the roof over his family's head, were being repossessed. So much for respectability! She had nothing to thank her father for.

The rented accommodation she'd finally found after rushing around yesterday like a demented chicken was on the top floor of a three-storey tenement just off Bethnal Green Road. It consisted of a living room hardly large enough to swing a cat, two tiny bedrooms and a narrow kitchen with hardly anywhere to hang washing. The only lavatory was a shared one in the back yard, so that they were obliged to trek all the way downstairs to it. The whole thing was thoroughly distasteful and embarrassing. Their only washing facilities were the kitchen sink and a tin bath that hung on the wall.

She had put down the required first month's rent with money from her own allowance, aware with a small pang that there'd be no more allowance from now on. All the family had left was their collective jewellery to keep them going for a while but that would take time to sell and once gone there would be no more.

She had suggested pawning it all for the time

being, but that reaped a horrified reaction from her mother. 'I wouldn't be seen dead going any-where near one of those dreadful places,' she had said, adding incongruously, 'I'd rather die!' But Julia had been far too worried to see the funny side.

Her father had even allowed his life insurance policy to lapse, and along with all the other problems with creditors and banks, she had no idea where they stood at the moment. It had left her reeling, on top of having to contend with her mother's grief, her sisters' helplessness and having to take James out of his private school with no money to pay for any further education for him.

She felt sorry for her brother, knowing that his school chums would be discussing among them-selves what might have gone wrong in his life. Having to leave school was a terrible comedown for him, on top of the shock of his father's death. Julia felt anger rise up in her. The whole situa-tion was a comedown for them all.

She let her gaze wander again around the warehouse, wondering why she'd bothered to come at all. There was nothing here but a collec-tion of odd boxes probably containing imported goods and, stacked in one corner, quite a few bolts of dress material.

Curious, Julia went over to examine them. There was cotton, sateen, muslin, velvets of all colours, as well as nainsook from India, a fine soft cotton fabric she found pleasing to the touch. There was silk too, fine silk, some plain, some printed, feeling smooth and slippery as she ran a finger along each bolt. There were others whose names rang bells in her head – voile, chiffon, ninon, tussore.

As she touched each roll of fabric an idea began to form in her head. Quickly she went back to the desk to look for any of the appropriate receipts. Papers appeared to have been stacked in neat piles but nothing more.

It all looked as if those who had worked here saw no point in coming back to work now that their employer was dead and his business bankrupt. They hadn't been paid and, with creditors clamouring for money, it didn't look as if they would ever see the humble colour of theirs.

Fred followed her gaze. 'I got back 'ere after the 'ospital took him ter see if there was anything I could do,' he said lamely. 'But it was all out of my depth so I thought best to leave it as it was.'

Julia nodded absently and he went on, 'Yer father seems to 'ave sent off a tidy batch of stuff the day before. That's why there ain't all that much stuff 'ere, I suppose. He might have bin expectin' more ter come in but I don't know much about it. I told his workers ter go 'ome and contact yer father's accountant who'd pay 'em off. And I telephoned his accountant and solicitor about the sad news, taking the liberty of looking up their telephone numbers in his address book there. That was afterwards. Yer see, I stayed at the 'ospital till yer father died, which was ever so quick...'

He broke off in confusion, adding quickly, 'Begging yer pardon, Miss Longfield, I didn't

60

mean...'

But Julia wasn't listening. 'How much of this stuff do you think we can move out of here?'

Fred broke off to stare at the stack of material. 'Why?'

'Because I think I could make use of it.'

'All of it?'

'As much as we can load into the car in say an hour.'

Fred pursed his lips in doubt. 'It ain't ours... yours...ter shift.'

'It is until the place is padlocked as far as I'm concerned,' she said almost in defiance. 'Now come and help me!'

'We won't get the boxes in the car,' he said as he moved to help. 'They're too bulky and take up too much room.'

'We don't need them. I know nothing about spices or whatever, but a woman knows something about material and that will stack far more easily.'

Getting the bolts of material out to the car at the back was a nerve-racking experience. Julia's heart was in her mouth lest someone of authority turned up. By rights this was no longer her father's property; it could be claimed by his creditors. Taking it might be seen as theft, but since some of it would have to be left as there was no more room for it in the car, what remained would probably appease them. With all that her father owed, surely a few bits of material wouldn't make any difference.

Maybe no serious inventory had been done on so little stock and she wondered why the place was so empty unless her father, unable to pay for other shipments, had been selling off all he could to help pay some of his debts.

As she worked, dragging the stuff from where it was piled up, she kept hearing the solicitor's first words to her mother as he'd broken the news: 'Your husband was financially over-stretched, Mrs Longfield. True, the banks had accepted his personal guarantees for all his company's debts but as his debt steadily mounted there was growing concern; and now, with his death, they are naturally looking to recover those debts.'

How could her father have been so stupid not to have seen how deep a hole he'd been digging for himself?

Tense laughter bubbled up inside her at the aptness of that thought. She immediately quelled it, bitter anger taking its place at her father's stubbornness in keeping his problems locked inside himself, doing his own bookkeeping, ignoring any advice of his solicitor, his accountant, his bank, and especially keeping her and her family in the dark. And now here she was, pulling and tugging at heavy bales of cloth like a navvy, in the hope of saving something from this mess. Although she had no notion of what she was hoping to achieve; nothing but a vague, possibly foolish, idea that was forming in her head – an idea probably every bit as foolish as those her father had harboured and which had brought his family to this plight.

So absorbed was she by the tension of it all, the fear of being caught, that she suddenly realized that for the first time since reading Chester's cruel letter she'd forgotten about him.

Casting the memory of him from her, lest she be undermined by it, she forced her thoughts back to her task. This wasn't the time to start crying. Tears would come later at some odd, unexpected time when she was alone.

She squeezed one last bolt of grey wild silk into the car. It broke her heart to have to leave the rest of the beautiful stuff behind but there wasn't an inch of space anywhere to fit in another. But all in all they'd done a good job.

The vehicle's interior was packed tight from floor to roof, leaving only space enough for the driver, so she had to call a cab while Fred made off with their ill-gotten gains. Glancing at her little gold wristwatch – which would soon join the jewellery she hoped to sell – she saw that the hands were creeping towards nine o'clock. Glad to be away at last she was nevertheless filled with satisfaction.

She had given Fred the address of the flat she'd found. Now that she had paid the first month's rent, it was hers to store in it whatever she liked. The material would be safe there, away from the prying eyes of those in authority. Whether or not removing it was illegal she had no idea. She knew that the family's personal possessions, items of jewellery, clothing and the like, could not be seized. Maybe bolts of cloth might be lumped in with these, but it was best to be safe than sorry.

Between them, she and Fred humped the heavy fabric up the dark stairs, leaving it in a heap on the floor in one corner of the living room. She would decide where to put it all later. There wouldn't be much furniture left anyway to take up room after the bailiffs had been at it.

As Fred drove her back for what would be her last couple of hours in her old home, the only home she'd ever known, she sat in silence in the back seat. The next few hours were going to be hard, trying to console her mother, comfort her sisters, and James too. He had been so very hurt by this turn of fortune, seeing his future falling about his ears, blaming his father, just as she too blamed him.

She knew little about her brother, separated as they had been from each other during their growing up years, boarded at different schools. How would she deal with him if he let himself be undermined by bitterness, by anger?

Julia felt her own anger rise. Damn his anger! She too felt bitter, all this her father's fault. And Chester had done nothing to help, in fact had moved out of the scene so fast that it had taken her breath away. She had been so confident she could rely on him. Well, damn them all!

She stiffened her back against the seat. She had to win through somehow. But if only she had Chester to support her, comfort her. She suddenly felt herself wanting his comfort so badly at this minute. Tears began to cloud her eyes, her throat closing up at the thought of him. She hated him with all her heart yet so wanted him. Unseen by Fred, intent on his driving, she fumbled in her little leather handbag for a handkerchief and let herself weep silently into it.

# Six

Closing the door on her lovely home for the last time wrenched Julia's heart enough to make her feel almost sick.

Standing in the hall gazing around at everything she'd ever known, so familiar, it had grieved her that for years she'd taken it all so much for granted that it had become virtually unnoticeable. It had always been there and so she had believed, without giving it much thought, that it always would be. Perhaps for the first time in her life she was actually *seeing* the furniture she was leaving behind. As she closed the door on it all there came a deep, slow sense of loss with the realization that she would never again see this décor, these lamps, the furniture she'd known so well.

At the gate stood their cases, with their personal items beside them. The two pieces of furniture her mother had been allowed to take, her little writing desk and a small dressing table that had belonged to her own mother, had been loaded on to a small van ready to be transported to the flat where they would live from now on. Her mother was crying, dabbing her eyes with an already soaked handkerchief, her body hunched, her head resting against Stephanie's shoulder.

Struggling with her own tears, Julia left the door keys by the iron foot-scraper to be retrieved the moment the taxi bore her family out of sight. She glanced at the car sitting at the end of the street, its occupants instructed to check the contents of the house to ensure that everything they had been ordered to leave was present.

Refusing to look back, though her soul ached to do so, Julia came to join her little family that now included her brother. He stood silent and tight-lipped, his young, good-looking features marred by bitterness, his hopes and plans for university now no more.

Mrs Granby was standing with them. She was going to her sister's in Hoxton, not too far away, and had promised not to lose touch with her former employer's wife. It had occurred to her that they were now on equal footing but she tactfully refrained from saying so. She'd tried to wave away the wage Julia's mother had pressed into her hand, protesting that she'd stayed on out of friendship, but had finally accepted.

'Here's me address, Mrs Longfield,' she said, handing her a slip of paper as they got into the taxi. 'Now keep in touch, won't you, Madam? If you need anything, please write. Me sister don't have no telephone.'

Neither will we any longer, Julia thought bitterly as her mother did her best to stifle tears. She knew just how her mother felt. The parting was overwhelming her too, but she held back her own sorrow.

'Thank you, Mrs Granby,' she said on behalf of her mother who was almost falling into the

66

taxi with Stephanie holding on to her. 'You've been a good friend and we will keep in touch. And thank you for all your kindness in staying on with us.'

'You're very welcome,' Mrs Granby gulped. 'Take care of yourselves, all of you.'

She remained standing there as Julia climbed into the taxi and the vehicle whisked them away. With a last wave, Julia settled in beside her mother and put an arm about her shoulders. 'We're going to be all right, Mummy,' she soothed. 'Nothing lasts for ever, not even horrible things.'

Her hopeful words made very little difference to her mother who was still weighted down with misery by the time they reached their destination. Nor was the first sight of their new home likely to improve the woman's feelings. Victoria's face creased again at the sight of the upper windows of the flat, situated above a run-down-looking haberdasher's in the street that branched off the western end of Bethnal Green Road.

With Stephanie and Virginia supporting her, and young James dragging his feet at the rear, it was left to Julia to pay the taxi driver. She turned hastily away from his sour expression at the size of her tip, reflecting that he was no doubt in better financial straits than they at this moment. Walking away from the taxi, she followed her family down the short alley beside the grubby-looking shop to a door that served the flats.

Stephanie's face was a picture as they entered the dark hallway to the stairs. 'Is this all our father's solicitor could come up with?'

'He didn't have to come up with anything,' Julia said sharply, but quickly mellowed, too unhappy to argue. 'He doesn't act for us now. We can't afford to pay him any longer. It was nice of him to find this for us.'

'But here!' Stephanie burst out. 'Surely he could have recommended something better than this? With father's business gone we didn't have to go on living this side of London. Couldn't he have found something nearer the West End?' Hating to face her old friends she now wanted to move as far away as possible, where no one knew her, reacting in a similar way to her mother.

'This was all we could afford,' Julia snapped as she began leading them up the stairs, the others helping their still drooping mother.

Yes, it was early days and grief would be with them for some time to come, thought Julia as she now led the way. But the sooner her mother began to face up to realities the better. What had happened couldn't be changed and lamenting the past wasn't going to help. It could even make things worse than they were.

She wasn't being hard. She too was nursing her own misery but she was not her mother and realized that she would never really know just how Victoria felt. She hadn't much loved her father, but her mother had and was now thoroughly lost without him. That much she could understand.

Two flights of stairs, passing the first-floor flat on the way, brought them to their own door.

Inserting the key, Julia opened it to step straight into the kitchen. Behind her she heard the shocked gasps of the others. And who could blame them, she thought.

'At least the place is furnished and in a reasonable condition,' she said quickly, but that didn't seem to impress her family as they stood in the tiny space, five people immediately becoming a crowd.

To add to the difficulty, it was made even smaller by having three doors: the one they'd just entered; another to the living room; and a third Julia knew led to the narrow back bedroom which she had already told herself would be James's. The larger front bedroom that led off the living room would be for the rest of them. Mother would be pleased! Julia almost smiled at the uncalled for thought.

Under the small kitchen window that overlooked a back yard was a stained butler sink and a small wooden draining board, next to it a black gas stove, clean but old and against one wall a small wooden table with shelves above it.

On a hook near the sink hung the tin bath. Julia looked quickly away, remembering the spacious bathroom in their old house.

'Through here,' she said before any of them could speak, and led the way through to the living room.

It could have been worse, she told herself fiercely as she gazed about, trying not to think of the spacious, cosy home they'd just left; the home she had thought she would never leave until her marriage. Her mind flew instantly to

69

Chester and she felt her eyes grow moist and her throat tighten.

'Dear God, but this is awful!' Stephanie broke out. Her sister, having helped their mother to the well-scuffed brown leatherette settee, was gazing around in horror.

Stemming her tears, Julia swung round on her. 'What were you expecting then, Buckingham Palace?' she spat.

Stephanie hardly noticed. 'Is this all you could find for us, Julia? Honestly, there's hardly room to have a good sneeze! Surely you could have found something a bit larger, a bit brighter, something more...'

'I had two days. We've hardly any money...'

'But it's awful...' Stephanie broke off as their mother began to cry. 'Mummy, it'll be all right. We'll find something better in a day or two,' she soothed, sitting down beside Victoria to put an arm about her shoulders while her brother and youngest sister looked on, silent and lost.

James was the first to recover. 'It's not too bad, considering,' he said, trying hard to sound encouraging. 'So, what are the bedrooms like? I hope they've got beds in them.'

He gave a forced chuckle to accompany the lame humour, but already Stephanie was staring at the pile of material stacked in one corner. 'What's all that?'

'It's from Father's warehouse,' Julia said, encouraged to see that her mother had recovered enough to follow her daughter's gaze with curiosity. 'I got Fred to put it all in the car for me and bring it here.'

Stephanie stared at her, aghast. 'You broke into Father's warehouse after it had been locked up? What were you thinking? You could have got us into terrible trouble. And why bring the stuff here?' She cast an arm in the direction of the pile. 'There's hardly room here for us to live without you turning the place into another warehouse and cluttering it up even more.'

She stalked over to the pile to glare at it as if it had done her some gross injustice, her hands now fists, her arms akimbo 'What on earth did you think you were going to do with it all? Honestly, Julia, you must be stark-staring potty!'

'Thank you, Stephanie!' Julia's voice was tense with rage. 'No one else but me lifted a finger to find us somewhere to live. And now that I have...'

'Please, dears,' came her mother's tremulous voice. 'Haven't we been through enough trouble? Please, don't start arguing, on top of everything else.'

'Let's see what the other rooms are like,' suggested James in an effort to break up the tension.

'I know what they're like,' Julia said almost childishly.

'But we don't. Two bedrooms, right?'

Julia pulled herself together with an effort. She nodded to the second door in the room. 'That leads to the main bedroom.'

'And where do I sleep?' he asked flippantly.

Julia held her temper. 'That third door in the kitchen takes you into the room you'll be using.'

'From the kitchen?' he echoed, attempting a laugh. 'Isn't that a stupid place to have a door to

71

a bedroom?'

'Go and look!' she snapped, in no mood for banter.

When he returned his humour had faded. 'You mean I have to go through the kitchen to get to my room and to go to the bathroom?'

'We don't have a bathroom,' she told him. 'The toilet's downstairs.'

'Downstairs?'

'It's an outside toilet – in the yard.'

'You mean we have to go down two flights of stairs,' Stephanie broke in, 'whenever we need to go in the night?'

'What about the bathroom?' young Virginia asked innocently.

'There's only that galvanized bath hanging on the wall in the kitchen,' Julia supplied, trying to disguise her wretchedness.

'You mean that's what we have to take a bath in?' Virginia cried. 'We can't! Everyone will see us!'

'We'll keep the doors shut or put up a curtain of some sort.'

'But what if James opens his bedroom door? What if he peeps?'

'James will *not* peep!' cried her brother indignantly.

'You could, by accident,' Virginia shouted at him.

'Why would I want to do something as daft as that?' he shouted back.

'Please,' their mother bleated, 'I can't take any more argument. So many awful things have happened I can't stand much more.'

72

Instantly the two girls hurried to comfort her, leaving James standing uncertainly, wondering what to do, while Julia fought to avoid being undermined by her mother's unrelenting distress. She wanted to tell her that this was what they would have to endure from now on and that they must try to make the best of it; that it could have been worse; that at least it was a roof over their heads, but she held her tongue. No use making it any worse than it already was. She turned her thoughts instead to how they were going to survive.

They must start by thinking how they were going to keep themselves. There was rent to be paid, coal and food to be bought, money needed to keep them decently clothed and shod. James was going to have to find a job, Stephanie and Virginia too. It was going to be hard for people who had never had to work in their lives but they'd have to adapt or go under. What going under meant she dared not begin to imagine.

As for herself she knew exactly what she was going to do. She glanced towards the bolts of cloth she'd stacked as neatly as she could in one corner of the room. If she was successful at what she had in mind, they might not only survive, they could rise. She hadn't loved her father, but one thing she did have in common with him was his business sense.

So long as she hadn't inherited his weakness for gambling; his reckless quest to double his wealth that had led to his own and his family's downfall. Even so, she reflected, all business was a gamble, so in a way it might be a good

73

thing if she had inherited a little of that side of him. It remained to be seen. But as she stood looking around the pathetic room that was now their home, she vowed that this wouldn't be the end. Rather, as her gaze moved again towards the small pile of fabrics that her sister had so scorned, she felt that it could be a beginning.

# Seven

It was harder than they'd imagined trying to settle into this new life that had been thrust on them, even for Julia who was determined to make a go of it.

She missed her friends while at the same time telling herself they weren't worth the missing. Despite what her mother had said, she'd risked writing to one or two about her changed circumstances in order to escape the deep embarrassment of telling them face to face.

Not one had replied. Those friends who had willingly come to console her on the death of her father had shied away from offering sympathetic support in her new plight, quite obviously fearing being asked for monetary help – something she would never have dreamed of doing.

Stephanie had had the same reaction from her own friends, leaving her taken aback and bitter. 'I hate them,' she had burst out to Julia. 'If I never see any of them again it won't upset me.'

But she was upset; they were both upset, but said nothing to their mother. There was too much else to worry about – not least their financial situation. What little money they had would soon be gone. They'd been here just under a week and already Julia found the money dwindling far more quickly than she had expected.

There was food to buy and money to be set aside for next week's rent and all the weeks after that. Then, a few minutes ago, Virginia had come out from the living room with a small bag of toffees, her cheek bulging as she chewed.

Julia had turned from the kitchen sink where she'd been washing up the few discoloured dinner plates that had come with the flat. 'Virginia, where did you get those from?'

The girl looked as if she'd been accused of grand theft. 'Mummy let me have a penny to get them.'

A penny! Twelve pennies made one shilling! What was her mother thinking of? They needed every last penny they possessed to live on. Julia could have wept at the feeling of degradation that swept over her. Counting pennies! Never in her life could she have imagined it would come to this.

Mummy!' she rounded on Victoria. 'We can't afford to go buying sweets. We have to be careful now.'

The uncomprehending look in her mother's eyes as she stood helplessly with a tea towel in one hand and a plate in the other made it all too obvious to Julia that she had no real understanding of the plight they were in. Julia's heart sank.

'A child needs a few sweets,' Victoria answered in a high, querulous voice. 'She hasn't had any for a whole week since we came to this awful place.'

'That's not the point!' Julia was exasperated. 'We don't have that sort of money to waste any more.' She addressed her mother with none of the filial respect that she would once have offered as a matter of course. She spoke now as if she were admonishing a thoughtless child. 'Don't you understand, Mummy? We need every penny we can find, just in order to live.'

'But we have our jewellery, yours and mine and Stephanie's,' her mother protested, 'though it grieves me to see it having to be sold, all my lovely jewellery. And it is valuable.'

Julia ignored her laments. 'And how long will the money from that last?' she demanded. 'It's not going to be easy to sell. I know how valuable it is, Mummy, but we'll never get back what it is really worth. And when that's gone, tell me, what do we rely on then?'

The confused expression on Victoria's face brought her up sharply. The next moment she was holding her mother, words of contrition pouring from her.

'I'm sorry, I shouldn't have shouted at you. I didn't mean to hurt. But it's all different now and we have to realize that. Someone has to think for us. James and Virginia are still too young. Stephanie is like you – she can't get her mind round all that's happened – and you're still too full of grief and shock from losing Daddy to think about anything else.'

She leaned back to look into Victoria's eyes while still holding her. 'Who's going to keep us together? It seems there is only me; and I have to make sure that what money we do have isn't wasted on buying sweets and suchlike.'

Her mother had become unexpectedly reflective while Julia was speaking. Now she returned her daughter's gaze. 'All it might take is a pennyworth of sweets to help a child over this terrible sense of upheaval she has found herself thrown into,' she replied in a quiet voice. 'Don't you think it worth that one small thing to help her over it, Julia?'

To that Julia had no answer except to realize that her mother in her quiet way was right. She felt suddenly subdued. Even so, they couldn't continue in this way for long, lurching from one day to another with no notion of where they were going. A decision had to be made and she knew it would fall to her to make it. But to seem to be taking charge could cause more upsets and disruptions and even animosity than it was worth. Her head had begun to brim with ideas but she thought it might be best to let a few days elapse before putting them forward. And this time it was important not to allow emotions to get in the way; she must make it seem as if she was seeking advice from everyone rather than dictating to them.

'Well, that wasn't too bad a meal, was it?' Julia said, trying to buck up everyone's spirits as she and Virginia cleared away the empty dinner plates. Sausages, mashed potatoes and baked beans – something her mother would never have dreamed of having for dinner once upon a time; something she would have considered more suitable for Mrs Granby, Mary and the other servants.

'It was so oily,' she'd complained. 'I'm sure it is going to disagree when I get to bed. I shall be up all night.'

'Perhaps if you think of something else, Mummy,' Julia suggested. 'Perhaps clear the rest of the table, it might help you feel better.'

Instead her mother said, 'I think I'll go to bed and attempt to find some sleep while I'm able. It's quite bad enough with the smell of cooking drifting into the living room from that kitchen. It's enough to turn a body's stomach before the meal's ever eaten. It lingers even in the bedrooms. I never dreamed that cooking smells could linger so.'

There were many things Victoria had never dreamed of, Julia found herself thinking; cooking and washing up afterwards to name but two. Most likely it had never before occurred to her to imagine the work involved in preparing meals, and in washing and stacking away the dishes afterwards.

Even now her daughters did the cooking and housework, the washing, ironing and bed-making, with Julia doing the shopping. Eventually though Victoria was going to have to turn a hand and do something, if only to keep herself from fretting. So far all she'd done had been a little dusting and some ironing, which she soon said made her back ache; she pronounced herself too old for this sort of thing. Julia refused to accept this; she'd seen women around here far older than her mother on their hands and knees cleaning doorsteps!

The trouble was that so far housework had usually led to squabbles about who should do this and who should do that. James stayed

79

quietly in his room while this was going on, apparently believing that, as the only male in the family, housework was not his responsibility. Young Virginia was willing enough to turn her hand to anything but Stephanie saw herself as being put upon and often failed to do her fair share of chores, leaving more for her sister to do. Virginia naturally resented this and quarrels would break out. To save their mother being harassed by it all, Julia frequently found herself doing most of the work while her sisters sat apart from each other, petulant and hostile.

The time had come for a family gathering. She had to make them all see that this was their life from now on and they must all pull their weight. What she had to say would stun them but first she must prepare her mother before springing this new shock on the family.

She found her opportunity a day or two later. 'I know this has all been hard, Mummy,' she said, 'but it will get better, I promise.'

Her mother looked unconvinced. 'I doubt I shall ever get used to this. I'm not as young as I once was and I feel so tired all the time.'

We're all tired, Julia wanted to say, but held her tongue.

'Nor do I think I can stand much more of this bickering,' Victoria continued. 'There was never a cross word in our old home. But here...'

This was Julia's chance. 'We need to have a family chat, all together.'

She saw her mother watching her hopefully. More and more, she realized, Victoria was look- ing to her for guidance, expecting her to take charge, trusting her to make all the right decisions. And if a decision turned out to be wrong, she would be the one to be instantly blamed; no one would stop to weigh against it all the good decisions she had made. The thought brought a brief feeling of resentment, causing her to say a little too decisively, 'Tomorrow morning then.'

Tomorrow was Sunday; nine days since they'd left the comfort of their old home, hardly a fortnight since suffering the sudden loss of their father. What was she expecting of this family? How could she think they could knuckle down to this new, strange life after such a grievous shock?

'Will you tell them then?' her mother was saying, with such timidity that Julia felt for her.

As the remaining parent of this family Victoria should have been taking up the reins herself but was only too grateful to hand them over to one of her children. It wasn't her fault; she couldn't help being what she was.

'Yes, I'll tell them,' Julia said gently and patted her mother's arm in an effort to give solace.

'This is silly!' Stephanie glared at Julia across the table. 'You can't expect us to go looking for work. None of us has ever had to work.'

'You will now,' Julia said harshly.

'What do you mean, I will now?' Stephanie snapped back. 'You mean I'm to turn into some menial? We once used to pay staff to do the sort of jobs you're suggesting.'

'Once, yes,' Julia reminded, trying to keep her

temper while her mother, James and Virginia looked on, all three seeing Stephanie as their spokeswoman. 'We've no money now for staff. We're going to have to go out ourselves to earn money, all of us. And as none of us has any skills, yes, we will have to knuckle down as best we can and do menial jobs, as you call them. How else are we going to survive?'

'You don't mean Mother as well?' Stephanie's question was meant sarcastically, but their mother gasped.

'Oh, darling, I couldn't!'

'Of course you couldn't,' Julia soothed, glaring at her insensitive sister. 'I'm talking about the rest of us.'

'Not Virginia, dear, she is just a child, hardly out of school.' Her mother's arm went about the girl's shoulders in a gesture of protection. 'In better times she would be going on to a college for young ladies, just as you and Stephanie did. It's too bad! I never dreamed we would all come down to this.'

Julia held her ground 'Lots of youngsters leave school at thirteen or fourteen to start work, Mummy. It won't kill her. It might even do her good.'

'That's if any of us can find work,' Stephanie put in sourly. 'With unemployment growing again, how do you think we can find jobs with no idea what to do?'

'We'll have to keep looking until we find something,' Julia said firmly. 'We've got to bring in money somehow. What little we have in savings isn't going to go far.'

'I don't want to have to go out and work,' Virginia bleated. 'I'll be so frightened. I won't know anyone and I've never been on my own.'

'You'll be with other people, maybe girls your own age. You were with other girls your own age at school.'

'But that was school...'

'And what about me?' interrupted James angrily. 'Dragged out of my private school, any chance of going on to university dashed, thrust out into the world unprepared and unqualified when I might have done well. I hope you don't expect me to start wielding a pick and shovel.'

Julia bit back a sharp retort to the sarcasm. 'There are openings for clerks in banks and businesses for boys like you.'

'Start at the bottom, you mean?'

'Everyone starts at the bottom.'

'If I'd been able to go on to university, I'd have had a good start.'

Julia made a huge effort to remain calm. She didn't want this to descend into a slanging match. 'You're clever,' she said evenly. 'Starting at the bottom will give you good grounding for climbing the ladder to promotion.'

She saw a surly tightening of his lips. 'If you think I'm going to...' he began, but Virginia broke in, leaping up from the table, her thoughts getting the better of her.

'And what about this place?' she began, flinging her arms wide. 'Living here – it's an awful, horrible place!'

'It's clean and it's respectable,' Julia said sharply, resisting an urge to tell her that a child her age should have no say in these matters. But she understood how Virginia felt. 'It could be worse,' she could only say lamely.

'Nothing could be worse than this!' Virginia was very near to tears. 'Like the rest of this area, it's awful and the people are awful. Everywhere is dirty and grubby and the people are dirty and grubby.'

'At least they work, those who have jobs, to keep themselves out of poverty,' Julia said, trying not to raise her voice, 'which is more than any of us have ever done. But now that's just what we *have* got to do.'

Virginia retreated into silence but Stephanie turned savagely towards her older sister.

'And what about you, Julia – what work will *you* be doing?'

Julia gave her sister a long, cool stare. 'And who do you think is going to look after Mummy? She can't be left here on her own.'

'I could do that and you go out to work!' Stephanie blazed.

Julia turned a steady gaze on her. 'And you want to be the one to stay here and wash clothes and clean the place and cook the meals and do the shopping?' she challenged, pleased to see Stephanie go quiet.

She knew exactly what she was going to do. But now wasn't the time to tell them. In their present mood she feared her plan might provoke incredulity, even derision. Her glance strayed to the corner where the stack of material sat taking up space in the already cramped room. 'I'll pull my weight, don't worry,' she replied firmly. But for now all that must wait. The first thing was to get a little more money around them. Then she could start making plans.

The worst part of her family's reaction this morning hadn't been Stephanie's retorts, Virginia's small show of frustration or their mother's discomfort but the lost expression on her brother's unworldly face. The only boy in a family of women, he had been pulled out of the protection and security of school life into a world where it was everyone for himself. Here he would be expected to make his own way, stripped of the cushion of his parents' wealth and his father's business. Yet there was no escaping that this was to be his future. Well, Julia thought, hardening her heart, it was just too bad. That was the way things were now. She turned away from his bleak look.

James lay trying desperately to sleep. In the past he had always fallen asleep the second his head hit the pillow – unless, he remembered sadly, there had been secret tuck to share in the dorm with the others.

The thought of having to work for his living affected him deeply. His life had been turned upside down. Home had only ever been somewhere to spend school holidays; the start of a new term welcomed as the chance to return to his many friends. Now he was totally friendless.

At school he'd felt at ease with lads of his own age, his own sort, sharing confidences, enjoying sports and hobbies. When classes finished they would go fishing or into town to ogle girls and buy goodies. He was clever and as one of the older boys had held a position of prefect. He'd been looked up to, respected, had had a fine future ahead of him.

Then his father had died. Out of the blue he'd been torn from his friends and his comfortable life, back to a home and family he saw only four or five times a year. Now he was obliged to live with them permanently in a poky little flat Julia had bravely called clean and decent. And, even worse, he was now expected to go out to find work in some horrible mundane job, his dreams of a bright future in tatters.

Maybe it was the best Julia could find but, in James's opinion, the flat was situated in an area that was far from clean and decent. From everywhere came the smell of stale cooking and drains. The men, most of them out of work, were pasty-faced, wore old jackets and trousers, cloth caps and collarless shirts. Their wives wore none-too-clean pinafores over dreary skirts and blouses, their shoes shoddy, their coats shabby, while kids in grubby hand-me-down clothes hung about street corners. Now he was expected to go out and do the type of work they were used to doing and with no idea how to go about it and no one to tell him.

Lying awake he thought miserably of the university he would have gone on to from school. There he'd have made something of himself. What was there now for him? He couldn't blame Julia, she was trying to do her best, but he desperately needed to blame someone.

# Eight

July already. It had sounded so easy, saying they must all find work and start bringing in money. In practice it was proving nigh impossible.

First there had been a strong protest from her mother, protective of her youngest daughter, in support of Virginia.

'Julia, how can a child from a nice school and not yet fifteen go on her own to seek employment? She has no idea. You must go with her.'

None of us has any idea, Julia thought, but she consented to accompany Virginia in answer to the newspaper advertisement for a school leaver to fill the position of office junior in a small company.

'I'm scared,' Virginia whispered as they entered the building where several small companies apparently operated.

Julia pressed the girl's hand with her own. 'You'll be fine,' she whispered back, tapping firmly on the frosted-glass door to the company's reception office on the ground floor. 'I'll be with you.'

A young woman opened the door. 'Yes?' she enquired abruptly.

'We've come about the advert for an office junior,' Julia supplied.

'Come in.' The woman opened the door wider for them, indicating a row of seven chairs lining one wall. Four were occupied by young, anxious-faced girls around Virginia's age, the other three were vacant.

'Take a seat,' she told them. 'Mr Green, the recruiting manager, sees each candidate in turn, so you may have to wait some time. And no talking, please.'

The tone of cold efficiency alarmed even Julia and she glanced at Virginia as they sat down obediently. Virginia's face was pitiful.

'It's all right,' Julia whispered encouragingly and took hold of the cold, trembling hand. She would have given anything to be able to erase the past few weeks; for them not to have to be here.

To take her mind off Virginia's distress she turned to look at the other waiting girls, casting a small smile in their direction which all four ignored.

The door to an inner room opened suddenly, startling her. She felt Virginia jump. A rather drab, poorly dressed girl, looking hardly more than a child, came out, her expression a picture of forlorn hope well and truly dashed. Without looking at anyone, without even a thank you to the painfully efficient secretary now seated at her desk, she left by the frosted-glass door, closing it quietly behind her. The secretary, half hidden by an enormous, black typewriter, hadn't even looked up.

'Next!' she said, still without glancing up. 'Knock before you enter.'

The girl at the head of the row got to her feet and, walking hesitantly to the recruiting manager's door, knocked timidly.

'Come!' ordered a deep voice from within, muffled by the closed door.

Obediently the girl did as ordered, closing the door behind her. As if by some silent command, the next girl moved to the now vacated chair, the rest moving up accordingly. The secretary went on with whatever she was doing in the reception office, the quivering silence broken only by the occasional faint rustle of paper from her desk and, every now and again, a timid knock on the glass door to announce another applicant.

Julia smiled down at her sister encouragingly.

It was nearly an hour before Virginia's turn came. She looked up at Julia as the secretary muttered, 'Next!'

'You're coming in with me?' she pleaded.

'Just the young lady,' said the secretary.

'I'll be out here, waiting,' Julia encouraged. 'Don't worry, dear, it'll be over before you know it.'

She truly believed this. None of the other young applicants had taken long and none had come out looking very hopeful, so what chance did Virginia have, cosseted at home and at her private girls' school? The chances were that this fruitless exercise would be repeated over and over again until Virginia finally found a menial cleaning job, if she was lucky.

One thing in her favour though, Julia thought hopefully as her little sister disappeared into the great man's office, was that unlike any of the previous applicants, Virginia was wearing a good-quality skirt, blouse and jacket, a nice little hat, stockings and good shoes, purchased some while ago from West End department stores such as Peter Robinson's and Selfridges, in the days when they could afford to shop there.

Julia's mind returned to the now closed office door behind which her small sister was undergoing a trauma of interrogation. Her own insides were tightening up for her. But she had primed the girl very carefully.

'Tell him who you are. Speak up, the way you were taught at school. Remember, you are a lady. Don't dwell on the fact that you've lost your father and we have come down in the world. Don't apologize for where you live. Give him to understand that it is a respectable, comfortable, well-appointed flat. Above all, don't let him see we've hardly any money. Be courteous but hold your head up high, look him in the face. You have your pride, remember.'

Virginia had nodded and Julia could only trust that she'd remember to sit with a straight back and not hang her head or appear as nervous as Julia knew she felt. She prayed the girl would stand her ground and not show herself up. Julia had noticed the secretary glance up once or twice in Virginia's direction, her expression one of curiosity and guarded appraisal. Perhaps that was a good sign. Though, with so many more young hopefuls still arriving, Virginia's chances seemed to be dwindling.

Julia stood up as Virginia reappeared, already trying to read the girl's expression. To her relief it seemed composed, if a little dazed. 'How did it go?' she questioned as they emerged from the building on to Leadenhall Street, noisy with traffic at midday and sounding extra loud after the oppressive silence of the reception office.

'I don't really know,' Virginia answered in a tiny, distracted voice. 'I don't remember a lot about it.'

'What did he ask you?'

'I can't remember.'

Julia felt her patience wearing thin. 'You must remember some of the things.'

Virginia shrugged. 'It was all so muddled. I seemed to be in and out of there before I knew what was happening.'

'Try!'

Again Virginia shrugged. 'He said he'd let me know. They'll write to say if I've got the job. I think he said in about a week.'

'What else?' Julia had quickened her step towards the bus stop and home, and her sister was obliged to keep up with her. 'What questions did he ask?'

'He asked to see my school report,' Virginia answered breathlessly.

'Go on,' Julia urged.

'He said it was very good.'

'He did, did he?' Julia said, her heart lifting in new hope.

'He asked what school I went to,' Virginia supplied, warming at last to the subject. 'He seemed interested in that. I had to add up some figures. He said I'd got them right. He did say I spoke nicely. He asked me to write something and I remember he said I had a good hand. I can't think of anything else.'

It all sounded encouraging. Julia was beginning to feel that her sister might even get the position, but curbed the feeling, knowing how easily hope can turn to disappointment. She said nothing to Virginia of her hopes. The bus was coming and they both broke into a run and hurriedly boarded it. Julia's heart had quickened and not purely from hurrying to get on the vehicle.

Things weren't going so well for Stephanie or for James. He had been to three interviews so far and had heard nothing as yet.

'You need to be more assertive,' Julia told him. 'If I know you, you're behaving in front of them like a schoolboy who knows nothing of the world.'

'I don't,' he told her frankly, ruffled by her directness.

'Then *pretend* you do!'

'That's easy for you to say,' he retorted, becoming riled. 'You haven't gone hunting for work yourself yet. All you've done is sit back and tell us what we should be doing as if you were head of the family.'

Julia hadn't retaliated. It wasn't worth another family argument. She just hoped something would come up for him soon. There had been far too many arguments these past two weeks. Her mother, appearing frailer by the day, would stop her ears with her hands as soon as voices became raised, calling piteously for a little peace and quiet.

She wasn't adjusting well to her situation but nor were any of them.

The strain was starting to tell on them all and the money they'd brought with them was now dangerously low. They had had some luck selling their jewellery, though it had tugged at their heart strings to see it go. The proceeds had been put into a post office savings account.

As for her ideas for the material she'd brought here with her, so far she hadn't had the will or the expertise, she was coming to realize, to do anything with it. It still sat in one corner, a bone of contention with Stephanie.

'All I do is trip over it,' she complained continuously. 'The room's small enough without that clutter. Why did you want to bring it here in the first place, for God's sake?'

'You can only trip over it if you make a special point of going in that corner,' Julia retaliated.

'Well, it's still in the way,' Stephanie persisted. 'The table could go there if it weren't for that. It's no use to anyone and just takes up room. What on earth did you think you could do with it? Make dresses? You can't sew to save your life and anyway I'm not going to wear anything home-made.'

No, thought Julia, you'd prefer to spend our last pennies on dresses from expensive shops. But her sister had a point. Soon she'd have to do something about all those wild intentions of hers before they faded into thin air, though like James, she had little experience of competing in the world they now found themselves in.

James at least was trying. Stephanie, after two unsuccessful attempts to find a job, had apparently decided to give up.

'There just isn't anything,' she told Julia as she glared resentfully at her sister, 'unless you count serving behind grubby shop counters as decent work. I turned down both offers.'

Julia was shocked. 'You turned them down?' she echoed.

Their mother, sitting like one exhausted in the ancient armchair she'd claimed as her own, whispered, 'You can't expect a nicely brought up young lady to accept such dirty employment. It's bad enough being pushed out to work.'

'One awful man, a greengrocer,' Stephanie went on, encouraged, 'even had the cheek to say I had the wrong attitude for dealing with the public.'

'Anything would do for the time being,' Julia said, curbing a sudden impulse to remark that the man was probably right in his assessment of Stephanie. 'Later you could get something better. You'll just have to take whatever comes because you can't sit around all day moping. That money in the post office won't last for ever and if we don't start bringing something in soon, we could end up in a worse situation than we were before.'

'What do you mean, we?' Stephanie burst out petulantly, turning from the window to glare at her. 'I don't see *you* trying to earn money.'

'I have plans,' Julia began but Stephanie wasn't listening.

'It's all very well telling us what to do when all

you do yourself is sit around here looking after Mummy. Anyway, if I work behind a counter it will have to be in something like a boutique, or as a receptionist in a hairdressing salon. I'm pretty enough. I deserve better than handling dirty, smelly old vegetables or filling customers' bottles with vinegar or paraffin. No thanks!'

With that she bounced off into their bedroom to throw herself full length on the bed she shared with Julia, the other shared by her mother and Virginia. From there her angry voice floated back. 'I don't see anyone attacking James for not having a job yet, or Virginia for taking just a filing clerk's job.'

Julia smiled. Of course she wouldn't attack Virginia. She'd secured the filing clerk's vacancy after all. The pay wasn't all that good, even for a junior, but it was something. James wasn't allowing himself to be put down either. At this moment he was out searching for work, as he did every day. He'd had several opportunities but nothing so far had come of them.

Julia wanted to shout back, 'At least he's not giving up!' but held her tongue. There was no point in further upsetting her mother who sat with one hand to her brow.

But the petulant voice continued, 'And living here is like living in hell! The weather's so hot and I can't even have the window open because of the traffic noise!'

When there was no response from her sister she kept quiet, leaving Julia to sigh at the memory of the lovely peaceful road they'd had to move away from. The shared bedroom in the flat

95

overlooked Bethnal Green Road and was constantly invaded by noise. As well as cars and lorries, they could hear the occasional clip-clop of the few remaining horse-drawn vans and carts delivering coal, milk and bread, and the voices of people shopping. She understood Stephanie's frustration for she too was frustrated by it. She had always enjoyed shopping in busy streets, especially the West End, but having to endure the constant sounds of busy shoppers and street traders below one's own windows was maddening. Of course, she acknowledged, she was frequently one of them herself these days.

To get to the Bethnal Green Road shops meant going down the narrow alleyway beside the haberdasher's shop underneath their flat. The alley was usually cluttered with cardboard boxes and other rubbish from the second-hand shop on the other side of it. She hated that dingy alleyway as much as she did having to pass the first shop before the main road, also dark and dingy, with windows that looked as if they hadn't been washed for years.

A musty odour issued from its doorway, the interior so dark against the outside daylight that, if she did glance in, she could see nothing but the dim shapes of one or two people seemingly in deep conversation. She'd never seen anyone who looked as if they might be a 'real' customer enter or leave. What did the shop sell? The only merchandise displayed in the two small, grubby windows consisted of dated, cheap and showy jewellery and a few items of clothing that appeared to be stage costumes; nothing to attract an ordinary shopper's gaze. She'd never yet set eyes on the owner nor wanted to. In fact the place gave her the shudders as she hurried by.

Another two weeks passed. James at last found a job in a bank, with prospects of being promoted to a junior clerk if he did well. Julia would have rejoiced if Stephanie had been as successful. But Stephanie continued to linger about the flat moaning that everything she'd been offered was too lowly to accept and that Julia had no right to complain when she had done nothing herself to find employment.

Most of her time seemed to be spent lolling on the bed she shared with Julia, reading love stories in cheap books and magazines which Julia knew her mother was paying for from the little she still had left of her own money.

'You shouldn't indulge her,' Julia finally told Victoria one Monday morning after she'd noticed a couple of coins being furtively passed from mother to daughter.

Victoria shrugged. 'That's what mothers are for, dear, to make their children feel loved and indulged every once in a while.'

Julia smile tolerantly. 'Mothers are meant to guide their children not give way to them.'

'It's hard on her.'

'It's hard on all of us, but we've got to get used to it.' Any second she expected a query as to why she herself was doing nothing about helping towards the family income. Her mother had stayed silent so far, but Julia knew she was probably thinking along the same lines as Stephanie.

97

She knew they had a point. Soon she'd have to do something about the material she had salvaged before it became an even greater source of irritation to those trying to relax in one small room of an evening. James usually went to his own room, in search of solitude. Neither was their mother ever long out of bed, glad to retire and forget her circumstances, usually quickly followed by Virginia, eager to cuddle up to her.

Left alone, more often than not she and Stephanie ended up picking over the old sore of joblessness, needling each other in whispers until they too were glad of bed and, with backs to each other, sought the solace of sleep. It certainly wasn't the best of existences, leaving her constantly pining for the old days.

This morning, on her way to the baker's around the corner in Bethnal Green Road, she was still thinking of their life and all the problems it was presenting, trying to console herself that many were far worse off with this new wave of unemployment. At least for her family there was still some money left from their better days – if they went carefully.

Emerging from the alleyway, Julia as always quickened her pace past the shop downstairs but to her dismay she saw the door open and a young man emerge. Before she could look away he smiled at her and nodded.

'Good morning.'

Good manners demanded that she return the nod and she mumbled a response, immediately prompting him to step clear of the door. 'You're a member of the family who've recently moved into the top flat,' he stated.

His voice held no trace of the Cockney accent she had come to expect in this area. Instead he spoke very well. 'I've noticed you passing on several occasions. How are you finding it up there?'

There was no chance now to hurry on by. No matter how much she disliked his shop – for his she took it to be – she didn't want to appear rude.

'We're settling in,' she returned evasively, glad that her eyes and the top half of her face were pretty much hidden from him by the low-brimmed, mushroom-shaped hat bought last winter when life was sweeter. She was also suddenly conscious of the dress she was wearing – last summer's design. In voile, it felt uncomfortably flimsy before his gaze.

Now she wanted only to get away before he began asking questions she didn't wish to answer. But to her dismay he came forward, his hand outstretched.

'Welcome to the neighbourhood. I'm Simon Layzell.' It was the same name as the one above the shop; so he did own it.

'Pleased to meet you,' she responded negatively.

Obliged to take the offered hand, if only finger tips, she let her own fall quickly away. It would not do to get too familiar, yet what she saw in front of her was quite different from what she'd expected. This man was tall, slim and decently dressed, not at all the shabby person she'd imagined as owning the shop.

Reluctant to be drawn into any further conversation, she said as politely as she could, 'I have to hurry off,' adding by way of excuse, 'We're out of bread. My brother and sister had their breakfast and left only one slice and a topper for my mother, my other sister and myself.'

He frowned slightly. 'Five of you in that small flat...' he began but she interrupted him before he could ask where her father was. She wasn't prepared to air her business before a virtual stranger.

'I must go,' she said.

'Yes,' he apologized. 'I hope it won't be too long before we meet again.'

She moved off, embarrassed to find herself thinking how nice-looking he was, well-spoken and indeed well-mannered.

She was also aware that she hoped to see him again, though for business rather than personal reasons. It had occurred to her as they were talking that his shop did not appear to be doing all that well and, as she turned into Bethnal Green Road, now growing busy with early-morning workers, questions began to fill her head.

How long had he had the place? Did he own or rent it? With so few people ever in the shop as far as she could assess, did it actually pay its way? If not, had he ever considered closing it? In that case, it would make very good premises in which to start up some sort of business or warehouse. Her mind hovered around the pile of material cluttering up their living room. But could they afford whatever initial rent would be asked? And even then, could they keep up the payments? The next minute she was deriding herself for such thoughts. There was no way she would find money enough to buy or even rent such premises, run down or not.

Turning into the bakery, she fished in her purse for a couple of pennies to buy a small loaf, her mind only half on what she was doing.

# Nine

Virginia's eyes were shining as she came into the flat to throw her handbag and hat on to the sofa. She'd become a different girl from the one who a couple of months earlier had timidly entered Mr Green's office.

'Mr Green says I'm getting on really well,' she announced excitedly as she rushed into the kitchen to return with a cup of cold water from the single tap over the sink. 'Gosh, it's hot out!' She drained the cup in one gulp. 'Mr Green says that if I continue the way I'm going, he'll suggest promoting me to their post room.'

So far she was little more than a general dogsbody and tea girl. 'Mr Green says he'll speak to Mr Griffiths, our managing director about it.'

Plonking the empty cup on to the little dining table she turned back to her mother and two sisters, and went on excitedly, 'Mr Green says that if I continue to do well, I could be promoted to a proper department by the end of the year and given a rise.'

At last she paused for breath, allowing Julia a chance to get in a word. 'I'm so glad for you, Ginny,' she said, adopting the version of her name that Virginia's office friends apparently now used. 'We're all very proud of you.'

She gazed towards her mother and Stephanie for agreement, but Stephanie's lips had become a thin line and as their eyes met she turned and stalked off into the bedroom, closing the door with a sharp click to emphasize her feelings.

Their mother looked slightly taken aback by her daughter's apparent show of pique. 'Oh dear, that was really unwarranted. What is the matter with her? I would have thought she would be pleased for Virginia.'

'I know, Mummy,' Julia soothed, seeing Ginny's previously joyous expression change. 'She might feel a little resentful. You can't blame her.'

Stephanie still hadn't found a job. At least, she had found one three weeks ago, but had walked out after a few days, declaring it entirely unsuitable for a young lady and that she was being put upon. As far as Julia was concerned her excuse was totally unjustifiable with so many crying out for work, any work, to put bread on the table.

She had come home in a raging temper to bounce past her mother and Julia and on into the bedroom, her favourite place for sulking, saying as she went, 'I'm not a damn dogsbody for some prig of a boss who thinks he can say what he likes to me.'

'I thought you said it was a good job,' Julia said, following her in.

'Well, it turned out not to be,' was Stephanie's reply.

'Why?'

'Because I'm not going to be treated like a

dish rag, expected to wash up everyone's cups. I'm worth more than that. I thought I was going to be in charge of a counter.'

'Give it time,' Julia tried to reason, but there was no reasoning with Stephanie, even though she did her best to make her sister see how desperate many others were for a job of any kind, willing to do whatever was offered, even to cleaning drains, sweeping streets, clearing toilets.

'They *must* be desperate to do things like that!' Stephanie had huffed unsympathetically. 'I'm worth more than being expected to ruin my hands over a sink like some kitchen maid. I need to care for them and keep them smooth for when I get something really decent and genteel.' She'd lifted a hand to study it, delicately turning it this way and that. 'I expect my leaving will have its compensations, giving an opening for one of the *desperate* down-and-outs you spoke of,' she'd added airily.

There's no pleasing that girl, Julia had thought, but had kept it to herself. There was no point in causing yet another argument.

Pushing aside the memory, Julia went and gave her little sister a cuddle. 'Don't worry about her, Ginny. She's feeling a little bitter at not finding any work to suit her while you and James are obviously doing so well.'

'Then she should learn not to be so picky about the sort of work she *is* given!' Ginny said, sounding quite adult these days. She brightened. 'Anyway, James should be home soon. I'll come and help you to get tea ready for when he comes

104

in. I'm so very proud of my brother. Thank heaven at least two of us are bringing in money.'

The words were innocently said and probably aimed at her other sister, but Julia experienced a sudden stab of guilty conscience. She said nothing though. Virginia wasn't the vindictive kind and she was sure the comment was not intended as a criticism of her.

At the end of July Stephanie finally found herself a job she considered suitable – behind the cosmetic counter of Selfridges in Oxford Street. There was no end to her triumph. Maintaining that a pretty face, elegant appearance and return of her former confidence would go a long way towards helping her to secure the position, she'd dipped into her meagre savings, which Julia felt would have been better put towards her family's upkeep, for a fawn-coloured summer dress and hat for the interview, suede, Louis heel court shoes with clutch bag to match, and had her short hair Marcel waved.

To her delight she had been taken on, as a lowly assistant to start with, but with good money and the promise of promotion. She'd thrown herself wholeheartedly into the position, her only problem being the long hours of work.

'I've hardly had any time for myself,' she sighed, coming home to collapse into a chair after only two weeks. 'I never knew working could be so hard. And I feel so dowdy against others. My old dresses are out of fashion but there's so little left to buy more after contributing towards this family's upkeep.'

'Your upkeep too, remember?' Julia said and saw her sister pout. Stephanie had always put herself first. This had not mattered when the family had been well off. But now she had already got round their mother, pleading to borrow back a little of the money she'd contributed and being given it. Julia was exasperated with her mother for being so indulgent.

She'd now bought a couple of more fashionable dresses – admittedly, not as expensive as the previous outfit – and within two weeks had added a pair of glittery evening shoes, stockings and make-up. Victoria strongly disapproved of this last purchase but said nothing.

Fortunately James and Virginia were both giving up most of their wages, for Julia decided that while she herself was still at home it was best not to air her opinions to Stephanie. With her mother doing little but dwell in the past, hers was the role of cooking, shopping, washing, cleaning and running about for them all; some little compensation, she hoped, for not bringing in a wage.

Still on her mind was how to start making that horde of material work for her. Her remaining idea from all the discarded ones was taking shape – a long shot, needing careful planning and determination, along with a good deal of cheek, to make it work.

The dingy shop downstairs had held her attention for some time. She would pass it these days at a slower pace and over the past few weeks had made a point of getting to know the owner better. Surprisingly she'd found Simon Layzell a more likeable, intelligent young man than she had initially expected, despite his always looking slightly unkempt.

One Saturday morning, with the August sun shining straight into her face as she turned out of the alley, she saw him standing outside his shop door, his back to her, gazing towards the busy Bethnal Green Road. He didn't seem to be looking out for trade or expecting a delivery. His shoulders were slumped and there was a lonely air about him, as if he had no real interest in anything going on around him.

The click of her heels made him turn and as he saw her, a broad smile instantly transformed his glum expression.

'Hullo!' he exclaimed and then, noticing her ample bag, added heartily, 'Early-morning shopping then?'

'Our weekly shop,' she replied, and then, noticing a drawn look behind his sociable smile, added, 'How are you?' She saw the smile fade, saw him hesitate and the smile return – a little too bright to be genuine, she thought.

'Fine,' he said quickly, then again, 'Fine.'

'Good,' she said. That smile of his hadn't quite reached those blue-grey eyes, which held a guarded expression.

'I'm glad,' she added and started to walk on. But he held out a hand towards her, compelling her to pause. She gave him a questioning look.

'I'm sorry,' he began. 'The truth is, I do need to speak to you, urgently. I've been trying to summon up the courage for over a week now, ever since I realized I might not be carrying on this shop for very much longer.'

The news brought a wave of shock to Julia, followed by dismay; just the way it had been when long-standing neighbours in Sewardstone Road had moved away. She experienced the same vague sense of desertion; almost of betrayal. And yet she hardly knew this man, had spoken to him only in passing. She thought him pleasant enough but that was all. And there was also a sinking feeling of disappointment. She had taken it for granted that he'd be here for years.

'May I ask why you are giving it up?' Caught off guard she could think of nothing else to say.

His shoulders lifted briefly. 'I tried to make a go of it, but it just didn't come off. I gave it two years, but I suppose I'm in the wrong place for trying to entice theatre folk. Brick Lane's the area for this sort of trade, not here.'

'Then you should move to Brick Lane.' Why had she said that? He'd be even further away. She'd never see him again. Suddenly she wanted him to stay, and not only because her future could depend upon it.

He spoke rapidly. 'I can't afford to rent anywhere else. Every day I stay I'm losing money. On top of rent and overheads you have to buy in stock just to keep a turnaround but if you can't afford to buy much, you've nothing halfway decent to sell. When people see the same old stuff in the shop time after time they don't come back. All I'm doing is throwing good money after bad and it's time to call a halt. It's a shame. I had such high hopes.'

'But you can't just let it beat you!' Julia cried, seeing the vague ideas she'd had going down the drain. Yet, to her surprise, she now wanted him to stay for his own sake. 'What will you do?' she asked lamely.

'I don't know,' he replied. Then, more briskly, he added, 'But this isn't about me. I'm sorry to have gone on so. I wanted to warn you that the lease here is due to expire next year and the owner could very well put up the rent, not only on this shop but on the whole building. He owns it, so he can ask what he likes. And, of course, if his tenants can't afford to pay, they're out! No two ways about it.'

He gave her a wan smile. 'I'm sorry to be the bearer of rotten news but I thought you ought to know. As for the shop, another tenant might be able to meet the higher rent but not me. In truth I'd like to stay but what can I do if the shop just isn't paying?'

Julia was thinking fast. Suddenly this latest idea of hers didn't seem quite so implausible. Before she could stop herself, she'd blurted out, 'There might be a way for you to stay.' She saw him frown but before he could say anything, she added quickly, 'Let's go inside your shop where I can better explain.'

Still frowning, he gestured for her to go in ahead of him. The interior was dim and dingy and there was the musty smell she had noticed before. No wonder customers stayed away, she thought. She sat on a stool beside the untidy counter. It was strewn with a hotchpotch of gaudy trimmings, pieces of lace, flamboyant

109

buttons and costume jewellery: thick bracelets and heavy armlets, brooches made from cheap metal to resemble gold and silver and set with huge fake stones of all colours. From hooks hung a tangle of necklaces and dangling earrings made of coloured glass or clear glass cut to resemble diamonds.

He pushed some of it aside to make a space and, leaning his forearms on the surface, regarded her with interest. 'What did you mean, there's a way I could stay?' he said slowly.

'I'll try and explain,' she began, 'if you'll bear with me.'

Briefly she spoke of her father's death, avoiding too much detail about the financial distress it had caused to her previously well off family. 'It was left to me to seek some way out of the sudden poverty into which we'd been plunged,' she went on, hating the confession for it was still raw and deeply embarrassing. 'We couldn't keep our house and that's how we ended up living here.'

His blue-grey eyes hadn't wavered from her face while she'd been speaking, the expression in them full of sympathy.

Quickly Julia came to the point, explaining about the fine fabrics she had taken from her father's warehouse. 'I don't know if that was illegal or not but it was just lying in a corner, not wanted. It's heaped in our flat now, in everyone's way. I'm not sure what to do with it and everyone's complaining about it, especially my sister Stephanie, no matter how neatly I try to stack it.'

Now it was she who was talking nineteen to the dozen. 'It's quite valuable, fine silk mostly, from the Far East. I need to make it work for me and when you spoke about your shop I thought maybe, if you could keep this place going just a little longer, you could find room for it. I could pay you for storage and sell enough to buy in more stock of the same quality fine fabrics. I mean, real silk isn't to be sneezed at.'

She paused as a faint smile spread over his face at the unintentional pun, and found herself smiling with him. Suddenly they seemed to have become kindred spirits. But she needed to stay businesslike if she hoped to achieve her purpose and quickly resumed a more serious tone.

'What do you think?'

He paused for so long that her heart almost sank into her boots. Finally he spoke slowly. 'I think it could work though it does depend on how much material there is.' His face had become grave. 'And there's another thing – it takes money to start up a business, even if you've got enough stock to begin with.'

'But it's your shop. I thought you might be able to incorporate it into your business.'

'You mean take it off your hands and sell it for you? That's not a good proposition. Any shop owner would expect to get storage charges or else buy in at a low wholesale price so as to make a profit. That's how business is done – exactly as your own father did.'

Suddenly Julia felt like a silly little woman daring to face the harsh world of business with no experience of it. She felt like her mother,

111

who'd always hovered in the shadows, meek and apologetic, letting her husband make all the decisions for her.

Annoyed with herself, she spoke sharply. 'I'm quite aware of that!' she said. 'But I am desperate and so are you. I just thought our combined efforts might help keep this place going, if only for a while. I'm not a fool, Mr Layzell. All on my own I have so far managed to keep my family going when they might have ended up Lord knows where, and I've...' She broke off, reluctant to go into more detail about her family's downfall.

'We could have become destitute after my father died, but we didn't,' she continued. 'My brother and two sisters, who've never had to work before, have found work. We can now hold our heads up and one day I mean to start a business of my own. I know little about business but what I don't know I'll learn!'

'Learning costs money,' he remarked sceptically, but just as she thought he was about to turn her down, he straightened up and thumped the flat of his hand lightly on the cluttered counter. 'What the hell! Why not? I couldn't lose any more than I'm losing now. I'll give it a try, for the next couple of weeks at least.'

Julia could have hugged him. She'd had so many wild ideas for the material: making the stuff into dresses but she'd never been clever with a needle; selling it off bit by bit in Petticoat Lane but she hadn't the money for a stall licence; selling it to a stall-holder but he'd expect it for almost nothing. She had thought of

112

advertising it but buyers too would expect it for a song and the proceeds would hardly cover the cost of the advertisement. Even the cheapest storage was more than she could afford but the fabric couldn't stay in the flat much longer. This offer was a godsend.

'Do you mean it?' she gasped

His lips stretched into a wide grin. 'Of course I mean it.'

'But I never expected...' She broke off, lost for words.

He moved round the end of the counter and came to stand in front of her. 'I'll be honest with you, I'm thinking of myself as much as you. I could dress up the window with some of it once I've given the window...'

'...a good clean.' She laughed, suddenly at ease with him.

'You can do that,' he said flippantly. 'I'm no good at it. Cleaning is women's work.'

She made a face at that but let it pass. 'Women's work then,' she capitulated, now filled with excitement. 'And when they're bright and shiny—'

'I'll let you dress the window. You'll make a better job of it than I.'

'When?' she asked eagerly, still unable to believe this was happening.

'Right now, if you want.'

It was like a dream. 'I'll get my shopping first. My mother will worry if I'm late home. Then I'll come back here and we can start.'

He'd taken her breath away and as she hurried off her mind was racing, her thoughts very far

113

from the shopping. In the baker's she dropped coins all over the floor, in Home and Colonial she bought the wrong amount of margarine, nearly forgot to buy tea and almost left the milk on the counter and had to be called back for it. In the greengrocer's she forgot to pick up her purse and again had to be called back, and in the butcher's she couldn't think what she wanted, dithering for so long that the butcher cleared his throat loudly to alert her that there were others waiting to be served.

# Ten

'My dear, where have you been?' Her mother's words were panic-stricken as Julia came into the living room. 'You've been gone so long I thought something terrible must have happened to you.'

A stab of irritation tightened Julia's stomach as she took off her broad-brimmed straw hat and laid it on the dining table with studied care.

'What on earth could have happened?' she said, trying to keep her tone even. 'I've only been shopping.'

'But you might have been knocked down and I wouldn't have known.'

'If I'd been knocked down the police would have been here straight away and you'd have known soon enough.'

The sarcasm was lost on her mother. 'I've been here all on my own not knowing where you were. I didn't know what to do. Why were you so long?'

Julia's eyes strayed to the tiny oval clock on the mantelshelf, one she had picked up from a second-hand stall in Petticoat Lane market. 'I'm only twenty-five minutes later than I usually am.'

Twenty-five minutes! She hadn't realized she

115

had been talking with Simon Layzell all that time.

'But I wasn't to know, was I, dear? I was becoming so frightened. Where have you been all this time?'

Julia only just avoided an impatient tut and went to the pock-marked mirror above the clock to run her fingers through her short wavy hair. She'd have liked to retort that she did have a life of her own but that would only prompt an instant bout of weeping from her mother and she was tired of this dissolving into tears at the slightest provocation; of hearing the same old lament: 'If only your poor father were here. No one cares how I miss him, how lonely life is for me without him.'

To keep the peace, she said instead, 'I've been talking to someone.'

'Who?' came the response. 'We know no one around here.'

'*You* may not, Mummy – you've not set foot outside the door since we came here. But I see people when I'm out shopping and now and again I stop to pass the time of day with one or two of them.'

'So it doesn't matter that I'm left here on my own.' Her mother's voice shook with accusation.

'We should go out together now and again,' said Julia. 'This flat is so hot and stuffy in summer, I wonder you can stand it. You could do with some fresh air.'

Her mother shrank visibly from the invitation. 'I couldn't think of going out yet with your poor father so recently passed away. And I don't

116

really wish to know the people here. They're not our sort.'

Again Julia had to bite her tongue. What sort of people, she wondered, remembering the so-called friends who had shunned them in their trouble, were *our sort*? True, people round here didn't speak with the cultured, educated vowels of herself and her family; their Cockney accents were strong and vibrant. Maybe manners were not always quite what the Longfields had been used to, and there were some types one wouldn't want to get too close to. And, yes, there was the almost constant ringing of police car bells as officers sped to break up a fight or rescue some unwary who might have strayed down a side alley to be waylaid and robbed. But the women who shopped around the area were decent and law-abiding enough although, due to their straitened circumstances, they were not above sometimes taking advantage of a slightly suspect bargain.

Poor, scruffy and looked down upon by those who inhabited the better parts of London, Julia found them friendly and ready to help. She had found warm sympathy and support from two women a couple of months ago when she'd twisted her ankle stepping down from a kerb.

'Gawd, luv, yer nearly went fer a Burton then,' one had said, catching hold of her and gazing down at her ankle. 'Are yer 'urt?'

When she'd assured them she was all right, the other woman had added, 'You 'ave ter be so careful of these kerbs – they're all bleedin' un-even. Somfink ought ter be done abart 'em.'

'Just stand still fer a bit, luv, till it stops 'urtin',' said the first woman, who was still holding her steady. She smelled none too fresh to Julia, but her heart was obviously as bright and clean as kindness itself.

She had thanked them for their concern and laughed when the second woman had put a friendly hand on her arm and advised her, 'Best take a bit more water wiv it next time, dear!'

They had left her with a glowing feeling of warmth, yet here was her mother, a victim of her own imaginings, fearful and contemptuous of such people.

Victoria broke into her thoughts. 'Who were you speaking to for such a long time?'

'You wouldn't know them,' Julia said curtly, this time not bothering to hide her impatience. Her mother's attitude made it impossible for her to mention Simon Layzell so she headed for the kitchen, adding as compensation for her irritability, 'I'll make us a nice cup of tea.'

With excitement mounting in her breast as the days passed, she was many times on the verge of spilling her plans to everyone. But Mother's attitude to anything happening outside this closed family warned her that it would make far too awkward a situation to cope with at this present time. Best it remained her secret just a little while longer.

She had taken to slipping down to Simon's shop for an hour while her mother had her afternoon nap. An hour was hardly long enough to get much done and it did feel underhanded but, knowing her mother's temperament, she knew that her news would have to be broken gently, though how and when?

Even now she could visualize her mother's eyes filled with shock, her fingers to her lips in horror, could almost hear the words pouring out: 'Julia, my dear child, think! What would your poor father say if he knew what you are doing? What do you know of this man? Nothing. You must put a stop to it before it's too late.'

But it was already too late. She now trusted Simon. Her problem soon would be getting the bolts of material down two flights of stairs and into his shop, though no doubt everyone would be glad to see it go.

On Sunday, having first washed up the breakfast things, Julia went again to help Simon remove the last of his dusty display from the window before setting to work to clean the glass thoroughly. Having only Sundays free to work, it was taking longer than expected. But at least her mother had James and her two sisters there to distract her.

As she came back upstairs to help start dinner, her mother smiled contentedly at her but Stephanie's frowned.

'What've you been doing out there all morning?'

'Enjoying a bit of fresh air,' Julia lied easily. Time enough for them to know the truth once she began dragging that material downstairs. 'I'm surprised you haven't gone out too for an airing, being indoors working all week,' she added and saw her sister pout.

119

Stephanie had been in the bedroom most of the morning, no doubt reading her favourite fashion magazines and once again leaving Virginia to help her mother. James too was still in his room, probably also on his bed reading or gazing out of the window at the blue August sky, doing nothing in particular. But that was expected of most boys. Evening was his time, going out to enjoy himself with the new friends he'd made recently, to the pictures or to a dance, probably keen to meet a nice girl to take out. As a junior in a bank he now had a little money of his own in his pocket after handing over his portion of the housekeeping.

'It's such a gorgeous morning,' Julia went on.

'I'm going out this afternoon,' Virginia said. She, bless her, had already started preparing Sunday lunch, which people around here called dinner, making Julia feel selfish for having slipped off to help Simon.

'Not on your own, surely!' Her mother was immediately anxious.

'No, Mummy, with a friend from work,' Virginia replied patiently.

'What friend?' cried her mother and a look passed between Julia and her sister.

'Just a girl from work,' Virginia said evasively and went hastily back to cutting the cabbage while Julia peeled potatoes for baking around the small piece of pork.

As they washed up the dinner things together afterwards, Virginia whispered, 'Actually we're seeing a couple of boys whom we met during the week. There's nothing in it, they're just a couple

120

of boys, but don't tell Mummy.'

'As if I would,' Julia laughed, and they leaned towards each to hide their suppressed giggles.

As another week crept by Julia knew she would soon have to disclose her plans to the family. It was Friday. By next week everything would be up and running. Then she must face her mother, who was already asking questions.

'You're surely not going out again, Julia?' she appealed, letting her crocheting, now her favourite pastime, fall on to her lap as Julia put on a summer hat and picked up her handbag.

'Just for a walk,' Julia told her. 'I won't be long.'

'But you've been out nearly every morning this week. I can't see why you need to go out so often, dear.'

'I need to get some fresh air,' she said, hating the lie. 'It's such a lovely day.'

She and Simon now had the window ready for some of the silks to be tastefully draped. By next week the fabric would all have to be taken downstairs, and there was still the shop counter to be properly cleaned, some brass to be brightened up and the floor to be scrubbed. Together they had disposed of most of Simon's rubbish. The moment everything was up and running, she would tell the family, but not too soon – next week perhaps.

This morning she had washed up the breakfast dishes, swept and tidied the rooms while her mother sat crocheting, apparently not thinking to help. Julia had never condemned her for her thoughtlessness. She was after all still only recently bereaved and had been brought up to expect others to wait on her. And Julia acknowledged that at forty-three her mother was probably too old now to change.

Ginny sometimes grumbled when she was expected to do household chores after working all day but for the most part she was always ready to help. Stephanie, on the other hand, did as little as possible, protesting that housework spoiled her hands and damaged her nails, which would jeopardize her job. James had been ready to lend a hand but Julia knew their mother would have been horrified. In her eyes a man simply did not do housework!

Now Victoria regarded her daughter thoughtfully, her crocheting idle on her lap. 'How long do you think you are going to be, dear?'

Julia's heart began to race a little. 'I'm not really sure, but I'll be back as soon as I can.' She avoided her mother's gaze.

Victoria suddenly cast aside her crocheting. 'Do you know, dear, you are right,' she said. 'It is a lovely day and here I am sitting indoors in this dark flat day in and day out. Perhaps, if you don't mind, I can come with you. It's time I ventured out and became used to the area we are forced to live in. I could never go out on my own but with you I should feel safe.'

Her mother's words hit Julia as if she had been punched. Before she knew it she had cried out, *'No!'* Hastily she modified her voice as she fought for an excuse. 'Not today, Mumsy. I was thinking of going to Victoria Park and it's a tidy

122

walk from here. It might be too far for you. You'd get tired.'

'Not if we go by taxi.' Her mother's small face had lit up – the first time since losing her husband.

'We've no money for taxis, Mummy,' Julia said gently. 'And you wouldn't want to travel in a bus.'

The light died in her mother's eyes and she wanted to run and cuddle her as Victoria said, 'I expect you're right, dear. I feel safer inside. I don't like the people round here. So rough and uncouth, they frighten me. I hear them at night coming out of pubs, laughing and shouting and quarrelling.'

Julia surveyed her. She was like a little mouse, afraid of the world, hiding away behind a dark skirting-board. Would she ever change?

'I'll be home as quickly as I can,' she promised and hurried out of the room, through the kitchen and out on to the landing.

There she took a deep fortifying breath and immediately felt better.

Simon was waiting in his shop. It was looking so much brighter since she had got to work on it. The counter gleamed and sunshine now poured through a clean, uncluttered window. Soon it would display her lovely bright materials, tastefully draped, perhaps with a few of Simon's better brooches and trinkets carefully placed as extra decoration.

As Julia entered, his handsome features broke into a wide grin. 'There you are! I wondered if you'd decided not to come.'

123

'I was talking to my mother,' she said, explaining without going into too much detail what had transpired. The smile left his face.

'You're sure we're doing the right thing?'

'At this late stage, of course I'm sure,' she said hotly.

'But you still haven't told your mother, or any of your family.'

'I just don't want to provoke too many questions yet. Mother will only fret.'

She didn't add that her mother would be sure to disapprove strongly of her relationship with him. She didn't care what the others thought; it was her mother she worried about.

'I think they'll be only too glad to see the stuff gone. They've been going on about it cluttering up our room long enough but I didn't want to say anything until I felt sure of my ground – with you,' she added, instantly wishing she hadn't as she saw his brow knit in a puzzled frown. 'But we're wasting time talking,' she hurried on, 'and I'll have to be getting back soon. My mother worries...'

'Right,' he broke in and preceded her into the back room where a pile of what looked like discarded rubbish still lay – tangled ribbons and beads, tarnished costume jewellery, strings of fake pearls. He bent down and took up a handful. 'We can get this lot sorted out first. You tell me which needs dumping and which you think we might be able to keep.'

Julia felt a sudden pang of guilt as she detected a pathetic ring to his words. She was invading his territory, acting as if it were her own. She

124

hadn't given a thought to it before, but she was virtually trying to change his life and she had no right to do so. Then she reminded herself that he had been the one to offer the deal.

'Are you really ready to throw so much of it away?' she asked almost timidly. 'It was...it is... your livelihood.'

'Some livelihood,' he scoffed, calming her doubts. 'I thought I was on the right track when I opened this place but it seems I missed the point.'

He paused, a jumble of trinkets lying idle in his cupped hands. His face held a wistful expression, half rueful, half amused.

'Over the past two years I told myself so many times that I was being thoroughly silly trying to make a go of this place but I refused to be beaten. I kept hoping that the next six months would see me doing better but it wasn't to be. And there I was, thinking I knew it all.'

He let the handful of trinkets drop back on to the pile, and then with the toe of his shoe began idly sifting through it.

'I came out of the forces, spent two years at university, gained a degree in art but found there's no call for it, no jobs. No jobs anywhere. My family were deeply disappointed, those two years all wasted as they saw it. My father's an optician. I'm an only child and my parents had set their hearts on my following in his footsteps. When I didn't, Father...well, I wouldn't say he disowned me but he didn't try to stop me when I said I was leaving home to sort out my own destiny. They never write, and nor do I. It hurts

125

sometimes, but then I suppose I must have hurt them. Well...'

He sighed and ceased stirring the useless heap of merchandise with his foot. 'It's all water under the bridge. But I would like to have made a go of the business, if only to prove I could do it without them. But as I said, it wasn't to be.' He paused for a second, brightened and looked at Julia. 'And then you came along.'

For a moment she continued gazing at him sympathetically, and then quickly recovered herself. 'Yes, well, let's call it a turning point, shall we?' She leaned down and in turn ran her fingers through one of the piles of stuff to cover the embarrassment his story had provoked. 'I think if we clean it up a bit much of this can be used as decoration. It might even sell.'

She stopped, realizing how patronizing she sounded, but Simon broke into a laugh. 'I'm sure it will.' He laughed again. 'If you say so,' he added easily.

'I do.' She laughed too, and the tension was gone. This was turning into a wonderful morning, the two of them working companionably side by side. Tomorrow, if all went well, her materials would be gracing his shop window.

# Eleven

Victoria's voice was shrill. 'Julia, what are you thinking of? You hardly know this man.'

Standing on the narrow landing outside their flat, the furthest she'd ever ventured outside in the three months since they had lived there, she called frantically down the flight of stairs. On the floor below, her neighbours were peeping out to see what all the noise was about.

It was only the second time in those three months that their elderly neighbours had ever been seen.The couple spent their time closeted away in their tiny flat, though Julia had occasionally passed a middle-aged woman, perhaps a daughter, going in with shopping but they had never spoken. Now the pair stood gazing through the crack of the door, peering at the young couple who were attempting to manoeuvre several tied together bolts of material round the bend of the stairs.

'Julia, think what you're doing!' Her mother's voice was still calling down the narrow stairwell.

Last night Julia had finally told her family of her plans and her partnership with Simon Layzell. Her news had had the same effect as if she'd hit them all with a sledgehammer. Mother

127

had instantly leaped to the conclusion that Julia was carrying on a clandestine romance with a disreputable young man whom she had been too ashamed to introduce.

Stephanie of course had had plenty to say about underhandedness and gross unfairness to Mummy. She could talk! Julia thought. She was forever doing just as she pleased without a second thought as to how her mother felt.

James had also shown his disapproval, glaring stony-faced at her. For all his youth he saw himself as the man of the house now, especially since he had recently been given a promotion by the bank. In fact, it had occurred to Julia that he was beginning to behave a little like his father. It was a shame, she thought sadly, for she loved her young brother and the looks he'd given her last night had hurt her much more than Stephanie's contempt.

Virginia had tried to lighten the atmosphere by remarking cheerfully that at least they would see the back of the clutter in the corner. However, the others were more concerned about this suspicious young man with whom Julia had joined forces; a man about whom they knew nothing.

'Carrying on like you've been doing, it's disgusting!' Stephanie had huffed. 'How do we know what you both have been up to?

'We've been up to nothing, thank you!' she'd shot back. 'Unless you see doing business as being up to something.'

'*Business*, huh!' had been her terse retort.

James stayed silent but his disapproving expression spoke volumes.

Only Ginny supported her, saying quietly, 'Well, I think it's exciting.'

To which her mother replied sharply, 'You know nothing about these things, Virginia! There's something here that isn't as it should be and I am terribly upset and disappointed by your behaviour, Julia. I cannot believe that you have kept us in the dark about what has been going on, saying nothing to me, your own mother.'

And so it had continued. Finally, at the end of her tether, Julia had shouted at them that nothing untoward had been *going on*, as they put it. She tried to explain that she had been endeavouring to start up a business, for their benefit as much as for herself, to help them all out of this miserable situation into which they'd been plunged.

And at last they had fallen silent; a silence that seemed to fill the room until eventually Julia left them to go early to bed. Later, when the others came to bed, there had been none of the usual chorus of goodnights except for Ginny who whispered, 'Goodnight, Julia,' only to receive a quiet command of 'Go to sleep!' from her mother, whose bed she shared.

This morning, after Ginny and Stephanie had gone to work, and before their mother had got up, Julia and her brother were alone in the kitchen as she served his breakfast.

'Sis,' he said, buttering his toast, 'this person, how old is he?'

She paused in the act of pouring James's tea for him. *'This person?'*

'All right, the man you've been seeing.' James

129

kept his gaze on his plate. 'I know he manages that shop downstairs but I've never seen him. None of us have. We know nothing about him, but from the state of the place as I pass on my way to work, he doesn't seem the sort of person for you.'

'Then you don't know him,' she snapped, resuming pouring his tea. 'And I'm not *seeing* him in that sense. I told you, this is a business deal.'

'It's just that I'm concerned for you.'

Julia suppressed an angry retort. A boy not yet seventeen, behaving as if he were twenty-seven; how dare he take it upon himself to lecture her, giving himself airs and graces because he worked in a bank – how dare he!

'I'm not prepared to talk about it,' she said as evenly as she could, but was then unable to resist trying to present her side of the situation. 'I wish you'd give me credit for knowing what I'm doing. I'm not having an affair. This is purely business and at last I can pull my weight. It was I who approached him to ask if there was a chance he could find a small corner of his shop to store that material for us and it went on from there.'

Briefly she told him how things had begun to develop. 'It's no more than pure business and I won't have everyone reading anything into it other than that. We've discussed it and it might even develop into a good business.'

This was all she was prepared to divulge, and she ended the discussion by saying firmly, 'And now you'd best hurry off or you'll be late
130

for work.'

James finished his cup of tea and got up from the tiny kitchen table, dabbing his lips on the paper napkin she'd provided for him. He gave her a searching look. 'Be careful, Julia,' he said. 'You're my sister and I care what happens to you. You've done such a lot for all of us, kept us together. I don't want to see you done down by some unscrupulous business deal.'

For a second Julia found herself seeing another side to the brother she'd been judging so harshly lately. He was still the good-natured young boy she'd always been fond of and he genuinely had her well-being at heart.

'I know what I'm doing,' she offered in a sweeter tone. He was still looking at her.

'I hope so. But can I say that if things don't work out the way you hope, remember I'm here and I won't let anything bad happen. I don't know too much about business but being in a bank may count for something.'

A smile lit up his young face, eradicating any sign of pomposity. 'Now I must go or they'll have my hide!' he laughed playfully.

It was approaching nine thirty before her mother appeared from the bedroom to sit morosely by the living room window, staring stolidly out, not speaking except to decline breakfast.

'I couldn't eat,' was all she said.

'Then I'd best wash up and go downstairs,' Julia told her brusquely, to be met with silence. With a sigh she put on a jacket and went out, saying, 'I'll be back in a tick. I thought I'd bring

131

Mr Simon Layzell back with me. You remember, Mother, he's the owner of the shop I'll be doing business with. Then you can make your own judgement about him.'

With no reply forthcoming she had let herself out, returning moments later with Simon. But Victoria had retreated to the bedroom and locked the door. No amount of calling had enticed her out, so that Julia had been compelled to plead illness rather lamely on her mother's behalf.

It was only as they bore the last of the bulky material down the stairs that Victoria had seen fit to emerge from the bedroom into the hallway to lean over the banisters and call down the narrow stairwell after her daughter like a fishwife, for all to hear their business.

Filled with anger, Julia vowed in that moment that she would make a go of this venture if it killed her.

Already it was late autumn, with many a frosty, all-enveloping pea-souper making any movement about London difficult. Yet to Julia's delight business was going well, money was coming in, the theatre folk beginning to realize that despite being slightly off the beaten track, here was a shop worth visiting.

Julia had found a flair for window dressing and a way of using Simon's old, scrubbed up stock to decorate and add even more charm to her tasteful arrangements. Another added bonus was finding a skilled dressmaker.

Betty Lewis was about thirty, a widow whose husband had been killed in 1917. She, like

132

thousands of other women who'd lost their men to the war, had been desperately searching for work for months. A meagre pension, supplemented by what she could earn from bits of sewing for neighbours as poor as herself, hardly kept her in food, much less paid the rent. She'd leaped at this chance of work even though Simon could offer only a small wage.

'I only hope she can do all she says she can,' Julia had said when he had announced he had taken her on as a help to Julia.

Her heart had been in her mouth as she watched Betty cut a couple of yards of her precious beige Chinese silk – today's fashions being narrow and skimpy – before she could order her to use something less expensive for the trial garment. But she needn't have panicked. The high-class finish had her gasping in delight.

Betty was now proving a real treasure. Without her Julia wouldn't have known where to start, for she herself had no skill as a dressmaker. What she did have was a different, recently discovered skill – how to sell.

'I feel terribly embarrassed,' she said to Simon. 'We're paying her far too little for such quality work.'

'We can't afford more at this moment,' he told her. 'It's early days, and we need to keep our costs down until we're more certain of ourselves.'

He had done some advertising and people were starting to trickle in to have a look at the few beautiful garments that had begun to grace the two small windows alongside the tastefully draped luscious silks from the far side of the world. By the end of October there were even one or two people making purchases.

Most of the customers though were still theatrical people. 'Well, they would be,' Simon reminded her when, vaguely dissatisfied, she'd remarked that she thought they should by now be attracting a wider class of clientele from the outset. 'Most still come for the sort of stuff I've always sold.'

And then, noticing her ill-disguised anxiety, he'd continued encouragingly, 'But you notice they're buying for themselves personally, not just for the stage. And that's good,' he'd added on such a whimsical note that she'd laughed. He had a way of making her laugh at the oddest times with some quite simple remark.

On that occasion, and for no sure reason, she had suddenly thought of Chester, the man she'd been so in love with yet who had never in his life said anything amusing, or not to her. It had set her wondering how life with him would have turned out. As Chester's wife she would no doubt have been very much a lady of studied poise and cool composure, whereas these days she was rapidly becoming a girl who could laugh loudly and spontaneously without fear of attracting haughty stares.

'Of course it's good!' she'd quipped lightly and received a conspiratorial wink.

But news of his shop was beginning to spread more by word of mouth than any advertising. By late November Julia realized that it would only be a matter of months before her initial stock was exhausted.

'I must buy in more material, the same good quality as that first lot, of course,' she stated, unwittingly taking charge. Sometimes she almost felt that this was her own business. However, he had a knack of reminding her that it was more of a partnership, and each needed to consult the other before rushing ahead, without needing to say it in so many words.

'Remember, your first lot didn't cost anything, Julia,' he pointed out.

'I know, but...' she began, pulled up sharp by his caution.

'We still have to keep an eye on the pennies for a while yet.'

'I know, but we don't want to let the standard we've set slip now.'

'We also need some more decent-quality accessories,' he persisted. 'But there's still rent and lighting and heating and so on to find.'

His words were a gentle reminder that they were now working together, sharing everything evenly, outgoings as well as profits. And at the moment the latter were still a long way from being a fortune.

'So let's have a bit of a committee meeting, eh?'

There was no laughter in his tone, no gentle banter, and his expression brought her up with a small shock.

'Simon, I didn't mean to...'

'Of course you didn't.'

This time it was said lightly, accompanied by a quiet, relaxed chuckle, but it left her aware of

135

another side to him. It also left her with a new respect for him; and something else, a feeling that for a second she was unable to name.

And then suddenly she recognized the feeling; the sudden flutter in the stomach, the rush of breath, taking her completely by surprise. She was falling in love with him.

Simon slowly refolded the letter he'd picked up from among the morning post of bills, invoices and circulars and made for the back room they now used as a cutting and sewing room for Betty Lewis.

At the table Julia was selecting the paper patterns ready to be cut from the new roll of green crêpe de Chine she'd bought in. He held out the letter to her and she looked enquiringly at him as she took it. 'What's this?'

'It's from the landlord telling me the lease on this place is due to expire six months from now. He says he doesn't wish to renew.'

'Six months!' Julia gave him her whole attention now. 'How long was the lease?'

'Ninety-nine years. I bought the place just over two years ago, thinking that when the lease expired it would naturally be extended, as many are.'

He fell silent, toying with the letter. He suddenly looked so very vulnerable that her heart went out to him. Her heart seemed to react to him in so many different ways these days. She often found herself watching him, noting the way he moved, listening with a different ear to the things he said, taking in all the small gestures

136

that made him what he was.

He seemed for the most part unaware of her attention though every now and again she would see him looking at her, and then looking quickly away on catching her eye.

'What will you do?' she asked. It was all she could think of to say, making him smile at her naivety – a smile that again touched her heart.

'Just have to find somewhere else.'

'Can we afford to?' Julia realized she had automatically taken it for granted that she was being included in his plans. What if this turned out to be the end of a wonderful episode after all? She waited anxiously for his response.

'We're going to have to,' he said slowly. 'It all depends on how the profits go in the next six months. One thing's certain, we mustn't say too much to anyone. If they realize the place is up for sale or changing hands, they'll stay away. People always do. So we must watch what we say.'

The word 'we'! She almost threw her arms around him but refrained. There were more important things to deal with now than her feelings.

'Then we'll have to concentrate on even better profits,' she declared forcefully to allay the silly impulse she'd had. 'We should start by doing a lot more direct advertising.'

'We do that now,' he reminded her.

'I mean physical advertising, modelling, showing what the garments look like on real people. We need to actually *demonstrate* them to customers and have a proper showroom.'

'That will cost...' he began, but Julia already

137

had the bit between her teeth.

'It needn't be anything too elaborate or expensive. We'll need a model. I can't do it because I'd have to run the show – and besides I'd be too embarrassed. But my sister Ginny might like to try. She's so slim and beautiful. She'd make a perfect model. She'd love something like that, I'm sure. I'll ask her.'

'Steady, love!' Simon put his hand on her arm to stop the headlong rush of words.

For a long moment their eyes met and held. Slowly his other hand reached out to rest on her other arm. Then, before she could take a breath, he had drawn her to him to kiss her full on the mouth.

There the two of them stood, in full view of a surprised Betty Lewis who was busily working on an exclusive-looking silk day dress. Her discreet cough made them step hastily away from each other. But she had already returned to her interrupted task of pinning sections of a paper pattern to the double layer of crêpe, de Chine for all the world as if she were the only one in the room.

# Twelve

Five weeks elapsed and Simon made no further move towards her, leaving Julia unsure where she stood with him. It wasn't that he was brusque or stand-offish or even taciturn with her. If anything he seemed vaguely embarrassed, taking care to confine all discussion between them strictly to mundane matters. And all the while her whole being cried out to be held close, to be kissed by him again.

Sometimes it seemed to Julia almost as if that lovely moment of closeness between them had never happened; that she had dreamed it. But soon she had too much else on her mind to spend time fretting about Simon. As the expiry date of the lease drew closer the task of developing their business plans grew more urgent.

It had taken nearly a month to approach Ginny with her new plans. She was afraid she might turn down the idea, seeing it as another of her sister's wild schemes. In fact it seemed to her that the whole family had taken her business venture for granted. If they suspected there was more to her relationship with Simon than mere business, nevertheless they said no more. James and Stephanie were caught up in their own lives and work and Ginny too was now pretty well established in her job, making friends and socializing. Why would she want to change direction now?

Julia's approach was to emphasize how well Simon's business was going and their intention to expand. She thought it better not to mention the problem of the lease not being renewed at the end of April. There was no point in alarming anyone.

'I've been so lucky going in with him,' she said to Ginny late one night as they sat in the living room together. Ginny had just come in from an evening with friends, the other two were still out and their mother had gone to bed at ten as she usually did.

'The business is going really well,' she continued, 'and I'm so fortunate that I had to put so little into it other than the material. I still can't believe my luck. I'd never have found the money to go into business in the usual way and I'm so grateful to Mr Layzell for his generosity.'

Ginny was responding only half-heartedly to this enthusiasm, obviously anxious to return to reading her magazine.

'The thing is, Ginny, we're thinking about finding ourselves better premises where we can have a showroom. Of course, we will need to get someone to model my dresses and I was thinking, how would you like to be that model? I could pay you well because we're not doing too badly at all.'

Magazine forgotten, Virginia regarded her with shocked surprise. 'You want *me* to model for you? But I've got a job, and I don't really want to give that up.'

'You wouldn't need to. This would only be every now and again and it would put a little extra money in your purse.'

'I get decent money now. I've had that two-shilling rise this autumn and Mr Green says that as I'm doing so well, he'll try to give me another in the New Year. I can't see that I need another job as well. And it wouldn't leave me with all that much time to go out with my friends.'

Julia couldn't help being struck by how quickly her brother and sisters had accepted working for a living as normal. It wasn't so long ago that the mere idea of such a thing had been unthinkable. How different life was now for them. They had brought themselves up from the awful poverty that had all but overwhelmed them to this moderately comfortable life they now led. They were like new people; only their mother still left to lament her lot and pine for the husband who in life had hardly noticed her.

'Ginny,' she pleaded as her sister continued to look doubtful, 'it won't be every day, or even every week, just on the rare occasion. We won't be starting up for a few months yet and even then it would only be a few times a year. Later we'll have professional models. This business could go such a long way, so please say you'll step in and help.'

She wanted to add, 'Please help me as I helped all of *you*,' for where would they have been without her guidance, her energy, her plans? She had taken up the reins when her mother had not dared to do so, She had kept them all going. But she said none of this.

Virginia was beginning to look thoughtful, an encouraging sign. Julia let the minutes tick by in silence, watching her sister, allowing her to consider the offer. But eventually she couldn't keep silent any longer.

'Think how lovely you'd feel dressed in silks and satins, parading up and down in day dresses and evening dresses, all the height of fashion.'

Virginia's face changed. 'Parading?' she echoed. 'You mean walking up and down in front of people, strangers?' She gave an emphatic shake of her head. 'No, Julia, let Stephanie do it – she enjoys showing off. I don't.'

'Oh, Ginny...' Julia felt suddenly close to tears. All the months of worrying and striving and scrimping to keep the family going began to overwhelm her. 'I'd never ask her! It can only be you. You're the only one who can do it. Without you...'

She choked on her words as the tears overflowed. The next thing she knew, Virginia was hugging her, the magazine fallen to the floor.

'Julia, don't cry. I'll do it – for you. I know how you feel. I'll do it.'

Slowly Julia recovered herself and apologized for her foolishness.

Virginia sat back in her seat and grinned at her sister. 'Stephanie's going to be so jealous!' she said.

Stephanie was almost beside herself with indignation. 'Why? Why couldn't you have asked *me* first?' Giving her sister hardly time to reply, she plunged on, 'I know more about these things than she ever will. What is she? A little junior in some office! I deal all the time with clothes and cosmetics in a huge department store. I am often consulted by some really important customers and well thought of by the management.' She held up an angry hand as Julia opened her mouth to speak. 'I'm rubbing shoulders all the time with the wealthy and know how to behave with them, yet you chose her over me! What's so special about her?'

'I'm sorry, Stephanie,' Julia began but Stephanie was in no mood to hear apologies.

'You two have always been as thick as thieves,' she railed on. 'Don't think I don't know. You're always rowing with me, never with her. And what does an office junior, not even sixteen yet, know about how to display dresses before a discerning public? Well, all I can say is, don't come crying to me when she makes a mess of it!'

Running out of steam, Stephanie gave her sister a long, hard look and made for the bedroom, banging the door behind her. As she did so she heard their mother's gasp. Too angry even to burst into tears, she flung herself on the bed. If her mother should come in now to try to pacify her, she knew she'd yell at her, unable to stop herself. But no one came.

She lay on the bed straining her ears to the silence on the other side of the door. Were they whispering about her? What were they saying? Her mother should have taken her side but instead had sat looking from one to the other with

143

that usual pained expression whenever any of them didn't see eye to eye. At one time she'd been her favourite daughter. Her mother had bought her clothes, sometimes quietly supplementing her allowance, always there to listen to her when things hadn't gone quite right. But since they'd lived here it seemed to Stephanie that everything had changed. Julia was now her favourite, creeping around her, looking after her and the flat, taking charge, forcing everyone else out to work while she took it easy, earning nothing.

And all this talk about setting up a business, where had the money for that come from? Had their mother helped her secretly? Now this: Julia choosing Virginia over herself, and Mummy practically agreeing with it. It wasn't fair!

Stephanie's pretty features crumpled, her eyes filled with tears as she stared blindly up at the ceiling.

'I hate them!' she said next day to Rosie Gower, a work colleague. They had become friends. She and Rosie and a few other single girls went most Saturday nights to one of the many popular dance halls in the West End.

During the week they'd go to the pictures to collapse with laughter at Charlie Chaplin or Buster Keaton, or to squirm with longing at the dark and flashing eyes of Rudolph Valentino; lured back again and again to blush and giggle at the Latin Lover in *The Sheik*, or shrink in fear for him in *The Four Horsemen of the Apocalypse*.

144

Standing near to each other behind the cosmetics counter, one eye on their supervisor in case they appeared not to be paying enough attention to any early-morning customer who approached, they conversed in whispers, managing not to exchange glances while maintaining the fixed, beckoning smile demanded of the counter staff by the management.

Stephie, as she'd become known to her friends, spent most of this quieter time talking about her sisters while Rosie listened with rapt attention.

'You said modelling?' she hissed surreptitiously from the corner of her mouth. 'How can you expect a young girl of fifteen to model? I do agree with you, Stephie, you should have been asked first. I don't know what your sister must be thinking of.'

As more customers approached the counter throughout the morning, conversation was brought to an end, but Stephanie felt better for having got it all off her chest though it still rankled. Perhaps she might still turn things her way once Virginia showed herself up modelling dresses far too old for her.

By Saturday night some of her chagrin had faded and her thoughts turned to dancing. The dancehall was already loud with the chatter and laughter of young people as Stephanie, Rosie and two other friends entered. The band was blaring out a recent jazzy number, 'Margie', and the floor was a gyrating mass of couples doing the one-step.

Rosie led the way towards a line of girls who stood hopefully waiting to be asked to dance.

Within minutes two quite passable lads, apparently chums, appeared. The taller of the two approached Stephanie for a dance and his friend asked Rosie, to the disappointment of other hopefuls. Neither girl knew how to one-step properly but that hardly marred their triumph at being chosen. Stephanie's delight faded somewhat though when she discovered that her partner could talk of nothing but football. As the number ended she made her excuses and escap-ed to the cloakroom.

Leaning towards the mirror to apply another coat of rouge to her cheeks, Stephanie glanced sideways at Rosie's reflection. Like herself Rosie was rake thin, her sleeveless dress revealing slender arms as she smoothed the fine line of an eyebrow. With brassieres made to flatten rather than flatter, their short dance dresses fell straight down over their slim hips, with the skirt finishing just below the knees. Like her own, Rosie's hair was cut short at the back, graduating slightly longer towards the front and combed forward to a point over each carefully rouged cheekbone.

'What do you think of them?' Stephanie asked, referring to the boys.

Rosie grimaced. 'A bit juvenile, I thought.'

'I did too.' Stephanie laughed. 'We'll ditch them and find some a little more mature, shall we?'

'If we can.' Rosie laughed too.

'We can only try!' Stephanie observed, replacing her rouge in the beaded, green silk handbag that matched her taffeta dress. And, with heads

146

held high, the two friends strode purposefully from the cloakroom.

It had been a wonderful evening. They had found a couple of mature young men who had suggested going on to a nightclub, an invitation which the girls had readily accepted. The only bug in the salad was that both needed to be home by an acceptable hour, a request with which the young men, Robert and Algernon – Algy to his friends he'd said – had complied with amused smiles. To the girls' delight, the men had arranged to see them again the following Saturday at the dancehall.

'I don't see why we can't be out a little later next week,' Stephanie had said boldly as Robert and Algernon accompanied them to the number twenty-five bus that would drop her right outside her home.

Rosie had only yards to go to her home and as the bus drew away, Stephanie saw enviously that she was hanging on to Robert's arm as if for dear life. She vowed that she would do the same with Algy when she met him next Saturday. She would also tell her mother that she wouldn't be home until the early hours and that she was not to worry. She had no idea what her mother would say to that and nor did she care. If Julia could take the reins then so could she!

She would never have dreamed last year that a working life could turn out to be so good. She'd been a year younger then and under her parents' keen eyes, but since their move she'd torn herself away from those Victorian restrictions. And, she thought proudly, she'd done it by her own endeavours. She preened herself a little, thinking of the wonderful position she'd obtained at Selfridges, when all around her were long queues of the unemployed, practically begging for work.

There were jobs to be had but not for the ordinary and the unskilled. There was money to be had too if you knew where to look. Businesses were thriving yet the dole queues continued to lengthen, which was strange. If you ran a business you were laughing. Like Julia, she thought, fancying herself with her big ideas.

And all from that material she'd calmly helped herself to from her own father's warehouse. There'd been no guilty conscience, no grief at having lost him; she'd just grabbed what she could! Yes, that's where the money was, with those who helped themselves – like Julia.

# Thirteen

It was two weeks to Christmas. The time had flown by, taking Julia by surprise. She still hadn't got her modelling idea off the ground and now not much could be done until the festive season was over.

It was going to be a strange Christmas, she thought. In their previous life Christmas had been a formal, restrained occasion. The family would attend midnight mass, arising the next day to an exchange of Christmas presents prior to sitting down to an excellent traditional dinner prepared by Mrs Granby and served by Mary, the maid. Finally they would settle down to a quiet evening.

Julia recalled how as children they would be sent upstairs to play with their presents while their mother and father sat before a roaring fire. As they grew older they would join their parents for a while before going off to bed early. Knowing no better, they had taken it for granted that this was how Christmas was spent in most homes. It was only when Julia had begun courting Chester that life had taken on a new aspect of enjoyment.

This year her mother would probably spend the day remembering and audibly mourning her husband. And although, with three of them working and Julia herself bringing in a little money from her own endeavours, they were by no means destitute, Christmas dinner wouldn't be anywhere near as fine as once it had been. And nor would the company.

James was planning to spend most of the day with a friend who just happened to have an attractive sister, and might be eating at their house. Stephanie too had said that she would be going out in the afternoon and might not be home until the early hours. That left Julia, Ginny and their mother to spend the rest of the day together. It would be very different from last year, with the family apparently split apart.

Julia didn't mind the loss of Stephanie. There had been a sullen and strained atmosphere for weeks between her and her sisters, with Stephanie dropping hurtful remarks that left Ginny feeling uncomfortable.

'I only said I'd model for you to make you feel happier,' she said to Julia.

'If you don't want to do it, I'll understand,' Julia told her but Stephanie's attitude had made Ginny all the more determined.

'I do want to! Otherwise I'll have her putting on her airs and graces and looking down her nose at me as not being up to it. In truth I'm relieved that she won't be here for most of Christmas Day. I can do without her!'

Julia was inclined to agree. She was glad though that Ginny would be staying loyally at home for the whole day. On a whim she'd invited Simon to come for dinner. Now she wondered if that had been the right thing to do. Stephanie was sure to be awkward and she didn't relish her sniffing and huffing at the table and ignoring him. It was just as well Stephanie wouldn't be there the whole afternoon.

Simon had seemed reluctant at first to accept her invitation. 'I can hardly intrude on your family,' he'd argued. 'They wouldn't relish a stranger at their Christmas dinner.'

'You're not a stranger.'

'Not to you but I am to them, virtually. Better I don't come.'

'I'll be the best judge of that,' she had retorted. 'We're working partners and you'll be my guest.'

*'Working* partners,' he repeated, pulling a rueful face. 'I rather hoped we were more than that.'

Taken off guard, she laughed nervously. 'What's that supposed to mean?'

For once he didn't laugh with her. 'Maybe it means only what you want it to mean. If you don't know, Julia, I'd like to make it clearer.'

As she stood there he took hold of her and pulled her to him, his lips closing upon hers. If she'd wondered about that first kiss so many weeks earlier, she was left in no doubt now about his feelings. She had melted into his arms, the moments going on and on.

With the delicious aroma of Christmas cooking filling the little flat, Julia's insides were all a-flutter as she tried to remove the beautifully browned potatoes from the dish they'd been baked in.

She was in love. Yet beneath that wonderful sensation she was prey to tiny stabs of doubt. Was Simon in love with her, truly in love? He had to be, he was an honest man. Not like Chester who had purported to adore her, only to vanish when things had gone wrong for her and her family. Simon wouldn't play her false. He wouldn't lie to her. Yet this past year she'd come to know just how easily and quickly some things that appear so wonderful can turn bad. She had learned to be sceptical. Having been bitten once, she had grown wary, even hard, and she didn't want to be hard. She wanted to be soft and pliable and in love.

'Julia?' Her youngest sister's voice made her jump and turn.

Ginny was looking from her to the flat metal slice that lay idle in Julia's hand while the baked potatoes remained stuck to the surface of the baking tray.

'Standing there dreaming,' Ginny went on as she resumed straining cabbage water from its black pot on to the meat juices in the meat dish to make gravy. The two pieces of pork and beef were already on their warmed plates waiting to be carved. 'The potatoes will be cold before we know it. What are you dreaming about?'

'Nothing,' Julia said sharply and began almost viciously to free the adhered potatoes from the dish, piling them on to a plate to be popped back into the oven to keep warm. She still had to carve the meat and serve it on to each separate plate with the vegetables.

This would all be done in the kitchen and

152

brought to the little table in the living room. It wouldn't be like last Christmas, with the meat carved at a large family table covered with a variety of vegetables sitting in tureens. This year there was no maid to serve the soup course – there was no soup course. Nor were there any fine wines to be poured for them, one for each course. Today there were two bottles of cheap wine to accompany both the main course and the plum pudding Julia had made earlier in the year. And nor would there be any maid to clear away the dishes afterwards, to wash them up out of sight and out of mind. She and Ginny would do that between them.

But there was a threepenny box of Christmas crackers to add a festive air, especially if they had the courage to don the flimsy paper hats found inside each one, as Ginny and Simon did immediately.

Julia wondered if she'd have nerve enough to put hers on her head with Simon here and suddenly wished she hadn't invited him after all. Her heart sank as she glanced across at her mother and Stephanie, both sitting there looking so alike with their firmed lips and straight faces.

She should have known it was going to be an uneasy atmosphere. Her mother sat in silence over the dinner table, leaving her struggling to encourage conversation. She felt a simmering resentment towards her, against Stephanie too, making a great play of ignoring Simon. It hurt her when within a few minutes he took off his paper hat and laid it beside his plate. It was a most uncomfortable looking gesture even

153

though he smiled which made her feel even worse.

Simon was her friend, more than a friend, and Stephanie and their mother could think what they liked. She was more than relieved when soon after they'd eaten, Stephanie went out, leaving her and Ginny to clear away and wash up while their mother retired to the bedroom to rest.

Ginny had been a treasure, chatting away to Simon, asking about his shop and how it was going, laughing as she said she was looking forward to being a part-time model; treating him as more than a guest, as part of the family, putting him at ease enough to help with the washing up. But for Ginny Christmas would have been a dismal failure.

'I'm sorry about my mother and Stephanie,' Julia apologized as they went back downstairs, both of them, she felt, glad to be away.

He hadn't stayed long after the washing up. Her mother had risen from an oddly short nap, which made Julia suspect that she was trying to make a point, to sit in her chair and pick up her crocheting as if he were not there – and after he'd brought her a bottle of fine port too, to have after dinner.

Her mother's wintry smile as she accepted the gift had made Julia want to throttle her, but if Simon had been put out, he hadn't shown it. He had even thanked her for her hospitality as he left, giving the excuse of having to go on somewhere else.

It was a fib, Julia knew, and she felt embarrassed and humiliated. For two pins she would have shaken her mother.

'It's a shame you have to go, Simon,' she'd said incisively, adding, 'Would your friends mind if I came with you?'

His face had lit up. 'Of course not! It's a party, open house,' he'd lied easily.

So here she was, snuggled in a warm coat, scarf, hat and gloves, arm through his as they wandered leisurely without direction through the streets, dawdling contentedly despite the bite in the air and the threat of snow.

He brushed aside her apologies for her family's rudeness. 'Wait till you see my family,' he said lightly and gave her arm a warm and purposeful squeeze. It was a promise of something more permanent to their relationship and made Julia's heart glow as they strolled back the way they'd come.

No longer did she feel angered by her family's conduct. In the shop's dim back room, with just the glimmer of a street lamp filtering through the open connecting door, they sat side by side on his bed in the alcove. With its curtain drawn across they talked of the future, what to do when the lease finally expired, the need to find other premises, how she and her family would fare, where they would go.

'You'll still be nearby?' he questioned anxiously.

'Of course,' she said, needing to whisper in this cloistered space. 'We've a business to run. It's doing well and soon we can begin to afford something better, and for my family too.'

'Yes,' he said, letting conversation die away.

They fell silent, but it was a silence that was comfortable and warm. She felt his arm gently encircle her waist and she lifted her face to receive an equally gentle kiss – a kiss that became gradually more ardent, then urgent, and she let herself sink back beneath him in complete trust.

It had indeed been a strange Christmas, unusual but lovely, and life was going to be marvellous from now on. Simon had been gentle, tender, taking care of her, and her trust in him was total. Yet so far there had been no talk of engagement. Maybe it was because of the need to find other premises, but time was flying by and already it was February, the expiry date of the lease only two months away.

Each day the sense of urgency was growing. Together they scanned 'To Let' advertisements in newspapers and Business Premises boards in estate agency windows with growing dismay.

'Everything's far dearer than I thought it would be,' Julia said as they gazed in one window.

Simon squeezed her hand. 'We'll find something soon, don't worry. It took me ages to find the one I have now. And now I'm due to lose it. I suppose I've been spoiled by the low rent on this present one. Thinking back, I made a bad bargain there.'

'You probably saw it as a good one at the time,' she consoled and felt him squeeze her hand a fraction tighter.

'Perhaps you're right. Come to think of it, in a way it was a very good bargain, because if I hadn't taken it I might never have met you.'

She resisted the impulse to say that he might have met someone else. Instead she reached up and kissed his cheek before again growing serious. 'I know you'd have liked something nearer the West End, my darling, but the further west we go the more expensive it gets.'

Buoyed up by the success of their business lately, he had suggested looking for something near the West End theatres but it now seemed they'd have to be content with the cheaper Brick Lane area.

'It would have been nice though,' he said dreamily.

'I know, but we can't get too silly, darling,' she warned. 'Not yet. If we keep going as we are, in a year's time we might find something better, but for now we just need something a little larger than what we've got. We ought to be looking for something with a kitchen and decent living room and a bedroom.'

She stopped, seeing him grinning, and realized she'd been speaking as if they were planning to marry. She half expected him to allude to it but when he didn't, she hurried on, her gaze glued to the agent's window.

'Where you are now,' she continued, taking care to allude only to him, 'you have a back room with one chair and a table to eat off, which Betty now uses as a work bench, and that tiny alcove where you sleep, and I know you eat in there as well, sitting on the edge of the bed.'

The thought made her smile, despite the awkwardness of a moment ago. 'That's no way to live,' she continued. 'And we shall need enough room for some sort of a showroom for modelling garments and things.'

This time it felt safe to allude to them both for this was essentially a business partnership. But would there ever come a time when it would grow into something more? Yes, they had made love, careful, gentle love, and he had said he loved her, but he hadn't actually spoken of taking their relationship further, and she didn't want to push him to do so. Suddenly she was filled with doubt as to where all this was going.

'Julia, oh my dear, read this!' Victoria held the letter out to her daughter. 'It says the landlord is putting the rent up by another two shillings! For a place like this, how could he? There's not enough money coming in that we can afford to pay so much. And there's been no work done at all on the place since we came here. Everything is falling down around us!'

Everything wasn't exactly *falling down*, Julia thought. It was true that there was a broken roof tile, which meant that a bucket had to be placed in a corner of the kitchen to catch drips when it rained, and the very ancient and faded wallpaper was peeling off in one of the bedrooms from damp. The kitchen tap too was slowly furring up and becoming hard to turn on and off. But all this was nothing the landlord couldn't have dealt with had he a mind to do so. Julia thought of the nicer place they'd have once a new shop was found.

She took the letter, pretending to read it slowly to hide her excitement. But there was also a touch of guilt at having thought only of her quest these last few weeks. She hadn't informed her family that any day they'd learn of a huge week-ly rise in their rent or notice to quit if they didn't pay. Nor had she mentioned anything about imminent expiry of the lease on the shop.

She had certainly mentioned nothing about moving to other premises. It would have sent her mother into a panic, wrongly imagining herself deserted. Even a year after her husband's death Victoria was still badly affected by the shock and by the loss of the home she had known all her married life. Another upheaval might have been too much for her. Julia had seen no reason to worry her too soon.

A rent rise of two shillings a week for this place was exorbitant and unfair, but despite what her mother had said, they could now afford it with four people all bringing in money. But to Julia it was the principle of the thing. She just prayed that once they found somewhere nicer to live, her mother might stop comparing her life now to the one she'd once known.

She also needed to consider that wherever they moved her mother's new home would have to be practically on top of the shop so she wouldn't feel isolated. But in time all the family would depart, leaving her on her own. Stephanie was of an age for meeting someone, marrying and set-ting up home; James too, and Ginny, though not for some time yet of course. But that eventuality needed to be faced. For herself though she couldn't ever contemplate the day when she would leave her mother completely alone.

She made herself frown at the letter and as if on impulse screwed the demand into a ball. 'We're not having this! This place isn't worth another shilling extra, let alone two!'

'But we'll be thrown on to the street,' Victoria wailed. 'It will be like last time all over again. And where would we go? I couldn't bear...'

'There are plenty of places,' Julia broke in. 'Mummy, please trust me. It's going to be all right, you'll see.'

For the moment it was the best she could think of to say. She tried to sound encouraging but with little more than a month to go, she and Simon would have their work cut out to find suitable premises, for them and her family. She didn't dare tell them that as yet nothing had been found.

'I don't know what we're going to do,' she said to Simon after another fruitless search. 'We could all be homeless in a couple of weeks.' She could not admit it to him but panic was beginning to set in, making her feel sick whenever she thought about it, which was most of the time now as things became more urgent.

Simon held her in his arms as they stood in the rear of the shop after Betty had gone home. 'We'll be all right,' he said quietly, but there was an empty ring to his voice that betrayed his growing unease. So much for all those ambitions!

# Fourteen

Ginny was all excitement as she entered the flat. She had been to the West End with a couple of friends to see an early show at the pictures.

'Julia, I've just seen a shop to rent! The sign wasn't there when we went past in the afternoon but when we came back it was.'

She had been keeping a constant eye out for her sister since discovering that the ending of the lease on the shop was forcing Julia and Simon to look elsewhere. 'It could only have been put up while we were at the cinema.'

Julia glanced up casually from her book. She'd not long been home herself. She and Simon had been to the pictures too, but locally, to see William S. Hart in the new Western, *Travellin' On*. They had sat surrounded by shouts of encouragement from their fellow cinema goers, as well as hissing and booing of the villain and sighs of *'aah*!' at a love scene. The audience's participation always helped the film along with only the pianist's accompaniment to add emotion to a scene.

She'd developed a bit of a headache staring at the black and white screen. Simon had brought her home, saying goodnight with one ardent kiss to wish her better. She had taken a headache pill and was savouring sitting alone. James and

161

Stephanie wouldn't be in until late and her mother had already gone to bed, so she felt faintly irked by her sister's noisy entrance.

'There are lots of shops to rent up West,' she said absently, turning back to her book. 'Every one of them is well beyond our means.'

'But this one might be just what you've been looking for.'

'Ssh!' warned Julia as her sister's eager voice filled the room. 'You'll wake Mother.'

Ginny lowered her voice but maintained her eagerness. 'It does look quite run down but the sign said it's a really low rent and it's in the heart of things.'

Julia became attentive but sceptical. 'That could mean anything.'

'It was on the "To Let" sign,' Ginny said, taking off her hat and jacket to hang them on a peg on the living room door. 'It was dark but I'm sure I saw forty-four pounds a year. That's just over eighteen shillings a week!'

Julia had been up since six this morning, dismayed to see it raining. All night, unable to sleep, she'd tossed and turned, annoying Stephanie. By seven thirty, having taken a taxi due to the foul weather, she had found the premises, well run down as Ginny described. If the rental had been on the board, as Ginny insisted, teeming rain had now partially obliterated it. Jotting down the few details left on the placard, she hurried the short distance to the agent's with mounting excitement, careless now of the heavy rain.

162

By nine o'clock she'd been standing outside the agent's door for over half an hour waiting for it to open. Sheltering in the porch, huddled under her umbrella against the wet and the chilly March breeze, she was relieved to see someone arriving to unlock. Finding her standing there the man gave her a mildly curious look.

'Sorry to have kept you waiting, my dear,' he said as he inserted a key in the lock. Julia didn't acknowledge the apology.

'You've a shop for rent!' she burst out, making him flinch away from her a tiny fraction.

'Er...yes,' he replied hesitantly, 'we do have a few. But, er, yes, do come in,' he finished.

Recovering his wits he turned the key sharply and opened the door, ushering her inside to stand in the centre of the reception office while he busied himself switching on the lights against the overcast morning.

'Take a seat, my dear.' He indicated a chair in front of one of several desks as she stood uncertainly. 'I shall be right with you.'

Hurriedly taking off his hat, coat and scarf, he hung the coat and scarf over one of the arms of an umbrella stand, his bowler over another, and dropped his dripping umbrella into the receptacle below. That done, he came and sat behind the desk to face her, reached into one of the drawers to bring out a thick, black-bound brochure and began flicking through the pages.

'Shop premises for rent, you say. What area?'

'My sister saw it last night on her way to the cinema. It's in Mitchell Street, near to Leicester Square. The sign wasn't there when she went past earlier so it couldn't have been there long. I've been there this morning to take a look. My sister said it looked like eighteen shillings a week.'

'Ah!' Laying the brochure aside he began sifting through papers on his desk, pausing to glance significantly at the wall clock as a young woman entered. Quickly she dropped her umbrella in the stand before hanging up her hat and coat and, with a timid apology for her lateness, sitting at her desk, the typewriter almost obscuring her from sight.

He turned his attention back to Julia. 'I apologize for the interruption, my dear, but I know the one you refer to. The vacancy was only made known to us yesterday morning. The tenant it seems has apparently skipped off, leaving his landlord in the lurch, and the tenancy has been put into our hands. The landlord was not surprisingly very upset and has asked us to find another tenant as soon as possible, hence the low rent.'

'Then when may I view it?' Julia asked, barely giving him time to draw his next breath.

He gave her a condescending smile. 'It depends on what you intend doing with it, my dear,' he said, in the tone of a father speaking to a child, or a man addressing a feather-brained little woman. His attitude reminded her of her father and the way he would invariably speak to her mother. She felt herself bristle.

'I have a business,' she answered, lifting her head so that her neck appeared long and slender and dignified. 'I design gowns. The premises I

164

now have are proving too small and I need to expand. This one might be suitable and able to accommodate a modest-sized showroom, not too large.'

She saw interest steal into his expression, and a certain eager gleam. 'I do happen to have quite a few far better premises on my books if you wish to view any of those,' he said.

That would mean larger rental and obviously more money for him. Julia almost smirked. 'I would like to view this one,' she said firmly. Before it's snapped up by someone else, came the urgent thought. 'My business partner should be here too, but if I find it suitable I would like you to hang on until I get back with him, which would be within half an hour. Would that be possible?'

A bird in the hand, she thought, and it seemed he was of the same mind.

'I will be happy with that, Madam – Miss...?'

'Longfield,' she supplied.

'Miss Longfield. My name is Bennett. If you would care to have a closer look at the property before speaking to your partner,' he went on as she acknowledged his name, 'I would be happy to take you. If it is what you are looking for, I will most certainly wait until you consult your partner in order for him to take a look at it, if that is convenient to you.'

At Julia's acceptance he fumbled for the keys to the premises, at the same time instructing his assistant to hail a taxi. In no time at all, Julia was standing in the centre of the shop, its floor littered with the debris left by its previous occupier –

broken items of shop furniture, torn circulars, crumpled newspapers, ancient bills, along with lots of unidentifiable rubbish.

'I do apologize for the mess,' Bennett said, but Julia was more taken by the amount of space; it was twice as large as Simon's present premises.

The back room was promising too, with a kitchen area, storeroom and office, each sectioned off by a flimsy partition. Cleared, the space would make a perfect, if modest, showroom for her garments. The problem then would be, where would the kitchen, storeroom and office go?

He seemed to read her mind. 'There's also upstairs accommodation – two floors, which could be sublet or kept for your own use. It seems the landlord is stipulating a lock, stock and barrel deal for the whole building.'

Julia looked at him in surprise as he went on, 'They are good-sized rooms, I gather.' His eyes narrowed cunningly. 'Of course, they command a higher rent than that being asked for the shop, you understand; two self-contained flats, maybe in need of just a little repair and redecoration. They've only been vacant for a short while. You saw the "To Let" notices in the upper windows?'

She should have guessed there'd be a catch to it. In her excitement at finding out about the shop premises it hadn't occurred to her to glance up at the windows above. She felt she'd been duped, and was disappointed and angry. Why hadn't he mentioned this at the start, the cunning devil? No, it was a sprat to catch a mackerel and she'd been the gullible one. How could she and

166

Simon afford the rent being asked on such a place? It was bound to be exorbitant. But slowly anger began to give way to thoughtfulness.

She forced herself to remain impassive. 'So how much *is* he asking?'

He frowned, his lips pursed contemplatively before he finally announced a figure. 'Of course, it is only an estimate,' he said quickly as Julia in turn frowned and pursed her own lips. 'It might be possible to persuade my client to negotiate a slightly lower figure.'

'Even so, what worries me is why the whole building is vacant,' she said, now suspecting he might be hiding some structural problem.

He looked quite put out. 'Maybe it's the times we live in, with so much unemployment, so many unable to meet rising prices, the mounting number of evictions.'

So it could be that the previous tenants, unable to pay the rent asked by a grasping landlord grown greedy like her own landlord, had been thrown out to shift for themselves and find somewhere cheaper.

Julia was beginning to feel a pang of sympathy for the two families but Bennett's next words showed that this was unnecessary. 'I believe the first floor was used as a stockroom by the proprietor of the shop, only the top floor let as private tenancy. I have to confess, I was told the top floor does need a bit of cleaning up and on that score alone I could perhaps come to an agreement for a lesser rental.'

Julia said nothing but her mind was already working fast. The top floor, cleaned up, could

167

house her family, the first floor kept as a stock-room with enough space for Simon to live, under better conditions than he now did. This might prove a good deal after all, for it could cost more to find another flat. She needed to speak to Simon.

But there was also the lease. Simon had been naive enough to take on a lease on the verge of expiring. She would not be caught like that. She reflected that not so long ago she wouldn't have had any idea what a lease was; this past year had taught her a lot.

'Can you show me the top floor?' she asked, trying to sound non-committal. 'How long is the lease?' she enquired as they mounted the echoing stairway from a separate door to the shop.

'The lease,' Bennett repeated, 'is ninety-nine years with forty-five to go.'

It would easily see them out. Julia felt her heart leap, only to fall again as the door was opened and a musty odour of mice droppings greeted them.

Trying not to breathe too deeply she let herself be shown through the flat, her heart lifting again. There were three bedrooms, a living room, good-sized kitchen and a partially enclosed balcony similar to the one she'd seen below. A cupboard housed a lavatory, which was dirty and smelled dreadful, but her optimism had grown – it could easily be cleaned up. It would mean no more running downstairs to the yard, no more having to use chamber pots.

Like the lavatory the flat too was filthy; the previous occupants appeared to have been un-

168

savoury to say the least. Little wonder the landlord hadn't found anyone to rent it from him. In its present state, with peeling wallpaper, grubby windows and limp, stained curtains, it would have turned any likely tenant off, especially with the rental that was being quoted.

Julia decided she would play on the fact that it would take a great deal of time and effort to get it clean and airy and sweet-smelling again. Containing her excitement she gave a grimace of disgust as she turned to Mr Bennett, who was looking somewhat abashed; he had obviously been as unprepared as she was for the state of the place.

'I didn't expect to find such appalling conditions,' she said haughtily. 'I am so disillusioned. Who on this earth would want to take on this place? No, Mr Bennett, I'm sorry. I had such high expectations, but regretfully...'

She broke off, worried she might have gone too far, that he'd shrug and say she could take it or leave it. Had she already shot herself in the foot?

He gazed at her for what seemed minutes on end, while her heart sank. Then he said, 'May I suggest we return to my office where I might telephone my client and see what can be done.'

Two hours later, Julia alighted from a taxi and hurried into Simon's shop to tell him her news. Her excitement had abated and now her heart was fluttering with misgivings. All she had been able to think about in the taxi was, how would he receive the news that she had taken it upon herself to view premises for their business without first consulting him? After all, he was the one holding the purse strings, and finding the money for the down payment would eat into what profit there was.

As the proprietor of his shop, he would expect to make decisions of this sort or at least share with her in the making of them. But if she'd stopped to consult him they might have lost the place since no money had yet been handed over. Now she needed him to go back there with her immediately in case someone else snapped it up in the meantime. Filled with anxiety she went into the shop.

Simon was with a customer as Julia, closing her still damp umbrella, entered the shop. The man was examining a pile of huge, showy tiaras and bead necklaces of assorted lengths and colours – some of the original stock that Simon had insisted on keeping back during the restyling of the shop last year.

The man was saying, 'It's not a great production but in hopes we live to fill the house. This is just what I need – gaudy stuff, something to make the audience sit up and take notice.'

As Julia perched herself on a stool a little to one side, he half turned to glance at her before going back to his prospective purchases.

'OK then, these I'll take. Those bits over there I will also take, and the feathers too.'

Having seen her come in, Simon nodded at her with a smile then said to the man, 'What about costumes? We've a good stock of fine material, good-quality fabrics, silks, and...'

'I should want good quality?' The man gave a deep laugh and spread his hands questioningly. 'For my performances I need cheap 'n' cheerful, big patterns, colour – lots of colour to make the audience sit up and...'

'Take notice!' Simon chuckled, his customer laughing too before he sobered a little.

'You got nothing like that no more?'

'Only what you see.' Simon too had sobered but still smiled. 'We made a few changes last year, I hope for the better. We hope to...'

The man cut in with another laugh. 'Then take my advice, you're in the wrong area. You want to sell high class? Go to the West End. Here you sell what show people around here are looking for. But this stuff,' he sifted the necklaces through chubby fingers, 'here it'll always sell. Take my word.'

'It's odd you should mention the West End,' Julia cut in, making him turn, his broad face interested. 'A shop like ours could do well there,' she added.

Here was the way out she'd been looking for, a way of telling Simon her news without it sounding as if she was taking over. But before she could say anything more, Simon put in, 'This is my business partner, Miss Longfield. We manage the shop together.'

'I am a customer of your...partner.' The man smiled broadly at her. 'Maurice Isaacs, an *old* customer, but for some months I have been in the north, busy with a small theatre I am in partnership with up there. So now I am surprised to come back and find this shop changed. That is

171

your doing?'

'Yes, I suppose it is,' Julia replied. 'We teamed up last summer.'

Mr Isaacs gave a little bow. 'A very attractive young woman, I see. In the West End, with your looks, you would do very well with your modern ideas and your fine materials. Here we go in for the cheaper stuff. It suits the customers, you know, they pay at the door to be entertained, to laugh, have a good time, and bugger the state of the costumes so long as they leave happy.'

He paused to look from her to Simon. 'You said the West End? You don't make enough money here? It's a cheap place, but cheap brings in money. East End artistes with not too much to spare come to you to buy.'

'The fact is we can't stay here much longer,' Julia defended before Simon could say anything. 'The lease runs out in three weeks and the landlord won't renew it, so we have to find somewhere else and we've been thinking of moving nearer to the West End theatres and starting over completely...'

Her onrush tailed off as she caught Simon's warning stare.

Mr Isaacs looked surprised. 'Have you then?'

There was a long pause. Their customer turned back to the counter.

'Well, I must be going. I have to pay you.'

The transaction done, he left with a small bow of his head towards Julia, turning up his greatcoat collar against the now dwindling rain. As soon as he'd gone, Julia turned to see Simon rounding the end of the counter towards her, his

172

lips tight, his expression alarming.

'In business, Julia, never let a customer know we're closing down. Word gets around. People stay away. And we need every penny we can get.'

'I didn't realize,' she said, chastened. 'I didn't mean...'

'I know. I should have stopped you sooner. But Maurice Isaacs is shrewd. He'd have seen through us. He's been a regular customer ever since I opened, and been a good one when he's in the area. I doubt he'll desert us now.'

'I'm so sorry,' she began, but he stopped her by taking her in his arms and kissing her.

'Nothing we can do about it, my love. But, getting back to business, now people knowing we're closing down, I'm starting to worry about where we can go. I don't want to admit defeat. We have to find somewhere.'

Julia knew she had to be cautious as his voice died away and he let go of her. 'I think I might have found somewhere,' she began tentatively. 'But I'm a little worried now whether you'll think I've taken too much upon myself by not consulting you first. I had no time, you see,' she rushed on, and rapidly told him what she had been doing that morning.

He listened without speaking until she fell silent, still wondering what he thought. Would he come and see the place now? Was he upset by what she had done?

The silence seemed to last an age before he finally spoke.

# Fifteen

His expression was one of confusion. 'You say you think you *might* have found somewhere? When was this? And why haven't you told me?'

She could have done that last night as soon as she heard about the place but she had needed to think before doing so.

'Virginia only told me about it when I was going to bed. I thought you might already be asleep and I didn't want to disturb you by bashing on the shop door at that time of night.'

It was a small fib. What she'd needed to do first was to go early this morning and look for herself before telling him and getting his hopes up. Now it seemed to have been a foolish idea.

'I hardly slept myself for thinking about it,' she hurried on. 'It could have been just a flash in the pan and we would have had to wait until this morning anyway.'

He was still looking confounded. 'But if you'd mentioned it we could have gone there together.'

'I had to get there quickly before someone else found it first. I needed to ask if the vendor would hold it for us until I came back with you.' That was the truth. 'I left here at seven, well before you'd opened. I didn't dare wait.'

Actually it hadn't even occurred to her to bang

on the shop door and wake him, though that would have caused even more delay in getting there.

Explanations tripping over her tongue, she told him everything she'd found out: how surprisingly cheap the rent was and about the vacant flats too; how the first floor would make a combined stockroom and living accommodation for him, the top flat would be suitable for her family, with her mother conveniently near; how the estate agent had promised to hold it for an hour or two until she could return with him.

As she gabbled on it seemed to her a whole day had passed and the place would surely be gone by now even though in reality only an hour and a half had elapsed. But had she waited for Simon it could have been too late.

'I never intended to go over your head, Simon,' she ended.

But the way he was looking at her with that strange expression, she knew he thought she *had* gone too far.

'You've not gone over my head, as you put it, my darling,' he said but his expression hadn't changed. 'Only I would have liked to have known about it, that's all.'

'All I intended was to take a quick peek at the place,' she hurried on. That look of his was tearing at her heart. 'But I was so excited. I know I shouldn't have given the agent the impression that we wanted it, but I suppose I didn't think. I got carried away. I'm sorry, darling. It was wrong.'

She was ready to do anything or say anything

to see that expression on his face disappear. Never in her life had she grovelled to anyone in such a manner. She might give way in an argument to placate someone like her mother, but for no one else. Now, for this man whom she loved, she was willing to swallow her pride to appease him.

It was with sinking heart that she saw him look away from her as if loath to reveal what he was truly thinking. Julia bit her lip. She couldn't bear this awful hovering, negative silence.

'Darling, say something!' she finally burst out.

He looked at her as she cried out the words. For a second or two he studied her, then that strange, hurt expression faded and he said quietly, 'Well, I suppose we had best go and see this place then.'

They didn't speak at all as they sat side by side in the back of the taxi. And, as her unhappiness grew into anger, Julia vowed that if he wouldn't talk to her she wasn't going to talk to him.

Her mind was in turmoil. What if the place had already been snapped up in the hour and a half it had taken her to get back home, wait for Simon to deal with his customer, and then explain herself to Simon and finally for him to agree to accompany her back to the shop? She suddenly felt like a foolish little woman.

Defiantly she kept her head erect, her neck long and stiff, the tiny seed of anger inside her beginning to grow like some perfidious weed. Yes, he had taken her into his business without any real cost to herself, but it was she who had kept his shop going with her contribution of those beautiful materials of her father's. She knew they had attracted more custom than he had ever had before. But for her he would have closed down and left ages ago. At the thought of his leaving, Julia experienced a sick feeling, knowing she would have lost him for ever. But she hadn't been in love with him then, just rather strongly attracted; she would have got over it.

If he had left though, where would she and her family have been, trying to meet extra rent with nowhere to go if they couldn't pay? She would never have had this opportunity to help them. She'd have had to take a job, paying less than her materials were reaping. They would never have been able to afford extra rent. Where would they be now? How strange, she mused, that one small incident, one small decision, can change a whole life utterly. If she had made a different decision all those months ago, she wouldn't have had Simon; she wouldn't have known what it was to have him make love to her, to have him ask her to marry him, even though that time still seemed as far away as ever.

She had him to thank for where she was now. Yet at this moment he seemed to be looking upon her as if she were no more than a head-strong and naive girl. But she did have a good head on her shoulders, and he wasn't prepared to acknowledge it, sitting beside her without saying a word to her. How would he react when they reached their destination? Well, we will see, won't we, she thought, determined to stand up to any negative reaction he might display. But the thought failed to bring any comfort.

177

Julia turned away to gaze disconsolately out of the taxi window at the passing shops, the pavements thronged with people shopping, at blank-faced business buildings, and finally at the theatres of Leicester Square. The taxi turned into a side street and stopped outside the building she had viewed earlier, still with its advertising placard, still with the 'To Let' notices pasted on its upper windows.

Simon paid off the cabbie. 'This is it then,' he said flatly.

She nodded but he was already walking up to the shop front, shielding his eyes with one hand and leaning towards the glass to see inside.

'It looks a decent-sized area.' His voice was as normal as if there had been no friction between them. Perhaps it had only been in her imagination all along. She came to stand beside him.

'The agent said the rent was only eighteen shillings a week because it needs a lot of doing up.'

'Did he say what he wanted for the other rooms upstairs?'

'I think he said something like twelve shillings and sixpence a week for the first floor and ten and six for the one at the top.'

'That sounds a bit steep,' he observed.

'We are in the West End,' she reminded and he laughed lightly.

'Then we'll have to try and beat them down a bit, won't we?' he said.

'Part of the ground floor could be a wonderful area for a showroom. Ginny is still willing to be a model until we can get a professional one.'

178

She saw him catch his lower lip between his teeth in a speculative gesture and though he said nothing she felt her spirits lift a little.

Her feelings of rebellion vanished like wisps of smoke in a spring breeze and she made herself stand prudently aside for him to take over the business dealings with Mr Bennett. It was more comfortable to stay in the background, listening to Simon talking business, behaving like a man of the world. It was a side to him she'd never seen before.

By the time the transaction was concluded, she'd lost all track of the conversation, glaringly aware of how sheltered a life she had led; she who had once been so sure of her ability to confront single-handedly this great big cold world of business and finance.

'Well, darling,' said Simon as they came away, 'we've done it!'

Julia smiled but now it was her turn to fall silent and fretful. Had they bitten off more than they could chew? She'd sat by as Simon engaged the estate agent in deep discussion. Bennett had proved to be a harder nut doing business with another man than he had been with her, a woman to be handled gently and politely. She had felt suddenly very inadequate, knowing she would either have lost her temper or wilted completely if a man had addressed her in the manner in which those two had spoken to each other.

Simon had finally beaten the rent down a fraction during the agent's long phone call to the vendor, which had involved a good deal of haggling and reasoning. Even a fraction was better than nothing and Julia had sat there, her heart pounding with anticipation and immense pride for Simon as he wrote a cheque for the down payment.

'I do so love you,' she whispered as they sat side by side in the taxi that brought them back home. He placed his arm around her and squeezed her lovingly to him.

Even so, the following two weeks saw her still plagued with doubts. It had all happened so quickly that it had taken her breath away. Suddenly they found themselves in possession of a whole building.

'Are you sure we can find enough money for all this?' she asked again and again.

'We will,' he kept reassuring her.

'It's not just rent we have to find. What about rates and all the other overheads, heating and lighting and supplies? What if we find we can't repay the bank?' She'd been horrified when he'd told her that he had negotiated a good-sized bank loan.

'A bank loan?' she had echoed in horror, remembering what they'd had to face after her father died.

It was borrowing so heavily that had got him and his family into debt. He had been so sure of himself, so keen on expansion that he had taken out ever increasing bank loans, borrowing from financial backers, speculating without listening to good advice. Finally, in desperation turning to his own life insurance policies, he'd lost everything.

180

'We mustn't get carried away with borrowing,' she warned anxiously, as she watched him sign yet another cheque. Their outgoings seemed to be mounting by the minute. 'You mustn't ask the bank for any more, Simon.'

He smiled reassuringly at her. 'Just enough to tide us over for a short while until we're up and running.'

'That's if we ever do get up and running. I'm beginning to think it will never happen.'

'Well, it's got to happen.' It was said not with anxiety but confidence and he gave her a mock-serious stare. 'So you, dear girl, are going to have to work hard on your side of things. I shall concentrate on the theatrical side of my wares just as I've always done but on a grander scale.'

'You should have prepared me months ago for this.' Her mother's tone was plaintive.

'We didn't know ourselves months ago.' Julia tried to keep her tone mild. 'I did warn you, Mumsy, that if the rent went up too drastically, we'd look for somewhere else to live.'

'But it's come on us so suddenly. These up-heavals upset me so.'

'It's not sudden, Mummy. We have been talking about it for ages.'

But her mother wasn't listening, as she sat in her chair watching Julia gather bits together to pack into cardboard boxes. Not that there was much to pack. They were going to have to buy new furniture – another worrying expense. Already they were going through money like fingers through water.

'Having to move the first time was bad enough. I never thought we'd have to go through all the upheaval yet again. That was nearly the death of me.'

'The first time we *had* to move,' Julia said, trying to ignore the sight of her mother slumped and demoralized in her armchair, her face constantly creased at all the upheaval. 'This time we are *choosing* to go.'

'But I've become used to living here now.' She had never got used to being there, had never ceased to lament the necessity of living among people she considered were not her sort.

'Think, Mummy, we are going somewhere far nicer,' soothed Julia, 'with lots more room, *three* bedrooms, so you can have your own, nice views over London, and near the centre of everything. You know you hate it round here. This will be in the heart of the West End. You'll love it.'

'Three bedrooms! What will all that cost?' she cried.

'Leave that side to me!' Julia said, so tersely that her mother finally subsided into brooding silence, her still smooth hands clasped in her lap, her head bowed; perhaps, Julia thought, so that she would not have to look at all the chaos surrounding her.

Everyone was helping except Victoria, but that was natural, she had never had to lift and struggle with anything heavy or bulky in her whole life, everything had been done for her. She could not be expected to start now. Julia and Ginny heaved sheets and blankets from the beds into cardboard boxes while James dragged the heavier mattresses and the beds themselves from the room.

Stephanie, however, had merely shifted herself enough to box up her own personal belongings instead of sweeping the place clean as she'd been asked to do.

'Stephanie!' Julia called to her as she went back into the bedroom.

Stephanie looked up from filling a small make-up bag with jars of vanishing cream and boxes of face powder, startled by her sister's raised tone.

'What?' The single word was sharp and loud.

'This is a broom!' Julia seized the thing from where Stephanie had left it propped against the door and held it out at arm's length towards her sister. 'It's what we use for sweeping!' she added sarcastically. 'It's something you said you'd do. We need to leave this place clean.'

'I don't see why,' Stephanie shot back at her, resentful of her sister's tone. She took the broom begrudgingly with a well-manicured hand. 'We're leaving anyway.'

'Exactly! And I don't want the next tenant thinking we're a filthy lot.'

'Does it matter what they think? We'll be gone and they, whoever they are, don't even know who we are.'

Julia turned away and went back to their mother who'd given a cry at the sound of raised voices and was now indulging in a little weep.

'I'm sorry, Julia, I can't face all this fuss with everyone shouting.'

183

'No one is shouting, Mummy. I just told Stephanie to...'

'It sounded like shouting to me and it's making my poor head ache.'

To her relief, Simon called up to her from downstairs, providing her with a blessed chance to escape before her mother could find something else to lament over.

It was frightening, all this settling in. She hadn't given a thought to all that went into setting up shop from a standing start; hadn't thought just how much would be involved in getting things up and running. With the previous tenant having apparently gone broke and allowed his business to fall away, his customers to dwindle, it was taking a long time to get the place back on its feet. There was so much cleaning up to do, as well as serious repair work and redecorating to the style that she and Simon had chosen, that two months had gone by and nothing was yet up and running. In fact they seemed to be teetering on the edge of disaster. With rent, rates, builders' and decorators' bills to be met, the money was flying out and nothing yet coming in, and there was still so much more to do. Julia's nights were sleepless from worry, the more so since some of their outlay had been partly due to her lack of forethought.

As soon as they'd arrived, transferring all their stock from the old shop to this, she had ordered more materials for her side of the business. She now realized that she'd let herself be carried away; she who had worried about Simon's

184

spending. Instead he had shown himself to be the steady one. Neither of them, however, could have envisaged the amount of work needed here and the way it would delay the start of trading. Meanwhile Julia watched the loan he'd raised from the bank dwindling alarmingly.

'We're not going to do it, are we?' she said quietly as they sat on their own together in the half-decorated back room. Her family were upstairs in their flat, content to relax. Young James had worked his socks off helping to get the place up to scratch. He'd been a treasure, while Ginny had helped with painting bits and pieces. Stephanie of course had done nothing at all to help. Julia was not surprised but nevertheless annoyed at her sister's selfishness

But none of them had any inkling of her and Simon's worries and she wasn't about to pop their bubble just yet. She dreaded having to tell them that she and Simon might have made a mistake. God, how would they take it, especially her mother? They were content with their lot. James was doing well at his bank job, now earning three pounds a week, a man's wage, he boasted. Last month Ginny had excitedly disclosed that her wages were now up to one pound ten shillings a week. Eager to show that she could go one better than her sister, Stephanie had immediately and carelessly declared hers to be almost two pounds a week.

'An assistant on the cosmetics counter of a high-class department store is expected to advise customers of what is best for them. It's an important position and of course I am earning good money.'

Although the other two were giving more or less three-quarters of their wages towards the family upkeep, Stephanie contributed only half of hers. 'My job calls for me to look the part and that takes more money than if you're just office staff. And James merely needs a suit, shirt and tie to look smart.'

It annoyed Julia that her mother meekly accepted the excuse, yet it was hardly worth making a fuss about since the combined income of the four of them was now more than enough to pay rent, rates and food, with enough left for clothes when needed. And now that summer was here there were no worries yet about buying coal. It was here, in the shop that the hammer was threatening to fall.

'We mustn't give up hope yet,' Simon said as they sat over a cup of tea at the small table in the shop's back room, as yet still to be redesigned and decorated. At least the shop was now looking good.

Simon had insisted they shouldn't try to trade while it was being done up. 'It's just the thing to turn customers away,' he had said, but the money he'd borrowed was running out far too quickly for her peace of mind.

# Sixteen

Betty Lewis looked up from cutting out a gold lamé evening dress to Julia's own design. 'This is lovely, just right fer these warm, end o' September evenings. Mind you, I don't exactly like these new knee-length hems, but I do like yer idea of this back panel. It sort o' flows, don't yer think?'

Yes, she did. After selling known labels Julia had tried designing her own dresses and had found herself quite good at it. Now suddenly the vogue was for skirts up to the knees and as a designer of sorts she needed to go along with the times. But this delicate panel she'd come up with, draped from the back of the shoulders to fall straight down to just above the ankles, rippled like a golden river and gave a wonderful effect as one moved. In fact these days she was full of new ideas, ever eager to see the finished product.

Betty was proving a treasure. She'd jumped at the chance to come with them when she and Simon had moved. Now in charge of a couple of girls who treadled away on sewing machines, Betty was the cutter for the clothes Julia was devising with growing confidence.

She was helped by today's fashion for simple,

straight lines and often wondered if she'd have achieved the same success twenty years ago when the fashion was for intricate gowns with wasp waists and figure-hugging drapes.

Surprisingly, despite their misgivings, the shop had finally opened for business and was proving a success. Julia had begun by making clothes for window display as she'd done in the old shop, to help sell her materials. Instead it was the dresses that had sold. Simon had helped by sending out leaflets to publicize them and now, six months later, she was being asked more and more often to design garments exclusively for a specific clientele.

Her first commission had been terrifying. She'd lost sleep worrying about it, visualizing her customer shaking her head in disappointment, she feeling a fool and never getting another commission. But the woman had been delighted. Julia had discovered a gift she never knew she had; incapable of sewing two pieces of cloth together she had now developed a talent for design, sketching away with surprising results. With Betty left to the cutting and overseeing of the sewing, they made a perfect team.

They had sectioned off the shop so that one side held Simon's fashion jewellery, intended for stage costumes but no longer cheap and cheerful. Instead were long strings of cultured pearls; slave bangles of silver or rolled gold; shoulder and corsage brooches, still paste jewellery but of much better quality; long diamanté or cultured pearl earrings, also of superior quality. He now sold stage make-up as well, and his counter was always busy.

Julia's side of the shop displayed beautiful silks, satins, crêpe de Chine and other lovely material, arranged on shelves and in cubicles or tastefully draped on one or two mannequins. The back room, now a modern fashion showroom with curtained fitting rooms, had soft grey carpet, art deco mirrors, lacquer-red and black cube design window drapes hiding the back yard, a glass show cabinet with a glass fountain, and a low-backed, comfortable, red and black sofa with several matching chairs, making it a quiet and peaceful place for customers.

The floor above now housed a workroom, stockroom, office, staff room and toilet. They'd considered subletting to help pay off the bank loan but there was no need now. Here too Julia did her design work. Part of the stockroom had been partitioned off for Simon's living quarters, a small bedroom and a living room. Though she was still living upstairs with her family, Julia would have her lunch with him though dinner was always taken with the family.

If she and Simon were going out somewhere in the evening, perhaps to a show or a cinema, they'd have dinner out. Simon had suggested some time ago that she could come down to his quarters occasionally to enjoy an evening listening to dance music on the wireless set he had just bought. Wirelesses were now all the rage.

When she had broached the subject with her mother, Victoria had been shocked at the idea of her spending whole evenings downstairs with Simon.

'Oh, Julia!' she had gasped in tones of such horror that Julia had not pursued the matter.

It was best not to rock the boat. After all, a whole summer had gone by – where it had gone she hardly knew – and Simon had so far not spoken of marriage or even engagement. Perhaps, she thought, it was because of the pressure they had been under to get the shop up and running. Yet she knew he loved her.

'You an' Mr Layzell be goin' out tonight?' Betty's voice broke through Julia's thoughts. 'Only, if you are, I shan't work late if that's orright.'

Julia came to herself with a start. Betty had a tiny one-roomed flat above a solicitor's a few doors away.

'Only I got a bit of a backache what's gettin' me down a bit.'

Julia made herself concentrate. 'Oh, I'm sorry, Betty! Do you want to go now?'

'No, that's orright, I'll finish at me usual time then go and 'ave a good lie down.' She would often stay late if there was a rush on. 'Sooner 'ere than be in me flat all on me own,' she'd say, though she did go off to a working women's social club quite often with a few friends she'd made.

'That's fine, Betty. And I hope you feel better in the morning.'

'Yes, of course,' was the cheerful retort, leaving Julia wondering as she left Betty to it, if she'd be as cheerful if she'd lost a husband in the war. How would she feel if anything were to happen to Simon? God forbid! Her mother had

190

taken their father's death very hard and still suffered. How would she have coped if Chester had died when she'd still been in love with him? She hadn't thought about him for a long time, but every now and again she was reminded of the humiliation of being cast aside; a vague echo not of love or loss but of resentment.

Julia turned her mind quickly to thoughts of tonight. She and Simon were going to the new Tivoli in the Strand, which was being called a super-cinema. But it wasn't the film Julia was thinking about, it was arriving back here, saying goodnight to Simon and having to go upstairs to her family's quarters.

It was an effort of will not to stay, not to linger over a nightcap in his room. He'd never take advantage of her, she knew that. No, she was afraid of herself; of her own needs overpowering her; of the consequences of giving themselves up to each other. If she were to conceive a child she knew he would marry her, but it would be a marriage tainted.

Often, as he kissed her goodnight, she'd remember the one and only time they had thrown caution to the wind on that hard little bed in the back of his old shop. It had caused such awkwardness between them afterwards she could still feel it. She was sure he felt it too since he had never let it happen again. Yet she often wondered if he ached for her quite as much as she did for him.

Unable to bring herself to ask him such a question outright, she had to remain content with ardent kisses, almost desperate embraces, before she would break away, saying that she must go upstairs. At that he would give her the dismal nod of agreement she hated. If only just once he'd take the initiative and say, 'Don't go,' she would stay like a shot. But he never did.

She told herself it was the constant string of worries that had spoiled any repetition of that one loving night: their minds concentrated on trying to make a go of the old shop; the dismay of realizing the lease wouldn't be renewed; the desperate search for other premises; the effort involved to get the new shop up and running; the worry of how to afford paying back the bank loan; the unceasing hard work ever since. Now, with two days to go to October, and Christmas once again on the horizon, she knew they'd probably be too occupied getting ready for the busy season to speak of personal matters.

Watching the cinema screen that evening, Julia could barely concentrate on the story or what the actors were doing. She could think of nothing but the end of their evening; of not going upstairs for once, instead letting him draw her into his bedroom, of lying in his bed, his hands gently, tenderly exploring her naked body, the heat of his kisses, she and he becoming one. But she knew it wouldn't happen. She might stay for a nightcap, maybe even longer, but as soon as she had finished her drink she would say she must go, that her mother would be wondering where she was. What if she didn't though?

With these thoughts going round and round in her head she returned home with Simon. They crossed the stockroom together, he with his hand in hers, she with her heart thumping in anticipation of what could be if she allowed love to take its course.

At the door he paused before opening it, turning to look at her. 'You'll have a drink before you go?'

Why did he always say it in that tone of voice, as if he thought she might turn and run for her life?

'Yes,' she said simply.

Already her heart had calmed for she knew what would happen. He would put his finished whisky glass on the little sideboard, take her almost empty glass and put that too to one side, then kiss her. Gently and lovingly at first, but as the kiss became a little more urgent, making her want to melt into his arms, she would feel her muscles stiffen and he would feel them too, and let go of her. Then she would move away from him, saying it was late, her mother would be worrying. Excuses, excuses!

For something to say to combat her unease as they stood in his lounge with their drinks, she said, 'I think Virginia is enjoying modelling dresses. I think that as it's only in the salon and for lady customers she feels safe. And she is so pretty and graceful and so slim that she attracts clients to buy...'

Realizing she was gabbling on, she let her words tail off.

He didn't respond. He hadn't even smiled. He stood gazing silently at her for so long that she laughed nervously. 'What is it?'

'I was just wondering when you were going to

say that in a moment you'll have to be going upstairs, that your mother will be worrying again.'

It was said so slowly and deliberately that it sounded more like a taunt, leaving her at a loss.

'I...wasn't...' she faltered, frowning at the brusque way he'd spoken to her.

But he wasn't finished. 'Only your mother may be wondering where you are if you stay too long,' he went on in the same tone.

Taken aback, and hurt by his accusatory tone, Julia found her voice. 'It's not that...' she began, then stopped, confused.

He still hadn't smiled, but his tone had soften-ed. 'Come and sit down for a moment,' he said quietly. Wordlessly she followed him over to the little two-seater sofa and they sat down together.

'We've known each other for nearly eighteen months,' he began.

'July 1922,' she interrupted. 'Nearly fifteen months.' To her relief she saw him smile at last.

'Then don't you think it's about time we got married?'

Julia found herself holding her breath. It had come right out of the blue and for a second she thought she had misheard him. But in the next second her breath returned with a gasp as she realized that she had heard him correctly.

He was still looking at her and it seemed to her an age had passed since he'd said the words. Now he took her hands between his and as she remained staring at him, he looked steadily into her eyes.

'Julia, will you marry me?'

194

'Yes,' she said in a small voice. And then, breathless with sudden, overwhelming happiness, she burst out, 'Oh, yes, Simon, oh, yes, *yes*!'

The next moment she was in his arms, all thoughts of leaving forgotten. Tonight she would not leave; tonight she would stay with the man she loved – and upstairs they could think what they damn well liked!

'It's disgusting!' Stephanie stalked back and forth across the large, well-furnished living room, her fists clenched, her pretty features tight. It didn't occur to her to feel glad for her sister, to feel gratitude for the lovely flat that they now lived in, provided for them by her sister, whose good fortune had been so generously shared with them.

'And you!' She turned on Virginia with a sneer. 'Surely you won't be going on working for her still, knowing what's been going on.'

Ginny bristled. *'What's been going on*, as you put it, is no business of mine.'

'It's all our business,' Stephanie raged on. 'She's our sister, and your daughter, Mummy.' She turned to her mother, who sat with clasped hands in the lovely brocade armchair that was part of the suite Julia had bought for them. 'And I certainly don't think it proper for Ginny to go on modelling for her, knowing what those two have obviously been up to.'

They'd been concerned when Julia hadn't come back upstairs after her evening out and Stephanie had been all for going down to

195

Simon's rooms to find out what was going on.

'For all we know she might have been knocked down on her way home and taken into hospital,' she'd said.

Her mother had said quietly, 'We would have been told. We were told straight away when your poor father...' she'd broken off, unable to say any more.

Refusing to be silenced, Stephanie had gone down the iron stairs outside to the back yard, returning a couple of minutes later with lips as tight as if they'd been welded together. 'She's there – with him! The lights are on in his rooms, so where is she? I'll tell you where she is, she's with him!'

James was philosophical. 'There's not much we can do about it. She's over twenty-one and can do as she pleases, though I hardly think she'll get much of a welcome up here from any of *you*.'

He deliberately excluded himself from his family's censure. Now that he had a girlfriend he knew how hard it could be for young people to rein in strong feelings. But he wasn't prepared to let these outraged women into his private affairs so he merely allowed himself to put on an indignant expression and went hurriedly off to bed.

'She certainly won't get any welcome from us,' Stephanie said after he'd gone. 'In fact she should be ashamed to show her face.'

'But she still lives here,' Virginia reminded her. 'And she's done so much for us and as James said, it is her business what she does.'

'You mean you condone her behaviour?'

'No! I just...well, she's...' Before her sister's glare she shrugged and let it go.

Sleep that night, at least for Stephanie and her mother, was disturbed by vivid imaginings of Julia's improprieties. It was worse for Victoria, who had brought up her daughters to respect their purity until marriage. When she finally slept it was only to dream of turning her daughter out. She woke up on Sunday morning to find her pillow wet with tears.

Later, when Julia came upstairs to tell them joyfully that Simon had proposed to her and they were planning to get engaged as soon as possible, she was met with total silence from her mother, her good news ignored. From Stephanie came the caustic remark, 'I suppose you've had breakfast with him as well!' to which Julia made no reply.

The only friendly words came from Virginia, who whispered, 'How exciting! An engagement! Congrats, Julia, I'm so pleased for you,' and then probably a little guilelessly, 'I *will* still be your model, whatever happens.'

There had been friendliness too from James, whose wry, knowing grin made her wonder what he, now eighteen, got up to when he was with his girl, Georgina. He appeared to be going steady with her, although he'd not yet brought her home to meet them.

It was an uncomfortable morning, one she was glad to see the back of. She and Simon planned to take advantage of a fine September day to have Sunday lunch out (she couldn't have borne to eat here at home), later to take a stroll in Hyde Park, dine out and spend the rest of what promised to be a fine evening wandering along the Embankment.

Last night had been so wonderful; he had shown such concern for her, making her feel safe in his hands. They had not yet decided on a date for their wedding. With a business to run it would have to be fitted in outside the busy times, such as the build-up to Christmas. Maybe in the spring, although that too was a busy time; so in fact was summer. Still, it was something wonderful to look forward to and she felt entirely at ease with whatever the future held. Even so, staying the night with him should not be a permanent situation; she had her family to consider. She ought to have known what their reaction to last night would be, and had to admit they were justified in their feelings about it.

She told him her decision as they ate lunch. To her surprise and relief he agreed. 'I don't want to come between you and them. After all, in time I'll be an in-law. Can't start off on the wrong foot, can I?'

'But we will be together some of the time until then?' she pleaded, in sudden fear that it might be a while before last night was repeated.

He took her hand across the lunch table. 'That must be left up to you, my darling. I want us to be together every night of the week, but think carefully. It would cause enmity between you and your family and I wouldn't want that. Only know that I love you.'

His declaration made her tingle with happiness

yet his warning also made her think as they lounged on the grass in Hyde Park, surrounded by other couples and families with children, all taking advantage of the September sunshine. But she and Simon hardly noticed the others as she lay on her back, her head resting in his lap, each of them entirely at ease with the other. How different it was from the only other time they'd made love, last year, when they'd both felt so awkward afterwards.

He began tickling her lip with a short grass stem he'd just plucked, making her turn her face aside and brush the stem away. 'Now I suppose I must get you an engagement ring,' he said suddenly.

'Not if you don't want to,' she said with mock haughtiness, pushing aside a silly twinge of uncertainty at the odd way he had spoken.

'I suppose it will have to be a good one,' he went on lightly. 'None of my shop junk.'

'I hope not.' She broke off the banter to gaze up at him in sudden foolish doubt. He was joking of course, yet it seemed to her he'd been a little too quick off the mark in telling her to be wary of going against social decencies and hurting her family. 'You are going to get an engagement ring though?'

Still being playful, he bent over and kissed her lightly on the nose. 'I suppose I'll have to. What would you fancy – a solitaire, a band, a cluster?'

Hardly giving her time to answer, he lifted her up from where she lay, and taking her in his arms, he kissed her, a lingering kiss, in full view of everyone.

'I love you,' he said deeply as they broke away, then instantly became playful again. 'OK, hopefully tomorrow when we close shop for lunch, we'll chase over to Hatton Garden and see what we can find in the way of a really lovely ring – one that will take your breath away.'

He sounded so youthful, like a schoolboy with a sudden new idea. Casting aside all her doubts Julia knew with a sudden rush of joy that her life as Simon's wife was going to be the most wonderful anyone could ever wish to have.

# Seventeen

'Mummy, we've set the wedding date for Saturday the first of March, before the spring rush begins.'

Julia's voice carried no enthusiasm and Stephanie knew why as their mother hardly glanced up from her armchair where she was darning a little hole in one of her lisle stockings.

She felt a tug of guilt that she was the one keeping alive her mother's repugnance of Julia's flagrant behaviour. That it was flagrant she had no doubt; her sister's expression gave her away, hardly able to meet her mother's accusing eyes, her face lowered in an effort to conceal the ugly truth there on her face.

Stephanie had known a few times herself when a kiss and a cuddle with some young chap after a dance had threatened to develop into a bit of a fumble. But she'd never let it go any further than that, and unlike Julia she managed to keep her bits of fun well away from her family's door, as any sensible girl should.

Smug at having a darn sight more sense than Julia had, she couldn't help a surge of satisfaction at her mother's indifferent response to her daughter's latest news. It had been the same when Julia had bounced into the flat with Simon

201

one morning six weeks ago to show off her diamond cluster engagement ring after having blatantly spent the whole night in his rooms. Mummy's disgust had taken all the bounce out of her, along with Stephanie's own reaction; she had made a big point of giving the lovely engagement ring no more than a contemptuous glance before going back to eating her breakfast.

Perhaps her behaviour had been a little too pointed. She had been taken aback to see Simon's happy face change to an expression of bewilderment. He and Julia had left; she in tears, he with a comforting arm about her, their happiness completely deflated.

Simon had not set foot up here again since that morning and Stephanie was haunted by the thought that she might have gone too far. She persuaded herself that Julia had brought this upon herself, by not bothering to think how her conduct might have upset others. She had given no thought to how unfair she was being towards her mother by not respecting Victoria's admittedly old-fashioned sense of values or her peace of mind.

Clinging to that thought now, Stephanie tried to ignore the insidious seed of jealousy that was growing inside her; jealousy of Julia who, when it came down to it, had done all right for herself since their father died. She had taken over responsibility for the family, with no thought of consulting anyone else, bossing them all into finding work as if she were queen bee, but doing nothing herself except dream of riches gained from that stuff she'd purloined from their

202

father's warehouse. Yet Julia had been the one to benefit most from their misfortune. Julia had landed nicely on her feet, acquiring a successful business and soon to marry a handsome businessman. She, on the other hand, was still at her boring, foot-aching, nine-to-five job behind a cosmetics counter, even if it was Selfridges.

Ginny too was doing all right. She had always been Julia's favourite sister and now, having been taken under her wing, she looked as though she too could go far, modelling. On one occasion last August Stephanie had gone down to the well-laid-out, modern fashion room to see how their younger sister was faring. She'd come away screwed up with resentment that it was Ginny and not herself parading up and down in front of a small but admiring group of customers like the Queen of England. She'd never gone to watch her again.

'Please, Mummy, be happy for us,' Julia was now saying, breaking the long silence. Even Ginny, still finishing her breakfast of toast and marmalade, had not said a word; she had just gaped, toast poised between plate and mouth.

All at once Julia's sad, pleading voice made Stephanie feel uncomfortable. It sounded so unlike her strong, self-assured sister. Perhaps her mother felt it too. She looked up at last with a heavy, tremulous sigh, her mending falling idle, her eyes glistening with tears.

'How can I be happy, Julia, when I know what's going on down there? Can't you see how it upsets me?'

'It was just that one time, Mummy,' Julia

203

broke in. 'You must believe me.'

'How can I?' came the quavering reply. A stronger woman might have raised her tone, but not Victoria. 'You spend your evenings with that man in his rooms, which is just as wrong. You are there until nearly midnight, time enough to...' She broke off, unable to voice her thoughts. After a moment she continued. 'Surely, knowing you'll soon be married, you could abstain from indulging yourselves for the sake of decency. You ask me to be happy for you. Do this one thing for me, resist the temptation to go to his rooms, and I shall be the happiest woman in the world.'

Stephanie saw anger steal into her sister's eyes; saw her head go up.

'What about lunch times, Mummy? We eat lunch together. But that's all right? Who is to say we don't do something else other than eat? We go to the pictures, the theatre, have dinner out. Why not take time to do what you say we do of an evening, maybe down some back alley or in a dark corner?'

It was so loaded with cruel sarcasm that even Stephanie's breath was taken away, while Ginny, who had looked on without a word, possibly quietly taking her sister's part, cried out, *'Julia!'*

For one moment Julia looked as though she was about to throw herself into her mother's arms to beg forgiveness. Instead she merely shrugged and stood stiff and erect as her mother clamped a horrified hand to her mouth, for a moment struck dumb. Then, without another word, Victoria gathered up her sewing with shaking fingers, got up from her chair as if in pain and went slowly out of the room, closing the door quietly behind her.

Stephanie couldn't help herself. She turned savagely on her sister. 'Now see what you've done! How could you speak to her like that? It was wicked – wicked and cruel.'

'No crueller than the treatment I've just received. I came to tell you all that Simon and I have set our wedding date. I didn't expect such a reaction from you, especially after I've done all I could for this family. Without me...' She stopped as if defeated, ending quietly, 'How would you have felt if you'd been given the same delightful welcome as I have received?'

'I'm not the one doing what you're doing,' Stephanie began but then stopped, her cheeks grown hot, remembering her own secret pleasures, even if she had not been quite as shameless as Julia. But Julia didn't seem to notice. She merely gave a small, tight laugh. 'Well, I've told you my news. Whether you want to come to my wedding or not is up to you. I couldn't care less!'

The dance band was finally packing up, leaving the hall with a strange, lonely air, filled only with the buzz of young men and women departing to catch buses, taxis, trains for home. Dancers filtered slowly out into the foyer and then into the street, couples and groups tired yet still lively. Among them, Stephanie clung to Jimmy Waring's arm as they emerged into the December night. An icy blast whistled around her legs below the short dress and coat, making her shiver.

'Cold?' he queried.

'Freezing!'

Freeing himself from her hold, he wrapped one arm around her shoulders so that she could snuggle up against his thick overcoat and scarf. He grinned down at her from beneath his trilby hat. 'Fancy going on to a nightclub I know? Be warm there. Afterwards you can go home by taxi. I'll pay.'

'Oh, yes, please!' The offer was too good to miss. To be bought a drink in a nightclub! Not many young men she'd met offered that luxury. Usually it was, 'Can I see you home?' and that was usually by bus, with a bit of a grope on the corner before she went indoors.

It was quite all right, she could look after herself. She was a modern girl, did what most modern girls did these days. So long as her mother didn't know. An off-putting giggle would soon shut off a boy's ardour, followed quickly by, 'Got to go, I think I saw my mum peep out of the window, thanks for seeing me home, 'bye!' As he hesitated, asking, 'Can I see you again?' she'd say lightly, 'We'll see,' if she didn't fancy him that much, but if he was gorgeous it would be, 'When?' He'd suggest an evening, to which she would usually agree. As yet there was no regular boyfriend, she was having too good a time for that. And if she got tired of them she could let them down, though she couldn't help feeling put out if one did the same to her.

206

But Jimmy Waring had really taken her fancy; she could really take to him as a regular boyfriend. He was a good-looker, slim, tall, debonair, about twenty-five and far more mature than most boys she'd so far been out with.

She'd met him last week when she'd been with a couple of girls from Selfridges. He'd been in a mixed company of about half a dozen, but as the dance floor began to fill he'd looked towards her and come straight across. The next thing she knew they were dancing a tango, he commenting on her grace and the ease with which she followed him.

He'd turned out to be a smashing dancer and after that had asked her for almost every dance, to the envy of her friends. After escorting her back to her seat though he'd gone back to rejoin his group, leaving her feeling a little deflated. This week he was here again and made straight for her. Now he was cuddling her against the cold and offering to take her on to a nightclub.

'But I mustn't stay out too late,' she told him. 'I need to be home at least by twelve.' It seemed to her that offering her a drink in a nightclub amounted to a first date and one mustn't look too eager on a first date.

'Then we'll make sure of it,' he said cheerily. 'One quick drink to warm you up, it's only a couple of minutes' walk from here. You won't even notice the cold after that.'

One drink became two, then three. Chatting and laughing with him, she didn't notice time passing. When she finally glanced at her watch Stephanie saw that it was one thirty.

'I have to go,' she blurted, and made to get up from the table where they'd been sitting, wobbling a little as she stood.

Jimmy was on his feet holding her steady. 'You can't go home like this just yet,' he said with sudden concern. 'Look, I'll get a hotel room where you can rest and recover.'

As tipsy as she felt, she wasn't so tipsy that she had abandoned all caution. 'No, thank you! I shall be all right. If you'd just get me a taxi...'

He was all consideration. 'Then it might be best if I see you home. You can't go alone as you are.' So he hadn't designs on her after all, she thought, relieved. She had begun to fear that he had deliberately got her drunk in order to have his way with her.

In the dark taxi he was so kind, holding her close, asking if he might see her again. She was only too happy for him to do so. He gave her his address in Kilburn and for once she was happy to give hers, an address that at last she could be proud of, in the heart of the West End.

Jimmy told her that his father was a stock-broker on the London Stock Exchange and that he worked with him. So he was pretty well off, came the unavoidable thought as Stephanie cuddled close to him. It didn't seem wrong for him to put his arm about her slim neck and kiss her quite masterfully on the lips; kisses she returned with pleasure, aware of his hand slipping down inside her coat, the top of her dress, beneath her bra. Other boys had done this but she usually put them off with a quick laugh, but this time she found the sensation pleasurable, the warmth of his fingers on her breast, gently manipulating the flesh, making her nipple stand up. In fact it was so delightful that, as his other hand moved up inside her skirt and between her legs, she actually drew in a sharp breath as the touch on that place that had never been touched by any boy before caused her senses to respond involuntarily – one second later, in fear.

Pulling her lips from his, pushing the hand away violently, she came upright, realizing she had let his body bear her down upon the seat. There came real fear that he could easily render her powerless, and her imagination suddenly ran riot. But to her surprise he also sat up, taking his hands from her with not even a sign of anger. He even gave a deep chuckle.

'You're a good girl,' he muttered. 'There are few of those about these days. I'm sorry if I worried you. It was quite unforgivable of me. Am I still permitted to see you again next week?'

'Yes, of course,' came her meek reply. She did want to see him again. Already gratitude for his understanding was overwhelming her, almost to the point that she wished she had let him go further with her. In a way she felt cheated, wanting it to happen again; that delightful sensation she'd never before experienced, could never even have guessed at. Just thinking of it made her tremble deliciously.

But there was something else. She'd nearly let him go on; something in her had wanted – needed – it to happen. And this need was making her understand, as she finally alighted from the taxi,

209

Julia's need to share with her fiancé that most natural thing, being in love and wanting to cement that love, with no care for what others might think.

Christmas came and went. She had shared the festive season with her family though Julia spent most of it with Simon. When she came to be with them she came on her own. At last Stephanie understood. She could think of no one but Jimmy, yet had to conceal those thoughts from everyone because like Julia she had allowed their natural feelings for each other to take over and she was happy to express her love for him in every way that a woman can. Each day away from him was a yearning torture; she could hardly wait for the New Year to be over when they could forget their families and be together and enjoy the love they now indulged in as well as the new, exciting life he was showing her.

Over the past weeks he'd introduced her to his friends, and she had enjoyed sharing in their escapades. She was truly one of the 'Bright Young Things' as the wealthy young gadabouts were called. Jimmy paid for everything, even her clothes. It was such fun, dashing about in cars, drinking cocktails and champagne, smoking cigarettes in long elegant holders. There were fancy dress parties, babies' parties where everyone dressed as a baby, dancing to wild music, party crashing, Underground parties where they all went round on the Circle line for hours, getting drunk until they were forced off. Best of all was going to bed with Jimmy. Who cared what her mother said about her staying out until the early hours? She was enjoying herself. She no longer minded what Julia and Simon got up to. It was natural, after all. Everyone was doing it with someone. Before long Jimmy would propose. Who knows, she thought, we might even have a double wedding.

The wedding had had to be postponed. Work was coming in thick and fast; so was money, but there was no time for making any plans other than financial ones. The February dock strike had paralysed every port in the country, holding up delivery of Julia's lovely silks from India. They cost half the price being asked at home and without them she was left worrying how to meet the growing demand from her customers for ever more exotic garments.

The finding of more treasure from the young Pharaoh Tutankhamun's tomb in Egypt had begun a 'Tutmania' craze for turban hats, Egyptian earrings and bangles. Colours were named Coptic blue, mummy brown, carnelian and lotus in honour of the Egyptian craze. The wealthy flocked to Egypt to see the wonderful treasures and take part in more discoveries. They returned home with yet more exotic ideas and Julia was at her wits' end to keep up with their demands for exclusive and exotic clothes. She spent hours searching for fine brocades, gold-embroidered taffeta, chiffon in deep Egyptian colours, Oriental silk, all to meet the demand for this new style. It was not the time to think of marriage.

'We'll try for the summer,' Simon said glumly

and Julia had no option but to agree with that. They were now living together virtually as man and wife anyway. Her mother said little and Stephanie had appeared to come to terms with the situation. They were being careful, not only for the sake of propriety but because a pregnancy could interfere with business.

James had tried to lecture her just after Christmas when she and Simon had stayed downstairs together instead of sharing the festival with her family.

'You are a silly ass you know, Sis! No one other than a raging idiot shits on their own doorstep.'

As Julia drew in a shocked breath, he grinned. 'Sorry about that, but it's the truth. I mean, did you really expect Mother to throw her arms about you? It's best to keep what you do outside the home well out of sight. As I said, you're an ass, Julia, and you only have yourself to blame if Mother hardly speaks to you.'

'I've done a lot for her,' Julia reminded him. 'I've done a lot for you all.'

'I know, but that doesn't give you licence to run roughshod over our mother's feelings. Yes she's old-fashioned and these are modern times but you should spare a little thought for her, Julia.'

Julia had wanted to say that her life was her own, but instead she merely turned away, counting James as another finger in the pie denying her happiness.

Simon told her not to worry about it. 'We'll be husband and wife by the end of summer,' he said, drawing her to him when she expressed her anger at her family. 'We might be able to make it September, if that's OK with you, darling, just before the Christmas rush starts to get going.'

It sounded a good plan but in her disappointed state Julia somehow couldn't see it happening as easily as they hoped. At least by April, with the date of their wedding come and gone, and with it much of her disappointment, she was already organizing an important fashion show in her showroom.

Ginny had given up her job to work full time with Julia and was as excited as a puppy with two tails. Almost seventeen she was growing into a beauty and always drew rapt attention from the women customers. Julia had hired another young model to help out at times but Ginny was the one they looked for. Husbands and fiancés accompanying their ladies obviously enjoyed seeing her too, and Julia was proud of her sister.

The dock strike was now over and a specially ordered consignment of beautiful Oriental-type materials was at her disposal. Julia was designing a whole host of the new styles, among them a Turkish trouser suit and an Oriental pyjama suit for house parties. Another evening garment was a sleeveless, straight-sided, Eastern-style embroidered silk tunic with a stand-up collar meeting edge to edge. There was also an evening cloak in black velvet embroidered with coloured silks and pearls inspired by an Egyptian drawing she had found. She liked one design especially, a beautiful evening dress with an Egyptian girdle, the ends of which hung down to trail upon the ground.

She planned to redesign the harem skirt. This time round she hoped it would be a wow, though it had not been popular before the war. But then that was before Tutankhamen had appeared on the scene! There was also a new innovation all her own, a straight-sided Egyptian-style dress in gold chiffon with a scooped neck embroidered with colourful zigzag emblems based on the Egyptian styles seen on paintings on the walls of Tutankhamun's tomb. Even the modern evening bandeaux currently being worn just above the brow would match the designs of those seen on the wall paintings of the tomb. It would mean a lot of work if her garments were to be ready to meet the July deadline Julia had set for herself, but any later would lose her the summer trade and that would be a disaster.

Betty, as ever, was a treasure, toiling well into the evenings and chivvying along the two young machinists. Simon had been busy ordering all the Egyptian jewellery he could find and had negotiated a price for printing and distributing leaflets for the coming exhibition. He was already receiving whole loads of encouraging responses. Julia just hoped everything would be ready in time.

And at least all this work had managed to dull those earlier pangs of disappointment about having to postpone the wedding. It no longer mattered because by September she and Simon would finally be married.

# Eighteen

The fashion show had been a roaring success. Since then Julia had given two more and orders had begun to flood in. Her exclusive but élite fashion showroom would soon become the talk of the town. She'd had to add two more sewing machines in one corner of the stockroom near the cutting area and take on two more machinists.

It was mid August. The wedding had had to be rescheduled for October owing to pressure of work and Julia's stomach felt as if small creatures were constantly playing tag inside it, lest this new date too fell through. If it did there would be no further opportunity this year with the Christmas season once again upon them. It was amazing where the time went.

She had already designed her own wedding outfit – a white wild silk dress with long sleeves, a low waist and a hem falling to just below knee length, worn with a lace, pearl and orange blossom encrusted Juliet cap that covered her whole head, its veil falling about her shoulders to trail the ground. She would wear white silk stockings and white silk Cuban-heeled, court-style shoes with a slim bar across the instep. The style was very English; the craze for all things Egyptian

215

was slowly diminishing. As bridesmaids her sisters would wear beige silk dresses with knee-length hemlines and their headdresses would be bandeaux of pink flowers to match their posies. Her own bouquet would of course be fashionably long and trailing.

But the October date wasn't to be. A show in September brought more orders flooding in and once again their wedding had to be postponed. This time they did not dare to set another date.

'I'm sure you never intended to get married,' her mother complained as November arrived. 'Too content living in sin! It's shameful, selfish and wicked! You've no care how I feel, the pair of you!'

Julia might have protested, but she was tired of her mother insisting on seeing it her way. She merely turned away, leaving Victoria to her whining. Her love for Simon wasn't wicked or selfish. More than anything she wanted to be his wife but circumstances seemed always to prevent it.

'Couldn't we manage a Christmas wedding?' she asked. They were sitting up in bed together just like an already married couple, he reading a few brochures, she a novel before they turned out the light and snuggled down together.

He put the brochures down on the counterpane and pursed his lips thoughtfully, then nodded. 'I don't see why not. There's little going on until New Year when it all starts up again. Yes, it would be just right. And this time, my love, nothing is going to stand in our way – I mean, *nothing*!'

The words were hardly out of his mouth before Julia dropped her novel and threw herself into his arms. 'Oh, darling, yes, this time, yes!' she squealed. 'My dearest, I do love you so.'

It was the most glorious night, making love, falling asleep exhausted in each other's arms, neither of them having thought to wind up the bedside alarm clock. Julia awoke next morning to find that they'd overslept. Calling him awake, she washed, cleaned her teeth, dressed, combed her short hair and applied a little make-up all in the space of ten minutes. There was no time for breakfast, she could eat later. While Simon shaved she went down to open the shop. No one would come this early but it would not look good if they didn't open on time. She had just come away from the unlocked door when its bell tinkled.

Turning back she saw Stephanie standing in the open doorway, her face pale and drawn, her lips working, her eyes brimming over with tears.

Julia stared at her. 'Whatever is the matter?'

Stephanie came forward, moving slowly, her eyes fixed on her sister. But before she came too close she stopped as though there were a glass barrier in her way.

'What is it, Stephanie? What's the matter?' Julia repeated, now fearful that something terrible must have happened. Her thoughts flew instantly to her mother. Had she collapsed, had a heart attack, a stroke, maybe fallen down the outside stairs? All sorts of dreads flooded her mind in that split second. 'What's happened?'

At her words, Stephanie ran forward and

almost collapsed into her arms.

'Oh, Julia, I'm in such trouble! I don't know what to do.'

Despite the girl's anguish, Julia felt a surge of relief. It was only to do with Stephanie, who was always in anguish over something. She had the capacity to make a big thing out of nothing – a bit like her mother, only Stephanie was more forceful.

'What trouble? Who's upset you now?'

Stephanie had drawn away from her. 'I don't know how to tell you. I can't tell Mummy. I had to come to you.'

There was a long pause and then Stephanie burst out, 'I think I'm pregnant.' As she spoke the last word her voice gave way, ending in a high squeak.

She stood in the centre of the shop, a forlorn figure. She was now beyond distress, appearing resigned to whatever fate awaited her.

Julia repeated incredulously, 'Pregnant?'

Her sister nodded dumbly.

'Stephanie, how can you be?'

Stephanie hung her head. 'Don't tell Mummy,' was all she said.

'No, listen! I asked you, how can you be pregnant? What makes you think you are?'

'I've not seen my periods for three months.'

That didn't mean much. Julia knew some girls were like that. Perhaps Stephanie was ill and hadn't realized it. 'Have you seen a doctor about it?'

When Stephanie shook her head, she hesitated before saying disbelievingly, 'Have you been with someone?'

It came out so crudely that she half expected her sister to burst into tears of outrage. Instead, Stephanie threw herself back into Julia's arms, sobbing as if her heart would break. Moments later she was pouring out the whole story of how she had met Jimmy Waring, how wonderfully he'd treated her, what a marvellous time he'd given her, introducing her to such interesting people and taking her to all sorts of crazy parties.

Endlessly repeating herself she told how considerate Jimmy had been, respecting her decent morals and not taking advantage of her.

'If he's never taken advantage of you,' Julia said, growing angrier by the minute, 'how can you be pregnant?'

The anger in her tone made Stephanie tear herself free of Julia's hold. 'If you're going to be like that, I wish I'd never come to you for help.'

'Well, you have, and now you've started you'd better tell me the rest of it or I won't be able to help you. You've obviously let him make love to you. How often? How long have you been seeing each other?'

'Don't say it like that!' Stephanie stormed, suddenly defiant again. 'We've been together since last Christmas. We loved each other.'

'*Loved*?' Julia noted her sister's use of the past tense. Her worst fear hung on that single word.

'I love him. And I thought he loved me. He was always so attentive.'

Julia ignored that. 'Since Christmas you say.

Has he ever proposed marriage, mentioned engagement or taking you to meet his family?'

To each question Stephanie's replies were a sullen 'No'. Her attitude became increasingly defensive and indignant. But when Julia asked if they'd taken precautions Stephanie's lips began to quiver again. 'He was always careful with me.'

'Careful with you,' Julia echoed. 'Did he use anything?'

'He did for a while. But then he began to say that he knew how to look after me without that. He said we needed to be free, that using things was restricting our love and he wanted our love to be perfect.'

Julia bit back the anger that was building up inside her. She was furious both at the heartlessness of this unknown young man and at the foolishness of her sister. 'And where is he now?'

'I don't know.' The reply tore at Julia's heart.

'Sometimes he was away,' Stephanie went on as if excusing him. 'He said it was stock exchange business. That was his work. I wouldn't see him for a few weeks. A girl I knew laughed when I told her and said, "Business, he calls it? Darling, you don't think you're his *only* bit of stuff, do you?" I didn't believe her. But when I told him I'd missed two of my monthlies, he was so angry and said he was going away for a while. I remembered then what that woman had said. When I asked him to his face he admitted that I was not the only girl in his life. He said the women he preferred were far more mature than I was and knew how to look after themselves.

I've not seen him since.'

And probably never will again, thought Julia. But her sister was still talking.

'He bought me such lovely clothes and bits of nice jewellery. We'd go dancing and to night-clubs and he paid for everything, so he must have loved me or he wouldn't have splashed out like that. I just hope he'll come round to feeling better about – about the baby. He did suggest I should get rid of it but then said it was nothing to do with him. Now I don't know what to think.' Stephanie was wringing her hands with indecision. 'Perhaps he'll come back. I do still love him.'

Julia resisted a strong temptation to call her a silly little idiot. 'And if he doesn't?' she said in an as even a tone as possible. 'How are you going to tell Mummy?'

She saw Stephanie's eyes widen with terror. 'I can't tell her!'

'You probably wouldn't have to. She will see as time goes on. But you shouldn't wait for that. You should tell her.'

'I can't face her. I'll kill myself! She'll hate me!'

'No she won't,' Julia said quietly, ignoring her sister's dramatics.

But terror had begun to turn to defiance. 'I only did what you and Simon have been doing. I thought, if they can do it, then so can I.'

'Simon and I are intending to marry soon. This Jimmy chap hadn't even proposed to you. You hadn't even had a promise of an engagement.'

'I thought we would get married.'

'Then it seems you were wrong.'

Fear had begun to shine again in Stephanie's eyes. 'I don't know what to do,' she repeated. 'I know he loved me. I'm sure he'll come back. He couldn't be so cruel as not to. He loved me. He said he did. I can't tell Mummy. She was so upset when you and Simon started to live together; she said that sort of thing isn't done and that she was so ashamed and could never hold up her head again. What will she say to me with no one to marry?'

Cupping her hands to her face, she broke down in tears again, sinking on to her knees and leaning forward so that her head almost touched the floor.

Julia's anger evaporated and she quickly lifted Stephanie up to hold her tightly, knowing that Betty and their workers would soon be arriving. She couldn't have them walking in on such a scene and wondering what was going on.

'Come on,' she urged sharply. 'Pull yourself together. Look, I'll take you upstairs to Mother and I'll do the talking.'

'No, I don't want to face her. I can't! I'll die as soon as I see that look on her face, the look she gave you when you went with Simon.'

'I wasn't having a baby,' Julia retorted. Even in this crisis Stephanie had the capacity to hurt without thinking. 'I'll take you up to the workshop. You can wait in Simon's dining room until I come back.'

'I can't go in there!' Stephanie gasped but her sister already had hold of her arm and was marching her to the stairs leading up to the stockroom, calling to Simon to come down to the shop.

Simon was mystified as he passed them but Julia motioned to him with a discreet shake of her head, mouthing that she would tell him later.

'Oh, it's you. What do you want?' Her mother's greeting was so cold that had Julia's errand been less urgent she would have turned on her heel and marched back down the stairs. Victoria was in her dressing gown and Julia guessed that she'd still been in bed.

'There's something I have to tell you,' Julia blurted out and then paused. This matter needed to be approached gently. 'Mummy, can I come in?'

She felt like a stranger standing at the door, her mother staring at her, unsmiling, with a querying look as if she were a casual caller.

'It's very important!' she urged, and at the tone of her voice her mother stepped back without a word to allow her to come in.

James and Ginny had already left for work and the flat was silent. Victoria sat down in one of the lovely brown Moroccan leather armchairs Julia had bought for her. She didn't invite Julia to sit down.

'So, then, what is it you want?' she asked, looking up at her daughter. 'You hardly bother to come up here these days.'

'That isn't my fault, Mummy.'

'In a way it is, Julia. While you persist in living with this man...'

'He isn't *this man,* Mother, he's my fiancé and

as soon as we can we will be married.'

'Then you are taking long enough to get around to it.'

Julia held herself very stiff and upright, refusing to be humbled, and came to the point. 'What I've come here to tell you has nothing to do with me or Simon. It may take a little time to explain so do you mind if I sit down?'

To the faint ring of sarcasm her mother gave a shrug and a deep sigh. 'I suppose you had better.'

As Julia sat down in the opposite chair to her mother's, on the other side of the small fire, a strained silence fell on the room. This was going to be even harder than she had expected; her mother's hostile attitude wasn't helping.

'It's about Stephanie,' she began carefully. 'She's downstairs at the moment. There's something very important about her that you need to know but she can't bring herself to tell you in person. I said I would speak to you for her.'

Her mother lowered her head, her lips a quivering pout. 'I'm afraid Stephanie is not the girl I hoped she would be,' she said, her voice shaky. 'She cares for no one's feelings, always gadding out to these awful dance places with their noisy jazz, kicking up her legs until all hours, tiring herself out. Heaven knows what they get up to, dresses almost above their knees. She spends all night sometimes with her idiotic friends instead of coming home. Like you, she pleases only herself.'

'Mummy, she's young,' Julia excused. 'It's a different generation from yours and...'

'This younger generation!' her mother cut in. 'Virginia and James are also the young generation but they don't gad about like her. I can rely on them. They care for me. If it wasn't for their thoughtfulness I'd be here all on my own for all you and your sister care. Your poor father...'

'Mummy, listen to me,' Julia interrupted. With her mother in this mood how was she going to explain Stephanie's predicament? Victoria would probably go into hysterics or faint clean away. There was no other way but to tell her as gently as she could.

'Mummy,' she began, 'Stephanie's in an awful state. She came to me early this morning, crying.' She ignored her mother's startled exclamation and ploughed on. 'She's been seeing a young man for nearly a year now and...'

'She's said nothing to me about it. Who is he? I hope he has money enough to...'

'I'm afraid he's given her up,' Julia began, but was again interrupted.

'How typical! No more than I'd have expected of her. What has she done to have him give her up as you put it?'

There was nothing for it other than to come right out with it. However gently said the news was going to be shocking.

'Mummy, Stephanie's pregnant!'

There was a stunned silence before her mother said faintly, 'What?'

'She's three months gone.'

On impulse Julia stood up and started to move towards Victoria to offer comfort but found herself pushed violently away as the woman was

225

galvanized into action. There was no frantic weeping, no spasm of swooning or even hysterical screams. But the push was so strong that Julia almost lost her balance. Her mother was now on her feet and making for the bedroom Stephanie shared with Ginny now that Julia had moved in with Simon.

Hurrying after her, Julia found her scrabbling through Stephanie's drawers, the floor already littered with some of her stuff.

'What are you doing, Mummy?'

'You can take all this away, all that belongs to her,' was the angry reply. Without even turning round to look at Julia she went over to the dressing table to drag the contents from those drawers too, sweeping the surface clean of any make-up belonging to Stephanie. 'She's no daughter of mine. Take it away! Everything! She doesn't live here any more.'

'You can't do that, Mummy. Where is she to go?'

Her mother was already moving to the wardrobe, dragging out skirts, dresses, blouses, jackets, coats, hats to be flung on the floor with the rest.

'She can go wherever she likes – go and find the man who got her into that condition and appeal to his good nature, if he has any. Or she can live with you, the pair of you well matched. Take all you can to her now. The rest will be outside the door.'

So it was that she and a sobbing Stephanie gathered up armfuls of clothing, jars and bottles of make-up, perfume and toiletries, all strewn carelessly outside the door, to struggle down the stairs from their mother's flat, up the other stairs and into the stockroom. Here they piled everything in one corner until a proper place could be found for it all.

It was arranged that for the time being Stephanie should sleep on the couch in Simon's living room.

'It's not ideal, but where else can she go at such short notice?' he said so quietly and evenly that Julia felt overwhelmed by his unselfish generosity.

'Simon, I don't know how you feel but I can't think about our wedding with all this going on,' Julia said. 'You do understand, don't you, darling?'

'I do understand, my sweet. Christmas has come upon us so quickly, what with everything else, as you say, going on.'

He didn't seem at all put out, which brought relief on the one hand and on the other made her wonder why he should agree so readily.

'I wanted so much for us to be married before the New Year.'

He drew her to him as they lay in bed, his arm tightening about her. 'I know, my love. I did too. But it's impossible now that you have your sister to look after. You've been so good to her, taking her in as you have. How can I pile more responsibility on you? It's just going to have to be postponed.'

'Yet again,' she whispered against his chest.

'Let's just sort your sister out. Then we can

make new arrangements and next time it will be definite, I promise.'

He was so understanding, so unruffled, even when Julia repeated to him all those horrid things her mother had spat out earlier. As far as Victoria was concerned there was only one decent child left in her life. 'And that child is James,' she'd wept. 'James will never put me to shame as you and your sisters have, all three of you carrying on like trollops!'

'There's nothing wrong with Ginny!' Julia had said indignantly. Ginny was a lovely girl, a good girl, kind and sweet and selfless, and her mother was being totally unfair to her.

'It's only a matter of time,' had been the un-kind reply. Julia had watched helplessly as she'd worked herself up into a rage.

'She works for you, displaying her body before total strangers,' Victoria had continued. 'Isn't that enough? I was never happy about it though I hoped she would come to her senses. But you were bent on leading her astray, drag-ging her down to your level. Stephanie too – if she hadn't seen the way you were carrying on with that Simon she would never have been tempted into thinking she could do the same. Now look at her. At least I still have James. He is the only one left to me.'

At this she had hardly been able to speak for weeping. 'At least he sets a good example of virtue. He wants me to meet his young lady though they are too young to become engaged, but she is the only young lady he has ever had. He is sober-minded and respectable like his father and I trust him as I trusted your father.'

Julia suspected her brother was not as lily white as her mother imagined, but she let that pass. In any case, Victoria had already continued on another tack.

'As for Stephanie, I want no more to do with her. She ran to you, not me, her mother.'

'Because she knew how you'd be.' Julia had been unable to stop herself but had immediately regretted her words as her mother's face twisted into an expression Julia still couldn't get out of her mind.

'In that case,' Victoria had said slowly, her anger grown cold, her voice dry and harsh, 'you may have the responsibility of her.'

Julia had been shaken and hurt by the scene She had broken down in front of Simon later as it all flooded out. He hadn't shown any resentment, had made no comments against her mother.

All he'd said was that Stephanie would have to stay with them until the baby was born, then he'd find a little flat for her. It had made Julia angry all over again with her mother for her unfairness in persisting in seeing him as self-centred and uncaring. On the spur of the moment she found herself vowing never to speak to her mother again.

She said so to Simon, who frowned and looked suddenly sad and said quietly, 'No, darling, you musn't say that.'

# Nineteen

'What are we going to do when the baby arrives?'

Julia had never seen Simon so gloomy, he who usually made the best of things even when they looked hopeless.

'She can't stay with us for ever when the baby comes.'

He sat toying with his breakfast, the two of them sitting side by side on the bed at a little table. With Stephanie there they could no longer eat breakfast in the living room with any comfort.

Stephanie was still asleep. She rose later and later these days, taking advantage of her burgeoning pregnancy. Julia would creep about the living room trying to get breakfast at the little gas stove while her sister lay oblivious to the rattle of pots and plates. She'd been sleeping on the sofa these past three months and it was becoming increasingly inconvenient for them all.

Julia worried how she could sleep there in such a narrow space with her distended stomach growing larger by the week. There were many other inconveniences. Simon saw her often about the place in a dressing gown, he was banished from his own living quarters while she took a bath, and the chamber pot had to be emptied because she couldn't or wouldn't get herself across the stockroom to the staff toilet. As her pregnancy progressed and the baby pressed on her bladder she needed to use it several times in the night. Julia felt embarrassed for Simon, having to see Stephanie lolling in one of the two armchairs, her stomach bulging. The place wasn't their own any more.

Their relationship was already being strained as it was. It seemed to Julia that the longer she and Simon spent together unmarried the more of a stigma it was becoming. She was sure they were being talked about among their friends in business. As if that were not enough, Stephanie's condition was starting to make her feel a little broody. Of course, a baby was out of the question while she wore no wedding ring. Nor could they very well adopt Stephanie's baby when it was born, for the same reason.

In the meantime she couldn't help the feeling that their love might be growing stale, their moments of love making becoming ever less frequent. Maybe it was the pressure of business but sometimes she felt it went a little deeper than that. By the time they did marry, all the sense of newness would have gone out of their relationship and she was already grieving for the loss, as if for a real person.

Stephanie's presence also made it impossible for them to express their natural feelings for each other. Perhaps that was all that was wrong, Julia reassured herself, nothing deeper. Once Stephanie had her baby and moved into the little

231

flat Simon had planned for her, life would return to normal, they'd get married and start a family. Stephanie herself was depressed and often in tears. There had been no word from Jimmy Waring since the day he'd walked out on her. His name was always on her lips, her emotions alternating between 'I loved him so' and 'I hate him, the bloody horrible bastard!' Julia's heart would thud to hear her sister, who had never used words like that, using them now.

When she wasn't pining after the man who had wronged her Stephanie was complaining at having to give up work. 'I shall never get another job as good as that one,' she would lament. 'I'll lose my looks and my figure. It won't ever come back.'

Julia tried hard to be encouraging. 'Yes it will,' she soothed, but was growing weary of her sister's constant whining. Stephanie was beginning to remind her of their mother and her lack of courage.

At nearly seven months pregnant she now refused to go out. She had stopped going for walks with Julia a couple of months ago when her pregnancy had begun to show. Even then the winter weather had meant that the walks had not been regular. Now it was nearly April and the weather had improved but Stephanie was ashamed to be seen out. She got no fresh air and hardly left the living room so that Simon found himself more or less confined to the bedroom.

'The place is like a prison,' he complained testily as he pushed away his half-eaten breakfast.

Not only a prison, Julia thought, more like a sentence with hard labour. As well as trying to manage a business she was finding her time being taken up running after her sister and her work was suffering.

'What worries me,' Simon was saying, 'is that when she has the baby she might assume she can stay here, expecting us to look after them both. I'm sorry to say this, Julia, but your mother should have done something to help her. You should have stuck to your guns and refused to take Stephanie in.'

That was easier said than done. 'How could I see her thrown out?'

'We could have got her a little place of her own somewhere. We could have afforded it.'

'She can't live on her own in her condition. I couldn't do that to her.'

'It seems your mother could. There was a time I felt sorry for her, a grieving widow unable to cope. I wanted to help but she turned on us both. She behaved in a thoroughly self-centred manner after all you've done for her. Turning out her own daughter, no matter that Stephanie had done wrong, was cruel and wicked. She's no mother as far as I'm concerned.'

Julia bore his criticisms in silence. She knew he was angry on her behalf. She also knew he was right, but even so it hurt coming from him.

The plight of her sister wasn't the only thing that concerned her these days. With the wedding now postponed indefinitely because of Stephanie's situation, Julia was beginning to wonder if they should bother with a wedding at all. She

233

had to agree with Simon that if her mother had been a little more forgiving, her own future would by now be settled. Couldn't the woman see that her attitudes and behaviour were causing problems to so many others, as well as alienating her from her children?

Julia had tried to reason with her several times since Christmas but her only response was, 'Stephanie made her bed, let her lie in it.'

'But haven't you any motherly feelings?'

'In this case, I'm afraid not.'

She'd never known her mother to be so firm. 'Don't you see, Mummy, you're hurting the whole family and yourself as well.'

'Then I'm sorry but I can't alter how I feel. You've hurt me with your goings on more than I can tell you.'

It was useless.

'Julia! Help me...help!'

Stephanie's distant scream rang through the building. Julia, who was showing several colours of crêpe de Chine to a customer, excused herself and rushed upstairs. In the stockroom she saw Betty making for Simon's rooms. The four machinists had stopped work at the awful screams.

'Betty,' Julia cried as she reached her, 'go down and take care of my customer. The rest of you,' she added as Betty hurried off, 'carry on with your work.'

She found Stephanie doubled up on the sofa, her arms clasped about her stomach, her face twisted in pain. Immediately Julia guessed the worst. Stephanie was only eight months pregnant. Something was very wrong. 'Stay here,' she cried needlessly and rushed outside to the telephone to call for an ambulance.

Stephanie lay in hospital, pale and exhausted. The baby had been a boy. The doctor and midwife had tried hard to save him but it had been a breech birth and there had been complications. The child was stillborn.

Once the ambulance had driven away, bell clanging, with Ginny accompanying her sister, Julia had torn upstairs to tell her mother. Victoria's expression was stony.

'I heard the ambulance, so I assumed she had started.'

'She should have another month to go yet,' Julia shot at her. 'She's only eight months and it could be dangerous.'

'She has probably miscalculated. It would be just like her.'

How could her mother remain so calm, Julia wondered. She who for years would break down in tears at the slightest provocation. 'The doctor who examined her confirmed there's still just over a month to go to her full term,' Julia went on. 'I think you should go with me to the hospital, Mummy. She'll need you to be there.'

Her mother's expression seemed to harden. 'She's nothing to do with me. She chose to get herself in this condition. I've washed my hands of her.'

For a moment Julia gazed at her, stunned. Then livid anger seemed to rip through her like a knife. 'What a wicked, wicked woman you really are!' she burst out, making her mother jump. 'How dare you? And if she died, which she could, would that not bother you either?'

'I've told you, Julia...'

But Julia wasn't finished. 'I never realized what an utterly selfish person you are. You've been weeping for years over your loss, never allowing yourself to get over it, and expecting all of us to rally round *you,* help *you.* It's time you had a little sympathy for others.'

Before her mother could reply she rushed on, 'She's your daughter, no matter what she's done. Forget *yourself* for once, help *her*! Be there for her, comfort her. Or do you not have a single loving bone in your body? If you don't do this, Mummy, you'll lose us all – we'll all see you for what you are. You'll end up friendless and spend the rest of your life alone!'

Her voice shook so much with emotion that she had to stop, but her mother had finally become subdued, making no reply.

'So, will you come?' Julia asked in a steadier voice.

A few minutes later Victoria was being helped into Simon's new little Austin, bought only three weeks ago. She sat in silence the whole short distance to the hospital, either because she'd never been in a motor car before or because Julia's words had shocked her into silence. Still without uttering a word she let herself be helped from the vehicle and up into the clanking lift to the floor Stephanie was on.

Outside the ward they were met by Ginny

whose face told them that something was wrong. But before they could question her a nursing sister swished towards them, her face, grave and efficient but kind.

'Ah, there you are! Who is the father?' she went on, the briskness of her tone moderating as she looked directly as Simon.

Julia spoke for them, talking fast. 'He's out of the country and isn't able to be here, but I'm her sister. I left a note for her brother,' which she had done, 'and he'll be along later, I expect. This is her mother.'

'Ah,' the woman said quietly, leaving Julia to suspect that she had gleaned the circumstances surrounding this particular patient as she took in the older woman's expression.

'I'm afraid I have to tell you, my dear, that your daughter's baby was stillborn. I'm so sorry. Your daughter is still very weak. She has had a very traumatic experience and will take some time to recover. I think it would be wise to recommend that she spend a few weeks in a convalescent home, if you agree. She is very low, and her body needs building up, you understand.'

Yes, they understood. Julia tried not to feel relief that Stephanie would be elsewhere for a while, for all she was shaken by the news.

She sat now by her sister's bedside. Her mother hadn't yet come in to see her. She was too distraught and was weeping in Ginny's arms. But Julia could feel no sympathy for her, felt she deserved none. She had grown hard and didn't care for the feeling it gave her.

Stephanie was asleep. When she finally awoke, Julia would compel her mother to come in and hold her hand. Maybe the contact would help things to get back to normal. Even if she never forgave her eldest daughter her way of life, at least she might forgive Stephanie and that was more important. The girl, like her mother, had lost something precious and needed a shoulder. As she was thinking these thoughts she saw her sister slowly open her eyes.

'Hullo, Stephanie,' Julia whispered. 'How are you feeling?' For answer her sister nodded sleepily, and Julia went on cautiously, 'Has anyone told you anything about the baby?' She half expected Stephanie to burst into great heaving sobs and feared this might weaken her further.

Instead, her sister closed her eyes and said softly, 'They said I lost it.' There was a short pause, a deep sigh and then, 'Just as well, I suppose.'

Julia wondered if she'd heard her right. But she had, and the shock almost robbed her of her voice. 'You don't mean that, Stephanie. You can't mean that!'

She expected some emotional reaction, some display of anger, but Stephanie merely closed her eyes and mumbled, 'I don't want to talk just now. I just want to sleep.'

She never once mentioned the baby again, and with no one else willing to bring up the subject, it was as if she had never had a baby. To Julia it seemed totally unnatural for a mother not to feel the slightest sense of grief at the loss of her baby, even if it was illegitimate. Many a time she

238

wondered if her sister didn't perhaps grieve inside. If she did though, she kept it very well hidden.

After Stephanie had spent several weeks recuperating in the convalescent home, Julia expected her to return to live with their mother, with everything back to normal. She felt a great relief that the months of having to put her up in her and Simon's room were over. She broached the subject with her mother the day before Stephanie was due to come home.

Her mother's voice was hard. 'She's a grown woman. When she is better she'll be able to find her own place.'

Shaken by the reply, Julia protested, 'But she has no money, no job. How can she be expected to find enough to pay for somewhere to live?'

'She'll soon be back to normal, as bouncy as if she had never had a baby; no contrition, no shame, no hint of regret, still as trim as ever and full of herself. She'll soon find work.'

'And meanwhile where is she to go?' Julia queried acidly. 'We can't go on having her with us indefinitely.'

But her mother merely gave a shrug and turned away, the corners of her mouth pulled down, a reflection of how set her mind was. No matter what Julia said she would not be persuaded to have Stephanie back home or to hear any more about it.

Simon shook his head in astonishment when Julia told him of her mother's hardness. 'We'll have to find her a flat ourselves,' he said.

'But she has no job and no money for rent.'

'Then we'll just have to pay her rent for her,' he said generously.

By the summer of 1925 there were more jobs to be had but Julia knew her sister. She'd never take just anything. Despite the trauma and stigma of having carried an illegitimate child, Stephanie had lost none of her self-confidence or vanity. Even while recovering her strength in the convalescent home she had continued doing her nails, making up her face and trying on her dresses. They still fitted her perfectly, her figure having returned to normal already. Her sights were set on rejoining the bright young things she had come to know and she was looking forward to the prospect of going dancing and having fun, only this time without Jimmy Waring whom she had now apparently got over.

'I'll soon find somebody else,' she said brightly, full of self-assurance. 'Plenty more fish in the sea and next time I won't make the same mistakes again.'

She took it for granted that she'd land on her feet and she did, with Simon of course offering to find and pay for a flat for her to live in.

Julia might have thought he was being taken for a ride by her sister, but she had no time to dwell on it. She'd had enough of worrying about her family. Work was coming in too thick and fast now for her to worry about anything else.

Julia would have spent all day in her small workroom, designing and draping the results on a plaster mannequin she'd had for years, if she hadn't had to keep up a mounting succession of meetings with shops willing to take her

240

creations, or go looking for just the right materials for her work. She now had the services of a small factory to turn out copies of her various designs to send round the West End shops, and she was slowly making a name for herself. Simon too was well occupied with his own side of the business; he was now expert at knowing just what the public wanted in fashion jewellery.

By September their present premises were beginning to prove too small for a business that was rapidly expanding. There was no doubt that the economic situation was having an influence; there was more money around, and fashions were becoming more and more outrageous, with day and evening dresses skimpy, hems the shortest in history, hardly hiding a stocking top.

Women's hair too was being worn almost as short as a man's, in styles known as the shingle, the Eton crop and the bob. These were mostly hidden under deep, head-hugging cloche hats that Julia now bought in specifically to match each dress she designed. Every moment of her days and much of her evenings was taken up designing ever more exciting styles to cope with customer demand. She was creating a label to be stocked in a few West End boutiques and needed to find another cutter to help Betty. In addition she was now employing six machinists. There simply wasn't the room to accommodate such a workforce and even Simon was getting worried.

'We're just going to have to find larger premises,' he said to Julia one evening in late September as they lay together in bed before falling

241

asleep. 'I'm tired of living over the premises anyway. We've enough in the bank to expand and start living in a decent flat, somewhere we can entertain without feeling ashamed.'

These days they needed to entertain business people, maybe a client or two, but always in a fine restaurant or nightclub.

'It would be so good to be able to bring people back for drinks, hold a party or two,' he went on, but Julia wasn't thinking of that.

'What about my mother?' she asked, sleep momentarily swept aside. 'We can't leave her here. I know she has James and Ginny but when they're not here, I'm only a call away. And she's not getting any younger.'

He put his arm around her and drew her to him. 'We'll find her something nice and roomy nearby and I'll pay someone to cook and keep the place tidy.'

'It'll have to be very near, otherwise she might feel she's being ostracized.'

'I don't see why. She was the one who threw Stephanie out, and you too, darling. She'll still have Ginny and James living with her.'

'One day both of them will marry and leave her.'

'Then she'd be on her own anyway, darling. Time marches on. You can't go on coddling her. She doesn't appreciate it anyway; she still sees us as living in sin.'

That remark, though made lightly, started her thinking that they should again discuss when they would finally set a date for their wedding. But before she could say anything, he had

242

laughed at his little quip and squeezed her tightly to him, kissing her, and she knew it was a moment to make love and not worry over anything else for the time being.

# Twenty

'I can't believe this is all ours!'

Julia twisted round and round with joy, flinging wide her arms as if to embrace the huge lounge. The flat, with its two large bedrooms, fine reception room and beautifully appointed kitchen also had a lovely bathroom. No longer would they have to run across a workroom to the toilet, or use a tin bath.

'I never dreamed years ago that we would ever live in any place like this,' she went on.

After four months of pent-up anxiety about whether or not they could afford it, the place was finally theirs. As well as the flat, they had purchased new business premises which boasted a large showroom, an inviting reception area, a workroom and all the facilities, a separate cutting room and good-sized office where business could be done in comfort. All this had diminished her and Simon's finances to an extent that had been terrifying. But it was done now and it was up to them to make a success of it.

She had no qualms on that score. These past four months had been productive, her worries about her family thrown aside to concentrate on her own future for a change. Compared to the well-established fashion houses, Jacques Doucet, Paul Poirot, Worth, Lucile, Callot Soeurs, she was still small fry but proud to have her creations known by the name Julia Layzell. Though she and Simon were still not married, who cared so long as a Layzell garment was the one to have?

She might never be up there with the names that were now breaking new ground, Elsa Schiaparelli, Coco Chanel or Madeleine Vionnet, but she could always dream that one day it could happen. And as she told herself, if you dream hard enough your dreams could come true.

Ceasing her gyrations, Julia threw herself into her sister Ginny's arms while Simon looked on, amused; it wasn't like her to show so much excitement, she was usually so calm and collected.

Julia ignored his amusement. 'Isn't it just wonderful?' She was almost crying with joy and relief that the anxious months of waiting and worrying were over. 'After all we've been through – now look at us.'

'You've done marvellously,' Ginny whispered so that their mother, standing nearby, wouldn't hear and maybe make some bitter comment.

Bitterness seemed to have become ingrained in her over the years. It had sketched itself on her features, the corners of her lips drooping as she stared around the lounge with its comfortable three-piece suite, its art deco drapes, pictures and ornaments.

There was no cause today for her to be bitter; her family were all here around her. As well as Stephanie, Ginny and Julia, James was there with his young lady, Caroline. She was a demure young girl who smiled a lot but said little. The couple were set to become engaged in May when he turned twenty-one.

They were all smiling except her mother, who was surveying the room as if trying to make up her mind just how to disapprove.

'I hope you never forget what we have all been through.' She echoed Julia's words as if from a distance. 'The suffering I had to bear, losing your dear father. I only hope he's looking down and praying you never get above yourselves with all this high life.'

Julia didn't respond. She'd long got over worrying about her mother's discontented outlook on life. The woman would never change. Refusing to move with the times, she still wore the long skirts and high-necked, dark blouses worn ten years ago. Her only concession to fashion was the ubiquitous cloche hat, but even there her choice was sombre and dull, reflecting her whole attitude.

She had seldom left her old flat, scorning visits to the cinema or theatre, refusing even to go for a walk on fine days, despite all Julia's persuasions. It was four years since her husband's death but still she had not even gone shopping, saying she wasn't ready to face the world; instead her groceries had been delivered. Lack of fresh air showed on her face, which was pale as chalk, the skin paper-thin, and life spent in the confines of a tiny flat was making her shoulders more rounded than they should be.

Her new three-bedroom flat was in Maddox Mews, off Maddox Street, just across from Julia's spacious apartment. She would have more room to move about here and maybe this would help her counter some of her premature ageing.

But all she said when asked how she liked it was, 'It's a bit rambling after what I had to become used to when we lost our lovely house.'

No word of thanks, and Julia had given up, saying perhaps a little too sharply and unkindly, 'Well, Mummy, if that's the case you can always stick to one room and leave the others to Ginny and James.'

'Virginia and James are hardly ever at home,' had come the plaintive reply. 'I shall feel lost in this big place all on my own.'

It was quite useless. Julia knew that Simon had splashed out much-needed money to get her mother this flat. She'd felt annoyed at her and embarrassed for him, but finally left Victoria to her own devices. The woman was totally unaware that she was slowly alienating herself from her entire family.

The next few months were too busy for Julia to worry much about her mother. James proved a stalwart, often bringing home Caroline, with whom his mother seemed taken, which was a relief. Julia was thus free to get on with her own life.

It wasn't an easy start. All the work she and Simon put into building up their new premises, planning and overseeing the fine décor, ensuring that everything was top quality, ate into their reserves at an alarming rate. Nevertheless, Simon seemed to be happy with things as they were going.

'I can't wait to see it all finished,' Julia said after yet another tiring day. 'I just hope we haven't been too extravagant. We're beginning to owe the bank far too much for my liking.'

Despite their success she still carried the memory of her father's downfall. What if it all fell apart for them as it had for him?

'Don't worry,' Simon told her. 'I know what I'm doing.'

Probably he did. She contented herself with that thought, but as the day of opening drew near with all its attendant anxieties, she felt as if the very elements were against them. February brought eighteen days no less of non-stop rain, deluge after deluge, with reports in the newspapers of terrible flooding in most of London's suburbs.

Simon's confidence was undiminished. 'It's going to be the sunniest day ever when we open,' he announced. 'It can only be fine after all this rain.'

But still Julia worried. She planned a grand opening in the form of a small fashion show, for which she intended to hire two models. This, her first real venture, made her heart race, her stomach queasy, and caused her sleepless nights. It was a nightmare getting together beautiful day dresses, stunning evening gowns, exciting party clothes, silk evening pyjamas, even pretty swimsuits with caps to match, all in bright oranges, shimmering blues, translucent greens and jazzy prints.

As for Simon, the days of selling cheap theatrical trinkets and bits and bobs were gone. He now concentrated on accessories to go with her creations; high-quality costume jewellery that was a far cry from what he'd begun with.

They went to great expense to advertise it all and though many of the invited buyers did attend, and the show was a complete success with plenty sold, February decided to vent the last of its foul fury on the day. The bad weather inevitably kept down the numbers and there were fewer customers than they'd hoped for. Ironically, the following day arrived with all that Simon had promised, a day of beautiful sunshine.

'It seems the gods are against us,' Julia moaned as they woke up to glorious sunshine on Sunday. 'Why couldn't yesterday have been like this?'

'Well, as I see it,' Simon said cheerfully, getting out of bed to gaze from the window at the quiet street below, 'after that great ending to winter we'll no doubt enjoy a good spring and summer. We didn't expect to recoup everything in one day anyway! Nothing else can go wrong now.'

She hoped he was right. But just as March and April began to bring a glowing recovery, there came the General Strike in May and almost the entire country ground to a standstill. With most of her workforce out, Julia was unable to complete orders.

'When they do finally return to work, they'll find their cards waiting for them,' she raged, but Simon shook his head.

'You can't do that. Half the country's workers are out in support of the miners.'

These had been on strike for weeks, seeking improvements to their pitiful wages and poor working conditions. They were still out and suffering, but adamant they would not give in.

'Thousands of ordinary workers are on strike for a good cause,' Simon went on. 'And if you sack your workers for joining them, you will be in the wrong. So we're over a barrel really.'

Julia hadn't seen it that way. Her only thoughts had been for her own business after the struggle they'd both had to get where they were.

The General Strike went on for ten days, with crowds descending angrily on any bus or train driver prepared to return to duty. Women and white-collar workers set to in order to keep coal and food supplies running, heaving postal mail bags, and risking being mobbed and in many cases actually falling foul of angry workers.

'If this goes on much longer we could be bankrupt,' Julia said. 'We've sunk almost every penny we have into this venture. If we fail now we'll have nothing.'

She was near to panic at the thought and Simon too, usually so calm and philosophical, was showing signs of despair. She wanted to add that they should never have let their earlier success go to their heads but that odd, beaten look on his face stopped her.

But just as she began to believe that all was lost, the strike ended as suddenly as it began. The miners fought on but the rest of the country went back to work. Julia had never felt such relief as she experienced when her own girls trooped back to their sewing machines, their pressing and their packing as if nothing had happened. She decided it was best to say as little as possible about the subject. With all this going on, it was June before the business took off, after six months of sheer panic.

Concentrating all their energies on making up for the loss of trade, they no longer saw the need to be married. There seemed to be no point to it. They were known by all their business associates as Julia and Simon Layzell. No one enquired into their precise status; all were merely pleased to be wined and dined by the Layzells and to attend exciting parties with them. Simon in particular entered enthusiastically into this new crazy life they were now living. And it was crazy.

Julia too found a quality in herself she never knew she had. Free of the responsibility of her mother and family, she found kicking over the traces great fun. She learned some of the gentler new dances, content to leave the more energetic ones like the Black Bottom and the Charleston to younger people. She knew all the current 1926 songs and the names of film and theatre stars; she even met a few of them as she mingled with high society. To her great delight, she had even been on the same dance floor as the Prince of Wales, if not quite swooning over him, then at least enjoying the sight of those women who did.

Simon was enjoying being able to buy all the newest gadgets for their smart flat. He had soon acquired the most up-to-date wireless set and a cabinet gramophone to which they would listen, either alone after dinner or with guests. Their home life had also been enhanced by the addition of a maid and a cook.

It worried her sometimes that he tended to spend money like water. Still haunted by the memory of her father's downfall, she became particularly uneasy when he caught the investment bug and began gambling on the Stock Exchange. Money was coming in steadily, the business doing marvellously well, but he seemed to be making sure it went out just as fast. He had developed a love of driving and bought himself a Rolls-Royce Phantom. Soon he began talking of holidaying abroad, taking Atlantic cruises, popping down to the South of France to the casinos. Julia felt it was time to make an effort to rein him in.

'Don't you think we should think a little more carefully about our finances?' she asked. 'We should be saving more than we do, just in case.'

'Just in case of what?' he asked, vaguely deflated by her lack of enthusiasm for his new toy and his exciting ideas.

'In case something should happen to bring down all we've achieved.'

'Now why should anything happen? We're on top of the world.'

'But we ought to be far better insured than we are against anything adverse that might happen. My father wasn't. And you know what happened to us because of it. Everyone needs adequate savings.'

'Then I shall buy some more stocks and

shares,' he said lightly and, seeing her catch at her lip in trepidation, added reassuringly, 'the solid gold sort, if you're worried. The worst that can happen to them is that they will yield very little.'

But she knew the big money came from the big risks, with the promise of huge gains. Her father had been seduced in this way and had either been deeply unlucky or ill advised. Whatever the truth of it, the result had been the same: he had lost everything and ruined his family. She could only hope that Simon might be shrewder and more fortunate in his dealings than ever her father was.

'There really isn't any need to worry,' Simon was saying happily. 'We are doing fine. I'm doing well on the stock market and we might even need to consider expanding the business still more.'

'I don't want us to expand. I'd prefer us to be content as we are.'

But discontent was beginning to creep into her life. It began in earnest in the spring of 1927 when Stephanie came to see her, hanging on the arm of a well-dressed young man. Proudly she introduced him to her sister.

'This is Edward John Tillington, Julia. Eddie. We've been seeing each other for nearly a year.'

She's kept that quiet, thought Julia as she shook the young man's hand, noting his firm grip and candid expression. Looking towards Stephanie as Simon took his turn to greet him, she caught sight of the flash of diamonds on her sister's engagement finger.

'Yes, we're engaged,' Stephanie blurted excitedly, noting the direction of Julia's gaze.

'Does Mummy know?' Julia asked quietly.

'No, not yet, but does it matter? We see so little of each other now, me with my flat and she in hers. But I will tell her. Eddie and I will be getting married this July and...'

'But it's already the middle of May,' Julia cut in, taken by surprise by the announcement. 'It's a bit sudden, isn't it? Why so quick?'

She saw a vague clouding of her sister's previously excited expression and guessed, with mounting dismay, at the reason for the haste. At the same time she tried to tell herself she could be wrong, was unnecessarily jumping to conclusions.

Stephanie was obviously put out by her question, protesting that after nearly a year together it wasn't a sudden decision, it was just that they hadn't announced it earlier.

Unconvinced, and unable to forget the look on Stephanie's face, Julia could only hope that she had misconstrued what she thought she had seen.

A few days later Stephanie popped into the fitting room of Julia's boutique. It was mid morning and a most inconvenient time for a social visit, but Stephanie insisted on taking her aside and asking if they could have a chat upstairs in Julia's apartment.'

'Well, I am a bit busy right now, Stephanie,' she told her, but there was something about the girl's eyes that arrested her attention. 'Look,' she said quickly, before turning back to her customer, 'go on up and I'll come as soon as I can. Give me half an hour. Make yourself a cup of tea.'

Stephanie's demeanour had been that of someone with a need to confess and it took a huge effort of will for Julia to give her attention to her woman customer's needs. Finally, the woman departed, satisfied and she hastened up to her flat.

'I couldn't help seeing the way you looked at me the other day, Julia, when I told you about our plans,' Stephanie began as soon as she came into the room. 'I knew what you were thinking.'

'Then am I right?' Julia asked bluntly, and was immediately dismayed by Stephanie's nod and deep blush. Seconds later though Stephanie had become chirpy and confident again, clutching both Julia's hands with hers.

'It's all right, Julia. Eddie is quite happy about it. The baby's not due until around December and by that time we'll be so well married no one will think of counting up, and if they do we'll just say it was premature. And no one will suspect at the wedding because I shall be hardly four months gone and not showing all that much. It's just that I had to come here and explain because you looked so surprised and worried.'

She seemed so self-assured, so happy, and left obviously feeling that all was well with her world. But Julia couldn't help fearing history could easily repeat itself. Eddie seemed a like-able, upright and honest young man, not at all badly off for money, and from quite a good family. But then so, apparently, had been the other one.

She continued to feel uneasy until the happy couple finally stood at the altar in all their splendour. The bride's mother, still unaware of her daughter's condition, had given her tearful blessing. Neither of the families seemed concerned at the haste of the wedding preparations and in truth Stephanie looked as sylphlike as ever as she and Eddie stood together at the altar. If, in the months to come, people started to notice her growing pregnancy and put two and two together, Julia felt she couldn't care less.

Yet she experienced a deep feeling of envy as the two went through their marriage vows. It should have been her and Simon standing there at the altar; the guests half filling the church should have been their guests. Simon should have been standing beside her as her husband-to-be, not giving her sister away in the absence of a father.

The feeling grew as she listened to the vicar's intonations; Stephanie's quiet responses, Edward's firm and confident; the church filling with sound as the congregation rejoiced for the couple; the organ playing quietly while the couple retired to the vestry to sign the register; then swelling again to the echoing, resounding strains of Mendelssohn's Bridal March as the congregation filed slowly out behind the newly-weds for the photographs.

Edward had bought his wife a lovely house in north London, not far from his parents. As the months went by and Stephanie started to show in earnest, Julia's envy grew stronger, as did a strange sense of longing; a slow realization that what she was feeling was broodiness. She had experienced this at other times in the past – an oddly miserable, empty feeling – but never as strongly as now. Somehow business had always seemed to get in the way before the feeling really took hold of her.

By the time autumn arrived Stephanie's pregnancy was becoming noticeable. She was so happy and proud, clinging to her husband's arm, and he in turn was so utterly besotted with her, that Julia's feelings of envy and longing grew in strength.

But she and Simon were not married. Few people were aware of this – she wore rings on many of her fingers, and the ring finger of her left hand bore a slim gold band with a single diamond that could have been a wedding ring. But whether others thought them married or not, a baby was a different matter, needing a father's name if it were not to be destined to carry the stigma of illegitimate birth for the rest of its life.

No. Babies were not on their list. Work and business were on their list. Simon was still full of ideas for expanding; she was still very much against expansion. These days Julia was unable to rid herself of strange premonitions of unexpected collapse and of pride often going before a fall. There was no longer any talk of marriage between them.

# Twenty-One

It was Christmas Eve, Saturday. Julia and Simon had driven through almost blizzard conditions to Brownswood Park in North London to spend the next few days with Stephanie and her husband. Stephanie was now near her time.

After much persuasion she'd managed to get her mother to come with them, though Victoria's fear of car travel caused her to draw in sharp gasps of breath whenever another vehicle materialized out of the whiteness from the opposite direction. Although told that a Rolls Phantom was the safest thing on the road, she refused to believe it until Julia felt her nerves in danger of being worn ragged.

It was important that her mother should be with them. Stephanie was unable to travel now that the birth was so close, James was spending Christmas with his fiancée and her family, and Ginny, not caring to spend a lonely, miserable Christmas keeping her mother company, had asked if she could come along with Julia to Stephanie's.

'I'll be all right here alone,' Victoria had said, her voice trembling.

'But you can't stay here on your own,' Julia had insisted, but her mother had at first been adamant.

'I'm getting used to being on my own,' she had bleated plaintively. 'If Virginia finds it a chore to stay and keep her mother company, let her go with you. I might just as well stay here by myself. After all, these days any Christmas to me is just another day without your father. It'll soon be over.'

'But we shall go down on the Saturday, stay Christmas and Boxing Day and travel home on the Tuesday. We can't leave you here all that time alone. I need to be there in case Stephanie goes into labour. She could have the baby any minute.'

'I can't help that,' was the comment, but Julia refused to give up.

'She has a lovely home. You'll be comfortable and there'll be lots of company for you. Edward's parents will be there on Christmas Day and his sister and her boyfriend.'

'I won't be able to sleep in a strange bed. I don't know his people.'

Julia had been near to losing her temper. 'Then shall we all stay here, Mummy, and leave Stephanie to her own devices if the baby suddenly decides to arrive? It's your grandchild, Mummy, your first grandchild. How can you not want to be there?'

'I'm frightened of travelling in a car.'

'Then you're going to have to get used to it, Mummy!' Julia blurted and would hear no more. So Victoria consented, allowing herself to be helped into the car as though she were an invalid, cringing in the back, yelping at every obstacle that appeared to her to be in their way while Ginny held on to her, murmuring words of comfort.

It was no better once they arrived. Christmas greetings over, she stationed herself in a far corner of the room in a comfortable armchair, sinking into it until she all but disappeared. There she remained, speaking little to anyone, making them feel awkward until they finally ignored her. Later she allowed herself to be assisted to the meal table where she picked unenthusiastically at each sumptuous offering until Julia wanted to shake her, fully aware that she was playing up deliberately.

Even so it was a good holiday and Stephanie managed not to interrupt it by going into labour. Julia would have loved to go back there for the New Year but decided it would be best to spend it with her mother. Stephanie had her husband's family around her and so was in good hands. There was still no sign of the baby though.

The following Wednesday, just four days into 1928, there came a telephone call ten minutes before nine in the morning as Julia was just about ready to go downstairs. It was from Stephanie.

'Julia,' a gasping voice sounded the moment Julia picked up the receiver. 'Nothing is happening. I keep having awful, really awful pains but nothing is happening.'

'Are you on your own?' Julia asked. 'Where's Edward?'

'He's visiting a client. He'll be home this evening.'

'Have you telephoned the hospital?' Edward's house had a telephone that he used to contact his office as a public accountant.

'I can't move!' come the cry. 'It's too painful when I move. Julia, I'm so frightened.'

'I'm getting a train and coming straight over,' Julia interrupted her.

Having raced downstairs to tell Simon where she was going, then back upstairs to alert her mother, she hurried off, finally arriving to find that though the front door was locked the back door wasn't. She found Stephanie huddled on the settee in a state of panic and pain.

'It's so overdue!' Stephanie wailed, doubled over with the pain. 'My doctor said it was due just before Christmas! Could it be dangerous?'

'It's only a week overdue if that's the case,' soothed Julia, but having no children of her own she had no idea if this was anything to worry about. She did, however, need to keep her sister calm with quiet and even words. 'Have you still not notified the hospital?'

Stephanie shook her head and moaned.

'Haven't you got in touch with Edward at all?

'I don't know where he is.'

'Well, his parents then?'

But again Stephanie shook her head. 'I was waiting for you.'

'It's taken me nearly an hour to get here. You mean that you've just been lying here, waiting for me, doing nothing, telling no one?'

'I didn't want to make too much of a fuss. I thought I'd wait until you came. Ooh...'

As her words broke off in a trembling cry of

pain, Julia rushed to the phone in the hall, yanking it off its hook, clicking the arm rapidly up and down until the exchange answered.

'I need the maternity hospital,' she yelled into the mouthpiece as the operator responded. 'I don't know the number or the name but I think this is an emergency. Can you put me through without having a number?'

Within a minute or two she was connected. Asked the details she was told that an ambulance would be there in ten minutes or so. Returning to Stephanie she found her still curled up on the settee whimpering like a tiny child, her cheeks almost lobster red as she bore down in response to the baby's need to come into the world.

'I don't know what to do!' Her voice was tight and squeaky amid new bouts of pain. 'It's worse than ever it was the last time. Oh, it hurts...'

Another breech, thought Julia, the memory of the last one sending her into a cold sweat of fear for her sister and for the baby. She needed to phone Edward's mother, but there was no getting any sense out of Stephanie, curled up and gripped by pain.

Between looking for a telephone number pad and trying to comfort her sister, she heard the ringing of an ambulance bell and offered up a prayer of thanks. Minutes later she was sitting inside it holding her sister's hand, soon to feel the sway as the vehicle swung into the hospital forecourt. Stephanie was carried off to the maternity ward and Julia sat alone, waiting. She had no idea how to contact Edward or his parents, and her own mother still refused to have a telephone in her flat. Simon was the only person she could get in touch with.

She phoned him, loving the reassuring sound of his light voice as he undertook to alert her mother and then try to contact Edward's office. Someone there would know where he was. She hadn't thought of that, in all the panic of dealing with Stephanie.

She seemed to have been sitting tensely in the empty waiting room for hours, silently praying that Stephanie and the baby would be all right. The arrival of Edward was a blessed relief, but without even saying hullo he asked from the waiting room door, 'Where is she?' Then, noticing a nurse passing by the door, he made off after her, giving Julia no time to reply.

She had half risen from her seat at his entrance but now sat down again. After a while a worried-looking young man, obviously a father-to-be, was ushered in by a nurse who was telling him that his wife was doing well. As she made to go, Julia leapt up from her chair.

'Sorry to bother you, nurse, but is there any news yet of my sister? She came in about an hour ago. Her name's Stephanie Tillington,' she gabbled on. 'Her husband is Edward Tillington. He went out to speak to a nurse a little while ago.'

'I'll find out for you,' the woman said briskly, leaving the room, the door closing behind her. Julia forced a smile at the young man but he didn't return the smile and she fell to waiting again, fighting the fears in her head.

The nurse did return, sooner than Julia had expected, and beckoned her out to the corridor. There was no expression on her face that Julia could read and she immediately feared the worst as she followed her. It was then that Julia saw Edward coming towards them, walking quickly, his face twisted with anxiety.

Before the nurse could speak he said, 'They've taken her for an operation.' There was fear in his tone. 'They say it's a breech birth. They say the baby isn't strong enough to come out on its own. They're going to operate to save it, maybe Stephanie as well.'

Julia felt tears form in her eyes, her throat grown restricted. 'Oh, Edward!' she whispered, but the nurse took her arm.

'She will be having a Caesarean section, there's nothing to worry about. She will be fine,' she said calmly.

Edward didn't seem at all comforted and as the nurse left them standing in the corridor he turned to Julia, his eyes full of reproach. 'I had no idea Stephanie had lost a previous baby,' he said quietly. 'She never told me. I had to learn of it from the hospital!'

It was evening before Simon could get away. Julia greeted his arrival with a flood of tears. 'Oh, Simon, what's happened is terrible!' she burst out, flinging herself into his arms. 'I've been here for ages on my own. I didn't know what to do. Edward left. I don't know where he's gone. Stephanie had a girl, but he doesn't know. I just couldn't explain to you on the phone what

264

has happened.'

Puzzled by her uncharacteristic outburst, telling her to calm herself, he listened while she composed her mind enough to inform him what had happened.

'Edward knows about Stephanie's other affair. He learned from the doctor that she'd had a previous baby. He didn't know. Now he's gone off goodness knows where.'

She clenched her fists and shook them in anger. 'How could she not have told him? The stupid, stupid girl! The poor man had to learn it this way from someone else! And he was in such fear for her, having to go through a Caesarean operation!'

'And how are they?' Simon queried.

'The baby seems to be fine.'

'And Stephanie?'

'I don't know. She's still sleeping off the anaesthetic.' Julia bit at her lower lip, uncertain what would happen now. 'I wish we could find Edward, explain to him. What if he can't forgive her?' She grew agitated again. 'What's going to happen to their marriage? She was so happy.'

Simon sighed and held her to him to stop her frantic outpouring. 'First we'll see if we can find him. He may have gone to his parents' house.'

'But I don't know where they live.'

'We'll telephone his office. They'll know.'

Julia clung to him, wondering what she would do if ever she lost him. Such a thing was unthinkable but nevertheless, seeing Stephanie's plight, she couldn't help wondering all the same.

* * *

Julia sat with the baby in her arms. Instinctively rocking back and forth as if she were the child's mother she let her mind wander over these past six weeks since the baby's birth, musing upon how a chain of circumstances could alter lives and send them along a totally different route, changing them completely.

Had her father not died, had their lives continued along the lines he had set, Stephanie would have been a different person from the one she now was. She would never have worked for a living behind a department store counter, spending her evenings dancing, looking for young men, looking for a good time. She would certainly not have got involved with a rogue who had got her in the family way, leaving as soon as he discovered her condition. She wouldn't be in this mess now.

It was ironic, Julia thought with a bitter smile as she gazed down at the baby in her arms. All her hard work trying to keep the family going after losing Father had been a waste of time. Her mother had become a miserable woman, allowing herself to age before her time, while Stephanie had got herself into this mess. Ginny had grown into a beautiful fashion model, parading herself before those chasing fashion – a lovely, kind-hearted young girl, but what sort of man would her lifestyle bring her into contact with? The thought was frightening and she vowed to try and guide Ginny, at least, away from some of the pitfalls Stephanie had encountered. She had no worries about James though. Of all of them, he had changed least, except to grow more staid, more like his father every day, a little pompous and remote.

The baby had begun to whimper, and then squirm. From gazing at the little face, lost in thought, Julia looked up at the baby's mother.

'Perhaps you had best have her now, Stephanie.' Even so she felt a slight reluctance to hand the child over; it felt so right to be holding her as if she were her own. She experienced a tiny pang of loss as Stephanie lifted the baby from her arms, the small weight gone, leaving Julia with a strange sensation of emptiness.

'She probably needs changing,' Stephanie said in a subdued voice.

It was amazing how she had altered over the past couple of years. Gone was the overconfident flapper she had been before picking up with that awful Jimmy, losing the baby and going through all her troubles. Meeting Edward had been her salvation. But now he too appeared to have become part of her past, her happiness dashed again as she was left to bring up her baby alone.

Julia had tried to talk to Edward, but it had been an impossible task to make him see that his wife, through no fault of her own, had fallen foul of a selfish brute whom she thought had loved her, who had spoken of engagement and tricked her into giving herself to him.

She had tried so hard to make him see that it had been he himself who had lifted Stephanie out of the mire she had made for herself. She'd striven to point out that Stephanie had tried to put the sad episode behind her; that she had never again referred to her desolation after that stillbirth, so why should she want to speak of it to him? Julia had asked him to put himself in Stephanie's shoes – prior to marrying her, would he have admitted to such a fall from grace if he thought it would wreck their lives together? In a way, meeting him had led to the only happiness she'd known. Why would she want to spoil it?

She had pleaded with him to forgive for the sake of his child as well as his wife, pointing out the harm his attitude could do, the effect it could have on his daughter if she had to grow up torn between separate parents.

During those six weeks since the birth and the separation from Edward Stephanie had been so ill that Julia had had to take time from her work to help with little Violet Julia, whom Stephanie had named after her sister.

On this particular Sunday morning a knock on their apartment door forced Simon up from lounging on the settee to answer it. He came back to the lounge grinning, followed by the broad-shouldered figure of Stephanie's husband.

'It's Edward,' he announced unnecessarily as Stephanie leaped up the moment she saw him.

Julia offered up a silent prayer of thanks that all her efforts had been rewarded, and then she and Simon quickly retired to the living room, taking little Violet with them, to give the couple some privacy.

As she picked up the child, Julia again experienced that discomforting sense of broodiness. Even more discomforting was the fact that Simon didn't seem in the least interested in the child. The question came to her, would he be interested if it were his own child – and would she ever be given the opportunity to find out?

When finally the two people called them back in it was to say that they were both returning home this afternoon. Stephanie was very quiet; Edward's eyes were on his wife the whole time, full of love and forgiveness. It turned out that he had not said a word to his parents about the temporary break-up. As far as they were concerned, the little family were happy.

His tact and discretion raised him further in Julia's eyes. Stephanie was a very lucky woman indeed and Julia found herself envying her in every way. She knew she was wrong to feel like this, but she couldn't help it.

Something in her own union with Simon was beginning to go horribly wrong in her mind. Lately he seemed to be evading the question of marriage completely. Maybe it was pressure of work. Or maybe it was simply that their union was going stale. She felt she was being treated far too casually these days and even their love-making was much less frequent than it had once been.

She thought of those early days when life had been so easy, so full of promise and hope. Where had it all gone? And if they did marry now, would it be an anticlimax; would their marriage be stale before it had even begun?

Having seen the happy pair with their baby downstairs to the street, where Edward had left his small car, Julia returned upstairs. Sighing, she closed the door of her luxury apartment upon her world of fashion, frustration and hard work until tomorrow morning when she must face it again.

# Twenty-Two

Fashion was changing, and changing fast. Julia had been caught out by it, knowing that she should have kept her eye on its eccentricities instead of worrying about Stephanie's problems.

Without her realizing, summer was here and in a matter of weeks hemlines had begun to drop alarmingly to below the knee, waistlines slowly rising from hip to waist level again. Evening dresses were no problem, they were mostly full length and elegant. The rapid change in daywear was the problem. An even slimmer look was all the rage, with women going on murderous diets to attain ever more sticklike figures. Hair was cut even shorter, vanishing beneath head-hugging caps. And while the rich flew off to find the sun, or like the famous Dolly sisters to gamble away fortunes, the few decent days in this year's dull and miserable British summer saw every young girl trying in vain to get a tan on a beach somewhere, wearing backless swimwear so that her backless evening dresses did not show a white line.

While top designers had kept abreast of things, Julia was suddenly aware that she had been left behind, her creations this spring already out of date.

271

'I'm going to have to scrap the whole lot and start again,' she told Simon miserably. 'At least, all my day dresses. All that work, those lovely designs, useless. Who'd want them? It's going to cost me a fortune.'

But already her mind was working on something that might help her keep up with the rest – day dresses, still hip-hugging and straight but falling to a wildly flared hem; another with a two-tiered one, both flared and fluted – she could use all sorts of computations. And although it wouldn't be long before someone like Chanel or Worth got hold of the idea, she'd be first on the scene. Even so, it took money and ate into the profits from previous seasons.

'Don't worry,' Simon pacified. 'I can get a bank loan any time I like if we need it. I don't want to touch my investments though if I can help it. At the moment it's a bear market but a little bird has told me it could soon be looking up quite substantially.'

Once on the subject of investments he would go off on his own road and when Julia tried to interrupt, hardly heard her.

'In a few months I shall be hoping to make a killing. So it's a time to buy, not sell. Next year we'll be laughing so don't worry over a few dozen dresses.'

It wasn't a few dozen dresses as he put it. It was almost her entire line; all her designs had to be thrown out, and starting on new styles cost money. The big fashion houses could weather sudden changes, but while she could certainly hold up her head in this trade she was still somewhat small fry compared to some. But Simon's eager remarks distracted her from her own problems.

'No, best not to dabble in anything at the moment,' she cautioned.

His dealings frightened her at times. He treated the stock market as a professional gambler might treat horse racing, studying form, one eye to the best studs, keeping a constant ear to the ground; so he kept his eyes on the ever-changing stock market, shrugging complacently when something didn't go so well, smiling with calm satisfaction when it did.

Now he was talking of buying more shares while they were low and waiting for a bull market to sell at a profit. He played the stock market just as her father had but he seemed far luckier. And where her father had kept his thoughts to himself, Simon talked incessantly of his investments, like a little boy looking for adventure.

'Don't worry the bank,' she cautioned again. 'I can always use some of my own money that I keep by in case I need it.' He was looking at her, smiling as a man might at a foolish little woman.

'I really find it amusing, darling, the way you hide odd shekels in that box of yours,' he chuckled. 'What is it now, a few hundred, if that? That'll go a long way! You should make more use of the bank, darling. After all, that's what banks are there for.'

She capitulated, trying to meet the slightly patronizing, if loving, smile. 'I suppose I won't be losing that much in scrapping my earlier designs. I can sell off the old stock to the high street shops. It's just that I hate seeing good money drift away.'

What she didn't say and what she had never told him was that she had an ingrained mistrust of all banks, dating from the time her father had left his family penniless. Because of it, she'd developed her own way of saving, vowing never to be put in such a position ever again. She did bank money, of course, but more for those day-to-day transactions that business demanded. It was Simon who took charge of the greater proportion of their finances, their business having been his in the first place.

He would go on gambling on the stock exchange and relying on banks for credit. It seemed to work and maybe her way was strange for someone in her position, but beneath the floorboards under the carpet in the corner of their spare bedroom was a small, locked metal box that was becoming ever more tightly packed with large, neatly folded bank notes, just in case something awful should happen.

She had never told Simon how much was in there and he had never asked, merely smiling tolerantly at her strange habit. Of course, such an emergency as she feared would never arise but in a small way it gave her a feeling of security and helped to assuage the gnawing fear of a rainy day should Simon ever go the way of her father. He was too astute ever to let that happen. Nevertheless, it was better to be safe.

In the back room, all was chaos. Her creations

were draped on hangers ready for the three models to change garments in split seconds, step into and buckle their shoes, change accessories and refresh their make-up before stepping out on to the catwalk. Out there in her modest showroom all was serene; gentle music, the quiet murmur of voices, appreciative applause from a few dozen invited buyers and a general audience.

Julia stood behind the blue curtains watching Ginny's measured walk, her movements leisurely and artistic, her head poised elegantly on her slender neck. At the end of the catwalk she turned confidently to retrace her footsteps, smiling gently at this person and that, no sign of hurry, no nerves; she was a confident and beautiful young woman, unafraid before all those eyes.

There came a small burst of applause as Ginny reached the curtains to be replaced by one of the other models. Julia had worked hard for weeks to get this show together and it looked as if it was paying off. She felt exhausted but thoroughly rewarded.

'Marvellous, Ginny, as always,' she whispered as Ginny passed her,.

Giving Julia a bright smile she hurried to where Betty waited with another garment for her, ready to be pulled this way and that, in several directions at once, in order to get the dress and its accessories just right, all in seconds.

It was an effort for Julia to tear her glance away from her sister to follow the next girl. The others too were lovely girls, tall and slender, but Ginny was the most beautiful. Sometimes the men, young and old and mostly from the fashion world, would eye her a little too long and closely for Julia's piece of mind. But Ginny hardly gave them a glance which was just as well. She seemed to have no wish to settle down, loving her life as a model, and after all she was still only twenty, wouldn't be twenty-one until November. There was plenty of time for her to put her mind to courting, though Ginny certainly enjoyed life, going to evening parties, to Wimbledon for the tennis tournaments, to cocktail and garden parties, and often driving out into the country with a group of friends. Lately she'd taken up cycling, going miles out of London exploring country lanes and country pubs, with a group of young men and women.

As a model she was slowly becoming well known and even had her picture in *Style*, one of the topmost fashion magazines, and had made scores of friends. But Julia couldn't help feeling responsible for her youngest sister, and was anxious that her success should not go to her head.

What if her head were suddenly turned by the wrong man? Stephanie had been caught like that, and Stephanie had been a woman of the world, or so Julia had thought. Julia could only hope that Ginny wouldn't make the same mistake. Though if she did there was little that she, even as Ginny's elder sister, could do about it other than keep an eye out for her and pray.

Everything seemed to be building up all at once as summer gave way to autumn.

Last March James and Caroline had announced the date of their wedding, Saturday the sixth of October. With only seven weeks to go, Julia was finding it difficult to get on with her own work, having to design and make the wedding dress as well as bridesmaids' dresses for Ginny and Caroline's sister Amy.

Then on Sunday Ginny brought a young man home whom she boldly introduced as Robert Middleton. 'He's proposed to me,' she announced, her eyes alight with joy. 'And I have accepted. We want to go out during the week to choose the engagement ring. You will give us your blessings, won't you?'

Shocked by the suddenness of the announcement, her mind full of suspicious thoughts, Julia quickly took her sister aside. But before she could get a word in, Ginny had burst out excitedly, 'His family live near Chingford, his father's business is based not far away and Robert is a partner.'

Changing tack, she said, 'He looks a little bit older than you.' She wanted to say he looked a lot older but hadn't the heart. But before she could say more, Ginny was off again.

'He's older only by about eight years. That's nothing. We met in one of those country pubs when a few of us were out cycling up that way. It was one of those places where really posh people congregate – you know, horses and hounds and cricket, that sort of thing. That was back in May and we – well – fell for each other.'

'Why haven't you told me about him before now, Ginny?' Julia cut in. 'You've known him for four months and said nothing to anyone. And four months is not long enough for two people to think of getting engaged.'

Ginny's happy smile turned to a frown. 'You sound just like Mummy! You're getting old-fashioned, like her. Why should four months be too soon for two people to know how they feel about each other? We're in love.'

Julia's thoughts returned to her previous suspicions, the awful thought still in her mind. 'Then why haven't you said anything about him until now?'

'I don't know.' Ginny shrugged. 'The time goes so quickly and there's always so much to do. We're mostly with lots of other people and, well, we just came together naturally. And anyway, why should I need to report to you?'

'It's not *reporting*, Ginny.'

'Well, I'm telling you now,' she rushed on, unaware that her retort might have sounded rude.

Julia didn't have the heart now to ask if her sister was 'all right' in that way she couldn't help wondering about. Ginny looked so happy. If she wasn't 'all right', surely she'd have a guilty look about her. But she was radiant.

It was Stephanie who announced herself once again pregnant and over the moon about it. 'I hope it's a boy this time. Eddie so wants a boy.'

Her joy instantly resurrected all those feelings Julia had thought she'd buried in her work as she warmly congratulated her sister.

'Have you told Mummy?' she asked.

Stephanie pulled a face. 'Not yet. I know what she'll say the moment I do: "I wish your poor father was with us to hear your news. To think he'd be a grandfather." Then she'll go into one of her miseries and say she's feeling poorly. I'd rather leave it for a while.'

These days their mother seemed to be continually ailing. She seemed almost to be giving up, complaining that all her children were leaving her. It was the natural course of things but she didn't see it that way. If only she could see it not as a family diminishing but growing. She'd have so many more people popping in to see her. It was this constant lamenting about the emptiness of her life and never letting them forget their deceased father that put them off, If only she'd realize that accepting their new lives with serenity would bring them closer, that it was she who pushed them away rather than they who were staying away.

As Stephanie said when Julia thought she should bring little Violet to see her grandmother more often: 'What's the point? As soon as she sees her she bursts into tears and says, if only Father had lived to see his granddaughter. Doesn't she see that if Father had lived I might not be married and have Violet? Eddie doesn't know what to say. It's embarrassing.'

It would have been the perfect wedding but for the rain, thought Julia as she stood with the congregation listening to the traditional resounding strains of the Wedding March

279

playing James and Caroline out of the church. Luckily, with no hope of snapshots in the open air, it had been arranged that photographs were to be taken at a nearby studio.

James had organized every last thing from beginning to end. But one thing he couldn't control – the weather. Julia thought she'd never seen such rain. Poor Caroline had arrived shielded by an umbrella held over her by her father. It was fortunate her wedding dress only came to just below the knees, following the current trend, and so didn't suffer much. But the trailing lace veil had to be bundled up unceremoniously by her mother, who held it at arm's length as much under the umbrella as she could while the two made a most unladylike dash to the church porch, followed by the bridesmaids, also under umbrellas wielded by a couple of uncles.

Even so, Caroline entered the church all smiles, ignoring the fact that those already in the church were filling it with the faint damp odour of mackintoshes and umbrellas piled up on empty chairs at the back.

Julia felt sorry for her brother more than for Caroline. He'd worked so hard. In that staid manner which had now become part of him he seldom smiled even when pleased, reminding her so much of their father in looks and attitude.

She only hoped Caroline would be of a stronger character than her mother and weather James's overbearing ways. Otherwise she could have a miserable life. But today she looked radiant despite the rain as she walked down the aisle on her father's arm while James rose from his seat to stand beside her.

Julia saw her feel for his hand, and saw James grip it briefly, and felt her heart give a tug of envy. Angry with herself for feeling so when she should be thinking of the happiness of those two, she had felt for Simon's hand, curling her fingers round it and feeling his curl around hers. 'Darling, we should get married,' she whispered and heard him whisper back, 'I know.'

The rest of the service became a blur in the euphoria that swept over her. Now though, posing for the official photographer, with the small band of close relatives arranged about the newly-weds in the studio all smiling fixedly lest the result blur, she wondered how genuine had been those two words of Simon's.

At the reception he was on the far side of the room – she could only glimpse him amidst the gathering, just beyond the wedding cake – and seemed oblivious to her. But if he'd meant what he said in the church surely he would be at her side now.

Her spirits drooping again, Julia smiled as Stephanie came up, champagne glass in hand though little of it had been drunk, and couldn't help glancing at her sister's waistline, already imagining she saw the first sign of thickening.

Eddie was at her side holding little Violet and a small, ugly, sneering thought went through Julia's head: 'A baby not yet out of nappies and she's pregnant again, it's disgusting!' Deep inside her heart though she admitted that it was not disgusting but that it was so totally, totally unfair!

281

# Twenty-Three

His investments were healthy, the business was doing well. 'Lately it seems we can't go wrong,' exclaimed Simon.

But all Julia could think of were those two words he'd said in church: 'I know.' Had they truly had the quality of a promise or had he merely been conveying that he'd heard what she said?

So many times she had been on the verge of reminding him of it but again work intervened. Christmas, despite thick snow, had brought a rush of orders and it wasn't until the festive season was over and they could breathe again that she found the moment to bring it up.

She did so one evening a few days after the New Year as they reclined on the settee hardly listening to the BBC's reports of terrible flooding in London, the result of a high tide combined with a sudden thaw. She snuggled against Simon who had one arm about her and was studying a jewellery catalogue he held in his other hand. As yet he didn't deal in precious stones but his costume jewellery was of the highest quality, designed to his specification, and was always in great demand.

Although he held her close to him, his mind

was obviously in another world; he didn't even look up when she began quietly, 'Simon, you remember at James and Caroline's wedding?'

'Mmm?' he murmured absently.

'What you said in church when I whispered in your ear during the service that *we* should get married?'

Glancing up from the catalogue, far too quickly for her mind, as if startled, he looked a little perplexed. 'Did you, darling?'

'You know I did. And you said, "I know." Don't you remember?'

He frowned and shook his head, but Julia meant to pursue her quest. 'It was the only few words we said to each other during the whole service and I need to know, did you mean that you know we should get married?'

'I'm not sure I remember what I said.'

It was as if he was deliberately evading her and she felt a sudden desperation to pin him down. She sat up away from him, snatching the catalogue from his hand and throwing it beside her on the settee.

'All these years together, the times we've promised ourselves to get married, to set a date, and here we are, the same as ever.'

'Aren't we happy as we are?'

'I'm not!'

The words were torn from her so forcefully he was left gazing at her in amazement and some apprehension. She almost read the question in his eyes: *You're not saying you want to leave?* But suddenly he smiled.

'Don't be silly, darling, we have everything
283

we've ever wished for. We're comfortably off, we've a nice apartment, and we have each other. We've...'

'But we're not married!' she broke in. 'Don't you want to be married?'

'Yes, of course, darling, as soon as we get the business really up and running.'

Her temper flared, surprising even her. 'How *up and running* does it have to be? Haven't we come up in the world enough? How far do we have to go before you consider it time you married me?'

She was trying to calm down, gain control of her anger. 'Simon, we've done so well. How much more do you want?'

She watched him get up and go over to turn off the wireless. The room was suddenly quiet, so that his voice, though soft, sounded almost too loud.

'I want us to reach the top of the tree,' he said evenly, 'to be up there with the big fashion houses – Chanel, Caret, Hartnell. I want your name to be the one that everyone remembers when they think of fashion.'

'And I want a baby! I don't want to climb to the top of any tree.'

She could hear the pleading in her own voice. 'We never have time for ourselves these days. That's why we never get around to the subject of marriage. I know you love me, Simon, but sometimes I feel taken for granted. I want to have a baby and I can't while we're not married. We never make love properly any more in case I fall pregnant. I don't know if I'm even able to have babies. We've never tried...'

She broke off. He was looking at her but his expression was obscured by the mist of her tears. Seconds later she was in his arms, weeping as if her heart were broken.

'Sweetheart,' she heard his soft voice in her ear, 'let's get the next fashion show over then I promise you, my sweet darling, we'll be married and this time nothing will stand in our way.'

She should have felt soothed, but it was as if she were seeing a rerun of a film, as sometimes happened in the cinema when the film would break and have to be restarted. How many times had he promised marriage and even begun to make the arrangements, only to have them all fall through as work interfered?

She didn't really believe it now but she let him carry on holding her, so confident he'd solved everything, really believing his own promises. Despite everything a small spark of hope hovered inside her that this time it would happen.

Julia stared at the expensive sapphire and diamond dress ring Simon had given her. The thought crossed her mind, maybe uncharitably, that this was to make up for last week. In the past, when they'd been struggling, he had often thrilled her with little gifts he could hardly afford. As they had climbed their financial ladder so his gifts had become more costly. But this was far too much. Even so she understood and kissed him ardently.

They were going out more as a couple too, to the cinema, theatre, dinner; just the two of them without the company of friends. But she knew work suffered and was sure that he too silently fretted over it. He was trying so hard to make her happy and she loved him for it; it was she who was now feeling guilty.

'We should be concentrating on next month's display,' she murmured as they lingered over dinner one evening after seeing a show. He smiled.

'Like you said, darling, we need some time to ourselves.' It sounded like criticism but he took her hand reassuringly across the table. 'We can make up for it the rest of the week.'

The rest of the week did see them hard at work, realizing how the time soon slipped away. Julia's next fashion show was still several weeks away. The cost of these shows often made Julia's mouth dry up with fear. The hire of the venue and the models, the cost of sets, lighting, music, and all else that went into putting on a fashion show could amount to around ten to twenty thousand pounds depending on its size and where it was held. The bigger fashion houses would pay even more. Bank loans usually paid for their shows, the money to be repaid by a certain time. So far they'd come out with a profit, such was the measure of their growing success.

Thoughts of work were always with them. As they sat together in a cinema one Saturday night their minds were elsewhere. It was only a matter of time before the next wave of new fashions descended on them. Already Julia was mentally preparing herself for the coming season's styles.

Her mind more on the clothes than the film, a talkie called *The Last of Mrs Cheyney*, she whispered to Simon in the hushed auditorium, 'I'm sure America's ahead of us in dress.' She was immediately shushed into silence, and glanced angrily at the shusher before turning back to gaze woodenly ahead.

She wasn't all that interested in the film, despite the fine acting of Norma Shearer and Basil Rathbone, two of the most popular stars, whose voices now held audiences spellbound. Many silent film stars had not survived the move to 'talkies', their high, scratchy tones putting off the fans who had previously adored them.

With the arrival of talkies just under a year ago the atmosphere in the cinema had changed. It was often difficult to catch the rapid American accents, so it was necessary to keep one's whole attention on the film. Consequently, the slightest cough, rustle of a sweet bag or the hiss of whispered conversation was a distraction. During silent films the place would have been full of open talk, crunching of peanut shells, shuffling feet and open comments about the film, with the audience even reading the captions aloud.

'Styles are changing. I'm going to have to keep my eye on them.' Julia risked another whisper and saw Simon nod his agreement in the pale glow from the screen, his eyes trained on the actors.

For the rest of the film, a stilted story without much movement to it, Julia's mind churned over the changing trends in fashion. Bosoms were making a slow reappearance; the wildly gyrating

287

dances popular a few years ago were now slower as dresses were becoming more ladylike and skirts lengthening. Belts were still at hip level but tops were now bloused, and hats had larger brims while still covering much of the face. Jewellery no longer dangled in long, garish strings and there was not a slave bangle to be seen. Everything was more elegant, the sleek, trailing, figure-hugging evening dress becoming ever more *de rigueur*.

As they moved towards the closing years of the 1920s she felt the new decade would be totally different from this one. A sense of eagerness assailed her as she stared vacantly at the screen. Already there was a change in the air. She and Simon would be ready for it.

It wasn't until they'd arrived back home that it came to her that the surge of eagerness she had experienced had temporarily pushed out all thoughts of marriage and babies. The realization made her look afresh at what she had now and what she'd achieved: this tastefully planned apartment, her wardrobe of lovely clothes, her expensive shoes, her jewellery, her beautifully manicured hands. And there was more: the inspiration that gripped her each time she entered her workroom, the exhilarating smell of new fine materials, the stimulating touch of tracing paper under her fingers. All this had become her life. Did she really want to give it all up? She couldn't imagine life without it. Was she really cut out for marriage and babies? Would marriage now in fact make any difference to her and Simon's lifestyle?

Suddenly she could not visualize herself bringing up a baby, nursing it, comforting it when it cried, bathing it, putting it to bed. With the money they now had she could afford a nursemaid and a nanny, but what would be the point? Perhaps Simon was right. Why worry him when they more or less had everything? No one could expect to have it all. She needed to learn to be content. She was a businesswoman. Babies and business just did not mix, she concluded sternly, and believed it.

Ginny burst into the cutting room. 'Stephanie's had her baby!'

Julia looked up from talking to Betty, still her number one cutter. But before she could speak, Ginny rushed on, her face alight with excitement.

'She went into labour in the night. Edward's just been on the phone. He wanted to speak to you but he couldn't wait. He had to get back to her.'

The old surge of envy and strange emptiness ran through Julia. 'Why weren't we told earlier?' she demanded as if Ginny were at fault.

Ginny didn't bat an eyelid. 'Because it started in the early hours and she only had it around seven. It's only nine o'clock now. Edward went in to see her afterwards and this is the first chance he's had to phone us, I suppose.'

Julia steadied her thoughts and tried to forget the empty churning in her stomach. 'I suppose so,' she relented. 'Did he say how she is? And the baby – what has she had?'

'He said Stephanie and the baby are fine. She's had a little boy, eight pounds.'

'*Aah*,' sighed Betty, laying her work aside for the moment. 'Have they a name for him, bless his little soul?'

'He never said,' replied Ginny, looking across at her. 'But he sounded over the moon.'

'He would be,' said Julia a little sharply but no one noticed as she went on, 'Well, I'm glad there were no complications. We'll have to go over there to see them when we can. But for the moment I've got to get on.'

Ginny went out, faintly disappointed that there hadn't been as much excitement as she had expected.

Julia had meant to ask if their mother knew. She probably did. Ginny was the only one of her children living there with her now. She no longer went out to work, being more than well enough paid as a model, so it was Ginny who kept their mother company, cared for her, listened patiently to her complaints and no doubt dreamed of the day she and Robert could be married, when she would be free of it all.

Robert had proved to be a really charming, caring young man. Ginny was lucky and said so more often than she needed to. 'I'm so very, very lucky! I can't believe how lucky I am to have him. I can't wait to be married.'

That would be next year, probably early spring, when she would be twenty-one. Julia already had it in mind to make hers the best wedding there ever was. She loved Ginny above both her other two siblings. A sweet and selfless girl like Ginny deserved nothing but the very best.

Stephanie named her second child Stephen Edward James. He was such a beautiful baby, so like his handsome father. Julia was asked to be his godmother, with one of Edward's aunts as the other and Simon as his godfather. As she held the little scrap at the christening she found herself wondering who a child of hers might take after. If it were Simon, that would be perfect.

Her heart thudded with longing all over again as she held him, before handing him gently over to be baptized and receiving him back, whimpering in protest at the water on his little forehead. She felt her heart break that he wasn't hers and drew in her breath with a huge trembling sigh.

'Are you all right?' Simon whispered as the mother took the baby for everyone to croon over. He was looking deep into her face but Julia smiled back at him.

'Of course I'm all right,' she said sharply, but later when they had returned home and sat together in their lounge listening to quiet music on the wireless, she said, 'When you asked me if I was all right, I was in a way but I did suddenly wish little Stephen were mine.'

'Mmm...' was the quiet reply. Seconds later he leaped up from the settee and went over to their glass and chrome drinks cabinet.

'Fancy another drink, darling?' he called over his shoulder.

'No, thanks,' she said curtly as she studied her

half empty brandy glass. 'I've still got mine.'

'Well, I'm having a top-up,' he said brightly, dismissing the subject of babies. He came back to sit down beside her and began talking of their next show in just over a month's time.

'It's coming along quite splendidly,' he said, 'don't you think?'

'Yes,' she said.

'You do such wonderful miracles with stuff. I don't know how the business would have expanded so well without you, darling.'

'No,' she said.

'I really do think this is going to be the big one, darling, don't you?'

'Yes,' she said.

The following March the Women's Wear Exhibition was held in London. Julia had lost sleep worrying about competing with so many stands. She needn't have done. Hers was proving far more popular with the public than she'd ever dared to hope.

Ginny was at the height of her beauty as she paraded in the shimmering sleeveless tops and equally shimmering pleated skirts that fell to just below the knee. Teamed with them she wore the new skull caps of silver and gold tissue that completely covered her ears and hid the whole of her short hair.

Julia watched with excitedly beating heart as Ginny posed elegantly for a moment on the edge of the fur-covered *chaise longue* she had placed at the end of the platform. Her legs were tucked neatly under her, her body lightly supported by one slender arm while her other hand delicately held a long, ivory cigarette holder. Occasionally she would put it to her mouth to allow a gentle trail of cigarette smoke to issue from her painted lips; then, rising nonchalantly to an outburst of applause, she would resume her slow, studied pacing of the catwalk, finally disappearing behind the curtain for Betty to dress her hurriedly in another of her employer's creations.

The necklaces she wore were Simon's designs to match each different dress, each different skull cap. Bracelets glittered like real diamonds; rings and earrings, looking like pure sapphires, emeralds and rubies, were now set in gold and silver to ape the real thing. Simon spared no expense to make them look so. Few people other than the experts would have been able to see the difference.

The exhibition was proving a roaring success and Julia felt her slender, figure-hugging evening gowns were a glittering triumph. The emphasis was still on the young, boyish look but she was keeping an eye on the bosom which she felt was about to make a gentle reappearance. She was sure this would be a welcome relief to the larger lady who'd been struggling for a decade to keep hers as invisible as possible. It seemed she was being successful at gently introducing it today.

Simon too had enjoyed great success with his costume jewellery but was growing restive. Usually it took twenty to thirty minutes to present a show, as opposed to the preparation which took hours. This time the show was to last a whole morning and continue through the afternoon, repeated over and over for the benefit of ever-changing audiences. It was exhausting and draining but it was imperative to keep going while other exhibitors continued to do so.

'I think I'll take a quick look around the other stands,' he muttered and Julia nodded, wishing she could too. But he would bring back reports of what he saw and that was as important to her as managing her own show.

As he moved off she put her mind to the reaction of the crowd. There were almost as many men at this exhibition as women, mostly with wives or girlfriends on their arms. Some were on their own, but they were usually buyers whom one could easily pick out. One such Julia noticed. He didn't look like a buyer though as he came towards her. There was something slightly familiar about him. She stared then moments later gasped as she recognized the face of Chester Morrison.

# Twenty-Four

For a moment he looked as startled as she. But seconds later his expression was replaced by a broad smile as he moved towards her through the groups of people, reaching her in a few long strides.

She had been standing by the curtain to the small changing area from where she could judge the reactions to her designs by both the public and, hopefully, buyers.

'What are you doing here?' he asked.

His voice still bore the energetic, amiable timbre she remembered and which now made her heart flip to hear. Why, she didn't know. At the same time came a resurgence of the old resentment at his callousness in breaking off their engagement the moment she and her family had found themselves in financial straits. But he'd been younger then and under the strong influence of his arrogant family. No doubt he was married now and his own master.

He made to step up on to the low, temporary catwalk but she stopped him with an almost imperious out-turned palm of her hand. It was typical of him to assume everywhere to be his domain. He hadn't changed. But at her signal he stayed where he was, forced to look up at her

from his position. She found that quite gratify-
ing.

'What am *I* doing here? I have my own a
business – I'm a fashion designer and quite well
known.' No harm in saying so and she was, to
some extent.

Julia lifted her head proudly and made herself
stand a little taller. She had noted a buyer hovering a few paces away, making notes as her
second model turned at the end of the catwalk to
retrace her steps with expert casualness back to
the changing area.

Chester looked suitably impressed. 'Glad to
see you doing well,' he said, but Julia had her
eye on the buyer. Chester's presence might prevent her from speaking to the man and he could
prove important to her.

And where was Simon when she wanted him?
She looked down at Chester. 'Excuse me for a
moment, will you?' She saw him step back a
little, obviously not expecting her reaction. 'I
have to speak to someone,' she offered as an
excuse as she moved casually off towards the
man making notes.

He looked up from his pad at her approach and
smiled, tilting his head towards her stand. 'Very
good,' he appraised. 'You are the designer?'
When she nodded he said, 'I am a buyer for...'
The name was drowned by a group of young
people passing close by, laughing noisily. But
Julia wasn't worried. She could ask him again
later. 'So you are Julia Layzell?'

'That's correct,' she answered calmly though
her heart was pounding rather surprisingly. She

296

had dealt with many buyers and was mystified why she should feel so on edge and excited this time.

'I wonder if we might have a small business chat,' he was saying. 'I have to be somewhere in a few minutes, but what do you say about having lunch together, say in about an hour, around twelve thirty, at the George Hotel? That's only just outside this exhibition, a small place but we can talk better there.'

'That would be fine,' she replied, all thoughts of Chester flown. 'I will need to bring along my business partner.'

'Fine,' he replied. 'I shall see you then.'

'And you are?'

He held out a hand. 'The name's Thompson.'

Julia nodded as they shook hands and watched him shoulder his way through the moving knots of people, realizing that she hadn't asked him to repeat the name of the people for whom he was a buyer. She would ask him later when they met in the George.

She returned to find Chester still where she had left him. He grinned at her and said, 'Quite the important young lady these days, eh?'

She ignored the remark. 'And why are you here?'

Chester shrugged. 'Just having a look around but it's an unexpected surprise seeing you here. I've often wondered about you. Have you ever thought about me?'

He paused but when she didn't answer he went on, 'It is delightful to see you again.'

No reference at all to the way in which their

relationship had ended. She noticed he was looking down at her left hand.

'Not married, I see?'

'No.' Why had she said that? Of course she wasn't married but she need not have stated the fact so definitely. She should have explained that she was in a committed relationship.

Too late to alter it now as he said in a light tone, 'Fancy!' He became thoughtful then said suddenly, 'Look, why don't we have a drink together?'

'Sorry, I'm needed here.'

'Yes, of course,' he said. 'I'm forgetting you're a businesswoman now. And business comes first.'

'Comes first before what?'

'Before being sociable to old friends,' he replied lightly.

Old friends! Julia blinked. She wanted to retort that old friends did not walk out on one another in their hour of need but she held her tongue.

'I'm sorry, Chester,' she said instead, as coldly as she could. 'I told you, I'm in the midst of exhibiting my garments and also expect my partner to return any minute. Then we are going to lunch with the person to whom I was speaking just now.'

Chester's smile widened at her high-flown little speech. 'Well, perhaps tomorrow.'

'I shan't be here tomorrow. The exhibition ends today.'

'Then I'll pop round to where you work and see you. I'll find the address easily enough and perhaps I'll meet your partner then.'

'No!'

She had spoken far too sharply and knew she had given herself away, for he gave a knowing little chuckle.

'No, I don't expect he'd be pleased to see me. Well then, what about a coffee together somewhere so I can tell you what's been happening to me since I last saw you? And you can tell me all that's been happening to you.'

He grew suddenly serious. 'I'm glad you seem to have done well, Julia. I've felt terrible for years, wondering about you. It wasn't really my fault, you know. But I'll tell you all about that when we meet. I'll be in my car at the end of the road where you work tomorrow, say around eleven? It's a white Bentley sports car. Please be there. I need to explain myself, get it all off my chest. It'll make me feel a lot better. And maybe you will too. Is it a deal?'

He really did sound so repentant that Julia found herself nodding agreement.

With a small but almost gallant bow, he turned on his heel and she watched him walk swiftly away until he disappeared into the moving crowds. She was left staring after him, in a whirlwind of emotion. What had she done, accepting his invitation so readily – far too readily? She was a fool!

Quickly she turned her attention back to her exhibition. Celia, her second model, had just returned to the little changing area and Ginny was now on the catwalk again. Betty, looking trim and efficient in her smart suit, had temporarily taken over from her otherwise engaged employer,

They had all managed quite well without her
and she suddenly felt very slightly redundant
and undermined. It was Chester's fault. When
she met him tomorrow, and she was now determined to do so, she would give him a piece of
her mind and send him packing. It would make
her feel better, much better.

In her most sophisticated attire Julia emerged
from her salon on to Maddox Street. Looking
both ways she saw the white Bentley parked at
the Bond Street end. A quick glance over her
shoulder showed only the two counter staff
inside the salon. There was no sign of Simon as
she hurried away, now caught up in feelings of
guilt. She had left a note for him to say that she
had an appointment to keep but had provided no
further explanation.

Yesterday, when he returned to the stand, she
had said nothing to him about Chester or their
appointment. There had been so much else going
on, particularly the promising meeting with the
buyer, who had hinted that he might be able to
bring them in a good deal of business.

When they arrived home, they had been busy
unpacking their stock and going over the orders
to be sent on to the factory to be made up in
quantity. Finally they had slipped out for a quick
meal nearby, after which they were only too glad
to take themselves, weary but triumphant, up to
their apartment, she to drop gratefully on to the
settee while Simon mixed them a nightcap.

In bed at last, they'd made love, afterwards

talked of the long-term business deal they'd clinched with Thompson, who was a chief buyer for Bourne & Hollingsworth in Regent Street. There was so much else to discuss as a result of their successful day that she really had no opportunity to tell him about Chester, even if she had wanted to.

As she reached Chester's car now, he got out and came round to hold open the passenger door for her. 'What do you think of the old heap?' he asked flippantly as she got in the splendid vehicle, which was anything but an old heap.

'Very nice,' she said non-committally.

Dropping into the driving seat with an energetic bounce, making the thing shake, he chuckled. 'So where would you like to go?'

'You said we would have a coffee somewhere,' she reminded, staring ahead. 'Anywhere will do as long as it's not too far from here. I need to be back by lunchtime.'

'Or you'll be in trouble with your Boss-man?'

'No,' she said sharply and haughtily. 'We are partners – fifty-fifty.'

Noting her tone he grew serious. 'Sorry. But honestly, Julia, it's so great to see you again. We'll have coffee nearby then, and tell each other all about ourselves. At least I'll spill the beans if you don't want to talk about yourself.'

He grew quiet and said no more. After a short drive he pulled up outside the Ritz. Julia's lips tightened in a derisive smile. Trust Chester to show off. But she smiled graciously as he helped her out while a doorman held the car door open for them with a polite salute. The car would be driven to an area set aside for the vehicles of patrons, leaving them free to enter the hotel.

Julia had to acknowledge that Chester had chosen a beautiful setting for their meeting. They sat at a tiny table near a trickling fountain, laid with white bone china crockery, silver cutlery and delicate napkins, and ordered coffee from an attentive waiter who treated them as if they were his only customers. Soft music played on an unobtrusive grand piano to add atmosphere. They might have been quite alone but for the faint muffled conversation of the other customers.

The waiter poured their coffee and offered sandwiches and cakes from a silver stand. Julia pointed to the ham and he picked some up with silver tongs and placed them on her plate for her, before doing the same for Chester.

As the waiter departed, Chester leaned forward with his elbows on the white damask tablecloth, his laced fingers supporting his chin, his blue eyes searching hers.

'Now, tell me about yourself, my dear, what have you been doing?'

It sounded as if he was ready to quiz her. When she said nothing, merely sipping her coffee, he straightened up.

'Then I shall tell you about myself,' he stated, also sipping from his coffee and pulling an appreciative face at the coffee's mellow taste before replacing the cup in its saucer and sitting back in his chair. His face was serious, almost sad.

'First I really must say how sorry I was that

things didn't turn out as we'd planned.'

Julia made no reply.

'I wanted so much to explain,' he went on. 'But circumstances got in the way. I had so many long arguments with my parents but I couldn't bring them round to my way of thinking, no matter what I said. Indeed I became quite a rebel.'

Not rebellious enough, it seemed, thought Julia, but said nothing and he continued.

'I got near to falling out with them completely, but you can't do that with families. In the end I had to capitulate and see their side of things.'

Julia found her voice. 'And what was their side of things?'

He grinned wryly and took a sip of his coffee, reaching for another sandwich to leave it on his plate untouched beside those already there.

'I suppose like all families of their standing, they looked to me, their only child, to make a good marriage, keep up the family name, you know the sort of thing. You remember my telling you that I was on the point of coming into my inheritance?'

Yes, she remembered – a very substantial one that would have seen their marriage off to a wonderful start. She had to admit she had been just as eager to enjoy it as he was.

'It was to be mine on my twenty-fifth birthday, two weeks after our engagement dinner with our families, you remember?'

Julia nodded silently.

'It was that which my father held over my head,' he went on, 'when things went...well...I won't go into painful details.'

No, don't go into painful details, her mind cried. Didn't he realize how painful it was having it all brought back to her?

'I wanted so much to find you,' he was saying. 'To tell you it wasn't me, it was...well, circumstances. I wasn't strong enough or equipped enough to fight my parents. I suppose I was weak. I don't know. But we'd have been left without a penny. I didn't want that to happen. Not to you.'

'But it did,' she burst out at last, unable to contain herself. Her raised tone caused those at other tables to glance towards her. 'It happened anyway. And I was left on my own, trying to cope,' she added, lowering her voice.

'I know. I was to blame. I should have come after you. I wanted to, so much. But I couldn't go against my family, I love them. My father threatened to disown me if I came after you, and I know him – he would have done. And I was selfish enough not to go against him or my inheritance. I'm sorry.'

Gone was the youthful smile, the debonair confidence; she had never seen him look so remorseful, so sad. She found herself trying to imagine a young man, an only son, lost under the onslaught of determined, ambitious parents, who had raised him and cared for him, and wanted only the best for him. And what good would it have done him or her had he come after her with nothing to support them – and she with a distraught mother and three younger siblings hanging on to her skirts?

Suddenly she wanted to comfort him. She reached across the table and took his hands in hers. 'Tell me how you've been since,' she said, if only to see him brighten a little. 'Did you ever marry?'

He seemed to have recovered a little, though no smile lightened the now serious expression. 'Yes. Eighteen months later. Someone my parents thought *suitable*.' His voice held the ring of scorn as he spoke this last word. 'She was very pretty and she came of a good family, just what they were looking for, you see. It lasted three years. I'm going through a divorce just now. Decree absolute should be in a month or so.'

He gave a quietly ironic chuckle. 'I don't live with my parents now. I've a flat here in London. I don't see them. They go their way, I go mine. Now isn't that a laugh? We could have married, you and I, and cocked a snook at them if only I'd been stronger. It's odd, isn't it, now you are the one with the money. My inheritance is all but gone. I tried starting a business but couldn't make a go of it. My wife loved spending and when my money gave out she went back to Mummy and Daddy, who see me as a failure. Now, isn't that ironic? My family saw yours as a failure because things went wrong for you – talk about chickens coming home to roost!'

His tone had become monotonic, and Julia listened, mesmerized. As his voice fell away she came back to herself.

'Look, let's leave here,' she said briskly. 'Let's take a walk in Green Park then I must be back before one o'clock. My partner and I always have our lunch together.'

She still had not mentioned Simon's name. She wondered why not.

They drank their coffee and waited impatiently for the bill. Their waiter looked mildly surprised at the untouched sandwiches and cakes but well pleased at the tip Chester left, though manners forbade him to handle it except to bear it away on its plate as if it had nothing to do with him.

Emerging from the quiet, cool air of the Ritz into the thin sunshine of late March they were instantly assaulted by traffic noise along Piccadilly. A few yards on they turned left in the direction of Green Park.

Chester had already tucked her arm through his in the most natural way, leaving her feeling somewhat disconcerted and wondering why she hadn't withdrawn her arm immediately as she should have done.

# Twenty-Five

'I have to go out for an hour or so, Simon. I'm seeing a buyer. I'll be back in time for lunch, OK?'

Simon glanced up from looking over a new consignment of costume jewellery made up from his most recent designs. He shook his head with a mild gesture of remonstration. 'I'm sure you're working too hard, darling. Don't overdo things. Let the buyers come to us.'

Julia felt a flush of guilt touch her cheeks and tried not to admit to the fact that she was being just a little dishonest. But what was so wrong in having coffee with an old friend now and again? She was only seeing Chester casually once a fortnight. What *was* wrong was not having mentioned it to Simon, turning it into something furtive. Worse, she'd begun to look forward to seeing Chester. She knew she should have spoken out at the beginning. After all, Chester *was* an old friend. But to mention their meetings now after two months would only make them sound suspicious.

'That's how it goes,' she lied as cheerily as she could. 'See you for lunch then, darling,' and hurried off before he could say any more, in her hurry failing to see the puzzled frown that touched his brow.

Simon stood staring at the door for some time after she had gone. She was impeccably dressed, as always, especially whenever she went to meet a buyer or anyone who might benefit the business. It was expected. He did the same: his shoes shone fit to see his reflection in, his suit brushed, shirt crisp, trousers well pressed, his tie exactly the right shade. Finally Julia would brush his trilby before he put it on.

So he was not surprised that she was dressed stunningly. What baffled him was the high colour that touched her cheeks these days when she hurried off to meet someone. She was not normally a nervous person.

A frantic ringing of the doorbell to their apartment awoke Julia. It was dark. She shook Simon awake. 'What...what...is it?' he stammered, hardly yet awake.

'Someone's hanging on our doorbell!' Julia shouted in his ear and fumbled for the bedside table lamp. She switched it on and glanced at the alarm clock. 'It's two thirty in the morning!'

It was Wednesday. They'd gone to bed early the night before so as to be ready for another exacting day packing buyers' selections to be made up at the factory they used – so many numbers per order and several orders coming in regularly over the weeks.

Simon sat up as the ringing continued, spasmodic and frantic.

'Some drunk?' Julia queried.

'I shouldn't think so. But it sounds urgent.'

She watched him slip out of bed, struggle into a dressing gown and slippers and make for the window that overlooked the Mews and the front door. He wrenched up the sash to lean out and she heard him call down. A female voice, high-pitched and frenzied, answered.

He withdrew his head and made for the bedroom door, calling back to her as he flung it open, 'It's Virginia. She says it's an emergency – your mother.'

In one leap, Julia was out of bed and following him. By the time she was down he was already at the front door, had unlocked and opened it. Ginny almost fell into his arms.

'It's Mummy! I think she's having a fit or a heart attack! I don't know what to do. Her skin's gone all sweaty and her eyes are rolling up into her head. She's as white as a sheet.'

'I'll call an ambulance,' said Simon, handing the trembling girl over to Julia and running upstairs for the phone.

Ginny was dragging her outside. 'I've got to get back to her. Come with me, Julia. I don't want be alone with her.' She was crying. All Julia had on was a thin silk nightdress but it was a warm night and Ginny needed her.

They sat in the hospital waiting room as dawn broke, slowly and begrudgingly brightening to a splendid sun whose light was dulled for them by the smoke-begrimed windows. Even in the warmth of May backstreet families still cooked on open kitchen grates.

Finally a grave-faced doctor came into the
309

waiting room to speak to them. Faces strained, wearied by lack of sleep, they looked up at him in hope. The sight of his expression dashed that hope even before he spoke.

'I'm sorry,' he said, but Ginny had already begun to weep silently. 'We did everything possible,' he went on, looking at the other two after a brief glance towards the younger girl.

Julia and Simon had stood up at his entrance. Now Julia nodded and said stiffly, 'Thank you.' Why was she thanking him? Yet she repeated her words. 'Thank you anyway.'

She hardly heard the information they were being given as she took Ginny to her; Ginny, the only one in the end who had truly given her time to their mother, and who, she supposed, had loved her far more than the rest of them.

Poor girl, she thought as they made their way home. In August she and Robert were getting married. It was to be a big wedding, and there were only a few things still left to do. The dresses were made, the cake and carriages order-ed, the church and hotel booked. How would Ginny get through it now? Without her mother there, how could it ever be what it was meant to be: a bride's happiest day?

'I did love her,' Ginny sobbed.

'I did too,' said Julia, holding her tightly, try-ing to still the sobbing.

During the funeral service and around the graveside, she kept thinking, Did I love her? Did I ever love her?

The question prompted a disturbing sense of having merely pretended affection for her

310

mother during all those years of caring for her, suffering Victoria's endless complaints about her situation and her refusal to move on after the loss of her husband. Julia alone had got her mother and the rest of the family through the bad times, always trying to get Victoria to find a little more courage to face the world as life improved. But she never had and her attitude had soured any love Julia had ever had for her. As she watched the coffin being gently lowered into the ground, she was shaken by a sudden realization; that all along there had lurked in her a tiny seed of resentment against her mother.

She confided those thoughts to her brother as the funeral party came away. It didn't seem appropriate to say such things to Simon. But all James said was, 'You did your best, Sis. No one could have done more than you've done for us.'

He had been philosophical about his mother's death, accepting it as inevitable, sooner or later.

'Thanks to you, Sis, Mother was at least comfortably off when she died, and had no worries to plague her at the end,' he said as the funeral guests said their goodbyes to each other to go their separate ways.

So that was it. Her mother was dead. The family would scatter with no focal point to keep it together any longer, though in recent years its members had found that focal point more a chore than a pleasure. James and Caroline had seldom come to see Victoria, and nor had Stephanie and Edward. They had their own little families to carry them onward.

Once Ginny and Robert were married, Ginny

would no longer work for her. As a newly married woman she would automatically give up work to take on the role of wife to the man she loved. Ginny though, unlike the other two, promised to continue to visit. 'We must always keep in touch, always!' she would say to Julia time after time, as if she regretted having to give up her modelling.

Even so Julia was already feeling deserted. Simon seemed to be taking her for granted more and more, that passion they'd once known dwindling into the commonplace. Would marriage to him make any difference now?

What did brighten her, guiltily, was the prospect of seeing Chester. Aware of her growing pleasure in these meetings she'd told him several times that she couldn't see him on a regular basis, emphasizing that they were merely old friends. But his agreement to that did little to quell the excited churning in her stomach as they drove to a little restaurant somewhere. She couldn't help feeling as if there were something grubby about their meetings, yet he never gave the slightest indication of having any ulterior designs on her.

To offset her own feelings she'd make a point of talking about Simon, her business, her family, or listened to him speaking of his life. She no longer felt angry with him; too much water had flowed under the bridge since the end of their relationship, and she was aware that he'd also had his share of trouble, compelled to submit to his parents' will and now going through a divorce. She even told herself that in the long run she had done better than he, and insisted to herself that they were just old friends. So why did she experience this churning excitement?

This afternoon she sat beside him in the car, the early June sunshine pouring down on them tempered by the slight breeze created by the moving vehicle. Taking the back streets, they headed towards the Ritz but a little beforehand he slowed the car and came to a stop by Green Park.

'I thought we might not have tea yet,' he said. 'It's a lovely afternoon. We could take a stroll in the park instead and have tea afterwards.'

It was such a splendid afternoon that she readily agreed. There would be no need for small talk; they could just walk and enjoy the fresh air.

They said little to each other; there seemed nothing much really to talk about, and she was beginning to think about getting back home. She even found herself wondering why she continued to see him, calling herself an idiot. She was on the verge of telling him there was no point in either of them continuing to meet, when he suddenly remarked, 'You must be feeling quite thirsty by now.'

'Gasping,' she said, smiling.

He looked about at the expanse of trees and lawns and pulled a face. 'There doesn't seem anywhere to get a drink.'

'We passed a kiosk as we came in,' she suggested, but he brightened.

'You know, we're not far from my place. In fact it's just over there.' He pointed towards their left. 'We're so near. Blow going back to the kiosk! We can have a proper drink.'

Julia bit her lip. 'I don't think so, Chester.'

'Why, for heaven's sake?'

'I have to be getting back very soon.'

'We've only been out half an hour or so. It's just a quick drink. It's so very hot. You'll feel nice and refreshed to return home. If I know you, you'll plough straight into work and won't drink anything at all. On a hot day like this, that won't do you any good. *Come on*,' he coaxed, laughing.

There was no hint of any hidden design in his laugh and she laughed in turn at herself for that fleeting touch of suspicion. And she did feel frightfully thirsty.

'Then we can walk back to the car. It's only a short distance,' he was calling over his shoulder as he led the way at a quickening pace, almost leaving her to trail behind. 'You'll be home again before you know it.'

His home was beautiful. It had the touch of a woman's hand on it. Whoever she was her photo was everywhere. There was one beside a great vase of roses on the grand piano in the huge lounge, another on the sideboard, one on the mantelpiece and another on a small desk in the corner. There was even a small one on a coffee table. Suddenly Julia felt deep sympathy for him. He must have loved her, maybe still did.

She touched one of the photos. 'Is this your wife?'

He nodded, then said, 'So, what'll it be, cocktail, brandy and soda? I have some wine or

314

would you prefer a long drink? Or there's coffee or tea if you prefer.'

He was questioning her far too rapidly. 'What's her name?' she asked. 'You have never mentioned her by name.'

'It doesn't matter. It's all over anyway. Now what do you fancy?'

Julia gave up. 'I'd like a long drink, port and lemonade if you have it.'

They sat side by side on the sofa, she with her tall glass, he sipping a whisky. He had turned on the radio. It was playing soft music. Julia listened without speaking for he was gazing ahead as if she were not there.

After a while she said, 'It a nice wireless,' more for something to say, to break the silence, than for any other reason.

'It's a radiogram,' he replied.

They fell quiet again. Then he seemed to pull himself together. 'Look, I'm not much company. I've turned into a miserable sod. Perhaps I should take you home.'

On impulse Julia took his hand. 'You're not a miserable sod, Chester. You must feel really down, you and your wife breaking up. You've never really told me about it. I don't know whose fault it was...'

'No one's fault, just didn't work out, that's all.'

She wanted to say that if that was the case, things might right themselves, but she merely continued to sit there silently, his hand in hers. Or now it seemed her hand was in his.

'You're such a good person,' he was saying in a low voice. 'I should have held on to you. I did

315

love you, you know, very much. I was such a fool.'

She realized that his free hand was covering hers and out of nowhere came that warm excitement, overwhelming this time. As she whispered his name he leaned towards her until his lips touched hers. In an instinctive move her arm went about his neck, holding the kiss as together they sank down on the sofa. She heard his voice in her ear but didn't know what he said. She felt him undo her clothing but made no move to stop him. Something in her wanted this. It wasn't love, it was a need. His hands were caressing her breasts, moving over her body to wring a responsive sigh of pleasure from her. But as the touch became more eager, she tensed. This wasn't love, only a sensation of love, and it was wrong. 'Chester...no!'

He stopped. 'What's the matter?'

'We mustn't. We really mustn't.'

'I have protection,' he whispered. 'No need to worry.'

Maybe not, but suddenly Julia had thought of Stephanie, of how free she had been with a man, or maybe more then one, and she felt ashamed. She had wanted to hang on to that delicious sensation, abandon herself to this need she'd felt but all she said was, 'I'm sorry, Chester. I can't.'

She had her eyes tightly shut as he lifted himself off her. She heard him go from the lounge and only then did she open her eyes, sit up and slowly adjust her clothing.

He had come back into the room to sit on the edge of an armchair, his hands linked together between his knees, his gaze on her. 'I am still in love with you, you know,' he whispered.

She didn't reply but sat, awkward and embarrassed, and then, feeling she had to take charge of the painful situation, said, 'I must go home.'

She saw him nod but he said nothing and she took a deep breath to compose her jangled nerves.

'I didn't finish my drink,' she said.

'No, you didn't.'

The heat of excitement had melted away and now she felt completely drained. Yet she knew she wanted to see him again, to feel his hands on her body again and maybe next time...No, she wouldn't think of next time.

He must have read her mind. 'Will I see you again?' he asked quietly.

'Yes,' she said.

'Here?'

'Yes.'

'Are you sure?' he asked slowly.

'Yes,' she said again. There was nothing more to say, but both were aware that next time would see the fulfilment of what today had been left uncompleted.

# Twenty-Six

It was July. She'd been seeing Chester on and off since March. She was sure she had set Simon wondering sometimes. Her cheeks would grow hot when he regarded her with that enquiring look he'd begun to adopt. He would frown but never once asked questions, which was all the more worrying.

If he'd thought her off colour surely he'd have asked if she was all right. He never did, and that made her certain he suspected something. She hated deceiving him. She still loved him. Yet it was Chester who fulfilled her needs.

The excuse of meeting buyers or clients had been used too often to sound convincing any longer, though of course she did visit shops, checking who stocked her labels, but her work was falling by the wayside – another thing to make Simon frown, make him suspect that something was very wrong.

'I don't know what I'd do if Simon found out,' she said to Chester.

From the start she'd allowed him to make love to her only infrequently and then not fully, afraid that one day they might become carried away and forget to take precautions. She was sure he would have the sense to be careful. He didn't

318

want an accident any more than she did, her primary concern always of Simon finding out. Deep down he was the one she loved.

'We shouldn't meet too often,' she'd said 'in case he does find out.'

'Are you worried?' Chester would challenge, too lightly for her peace of mind. He had nothing to lose, soon to be divorced. She had everything to lose. Even if he wanted to marry her after his divorce, did she want to marry him? What she wanted was to be married to Simon. The brief excitement of being with Chester wasn't what she really yearned for. In truth, all she was doing was jeopardizing her own happiness for an occasional thrill with a man who'd already let her down once, even though he swore he still loved her.

'This Simon isn't married to you,' he'd often reminded her.

But I love him, came the irrational thought. The idea of losing him made her go cold. 'It's all becoming too risky,' she now said inadequately.

Chester had laughed softly. 'It's a little late to be getting cold feet,' he had pointed out. But seconds later he'd become intense. 'I still love you, Julia. I made such a mistake last time. I won't ever make it again, my sweet darling.'

Today, enfolded in his arms, she almost succumbed to the need inside her but seconds later, as so often happened, Simon's image shot into her mind. 'No, Chester, not today.' How many times in the past had she said that?

But she wanted to be made love to. That overwhelming excitement was pounding deep inside her, lately becoming ever more frequent and urgent. These days her mind seemed to be in a constant whirl, affecting her whole concentration on ordinary everyday things.

On top of it all Ginny's marriage to Robert in August was rushing closer until Julia was near to exhaustion trying to fit in her own work as well as putting the finishing touches to the bridal gown and in the absence of her parents organizing the event with Simon. During the final week before the wedding Julia found it impossible to see Chester. All thought of him was driven from her mind; her only concern was for her sister, and Ginny's sadness that her mother would not be there to see her youngest daughter wed.

In church, listening to Ginny hardly able to say her vows for tears, Julia felt her own throat constrict as she in turn fought her own tears. Next to her, where their mother should have been sitting, was Stephanie, with her husband on her other side. Stephanie was staring ahead, eyes bleak but dry, with Edward's arm around her.

She was holding her baby son while little Violet, sitting beside her father, toyed happily with a doll. The child had hardly known her grandmother, she had so seldom been taken to see her. And Stephanie had the audacity to look sorrowful, Julia thought bitterly. Glancing at James and his wife further along the pew, he too seemed unmoved by the absence of his mother at the wedding and Julia knew he hadn't thought once about her.

Sadness, however, vanished completely amid the fun of photos being taken, wedding guests filling the rooms at the Savoy to be welcomed by the newly-weds, champagne flowing, the three-tiered wedding cake cut. The band played throughout the evening, dance music, slow fox-trots like 'Stardust', 'A Room With a View', as well as lively quicksteps such as 'I Can't Give you Anything but Love, Baby', waltzes, the first of which the happy couple started off, and of course jazz numbers. That year, 1929, was a good year for jazz and swing. There was lots of money for the rich to spend and investments were riding high.

Julia forgot all about Chester as she and Simon danced together. That night they made love and it seemed somehow different, new, full of passion and joy. Somehow Julia felt something happen in that moment of climax, though she couldn't have defined what it was even if she had wanted to.

The wedding had been five days ago and the couple were still away on honeymoon in the South of France. Already Julia was missing the sight of her sister's face.

Today she looked up from speaking to a client to glimpse what seemed to be Chester's white car pass slowly by the door to her establishment. She tried not to look on edge as her client continued discussing the new designs she was being shown, but after half an hour the business was concluded and the customer left, well pleased after having placed a substantial order.

Hurrying outside, Julia looked towards New Bond Street to see the white car standing there.

It could only be Chester.

Simon was out for the morning, his assistant Merriman keeping an eye on things in his absence. Her own helper, Miss Cleaves, was occupied neatly folding and putting away materials.

'I have to go out for a few minutes,' Julia called to both young people who glanced up and nodded.

Making towards the car she saw that the driver was Chester but when he greeted her it was not with his usual smiling face. He patted the passenger seat as she approached. 'Get in, Julia.'

She stood where she was. 'I can't go with you just like that,' she said. 'We have to make proper times to meet, you know that.'

'Please, Julia,' he interrupted. 'Get in. I've something I need to tell you. It's important. I can't tell you while you're standing there in the street.'

Wondering, she opened the door and slipped in beside him. It was a while before he spoke. When he did his voice was low and grave.

'Look, darling, I don't know how you're going to take this. But I need to talk about these meetings of ours. Things are going to have to change.'

Julia felt her body give a jolt, apprehension filling every part of her. What did he mean, things would have to change? But he was still talking – slowly, his voice low, yet buried within was a hint of excitement.

'The thing is, with this divorce on the verge of being concluded I had a letter from the solicitor yesterday. It's taken me until this morning to come and tell you about it – about you and me.'

Julia's heart raced. Was he asking her to marry him?

Conflicting thoughts were winging through her head, all mixed up. Now it came to it, did she want to finish with Simon and marry Chester?

If she refused the offer she was sure she was about to hear, she could be losing her chance of exciting love. Yet that night with Simon after Ginny's wedding had been every bit as exciting as any time with Chester. Of course though, they might lapse back into their old comfy situation. Did she want that?

And what of Simon, how would he feel when she told him what had been going on with Chester? He loved her in his way and as she visualized his face when she told him...no, she couldn't do that to him. But here was Chester...

She could hear him talking as if from a distance and forced her mind back to him.

'You see, darling,' he was saying. He was calling her darling. He had never done that before even at the height of their love making.

'It's like this. The moment I got the solicitor's letter I went straight round to see Helen, my wife, and we had a long talk. She told me she had broken up several weeks ago with the man she'd been seeing and asked me if I could ever forgive her. She looked so sad and I realized I still love her. I don't know how to say this but we've both decided to try and make another go of it. I've got to pick her up in a few moments and we're going to see our solicitors to sort things out.'

For a moment Julia's mind went blank and it took her a second or two to gather up the threads of what she'd been hearing. Then the meaning of his words crashed into her brain with such a force that she drew in her breath in one huge gasp, to release it in a sobbing, trembling shriek.

'You *bastard*!' She had never used a word like that in her life. 'You disgusting, evil bastard, you knew all along. You were just using me until...'

She broke off and began beating both fists against his shoulder and head, blind to passers-by on the pavement, who had been stopped in their tracks by her shrieks.

He held both her fists, pulled her to him. 'I didn't know, Julia. Please believe me, I didn't know. I'm so sorry.' His lips were against her cheek. 'I do still love you, Julia,' he was saying. 'I always will.'

In fury she pulled her face away but in the next second had pressed her lips to his. There was no response. She was making a fool of herself. With an effort she fought to control the uncharacteristic outburst that had so suddenly taken hold of her and fell back in her seat, suddenly coming to her senses, knowing she was humiliating herself. She wasn't prepared to let that happen.

She became aware that people were pausing, staring into the car for a brief moment before moving on, embarrassed. But one person still stood looking at her.

In a panic she clambered out of the car but Simon was already walking away. She wanted to run after him but all she could do was stand transfixed by horror. Behind her Chester's car revved up and drew away.

A whole week had passed. Simon hadn't said a word about the incident and it was torturing her. Every time she tried to make an effort to explain he would change the subject to some matter to do with business, or walk away. He hadn't resorted to sleeping apart from her but that made the situation even worse.

Tonight, as they had every other night since that awful day, they lay side by side, staring up at the ceiling, not speaking. He finally turned over and she did too, their backs to each other. Sleep refused to come and she knew it was the same for him; she was aware of him fidgeting from time to time, his breathing irregular. He even got up at one point and went into the other room, only to return to lie down beside her again.

She knew he was hurting, as she was, but for different reasons – he seeing himself as having been made a fool of, she screwed up with misery as the guilty party – and there was nothing she could do. It was a waste of time trying to speak to him in the quietness of the night but now she tried again.

'Simon?'

'Go to sleep!' His voice was muffled yet sharp.

But she had to say something. 'If only we'd been married...' She hadn't intended to say that. The words had come out all on their own.

To her intense relief they produced a reaction, even if it was tortured and sour. 'Would marriage have made any difference?'

Words now came tumbling out. 'I wanted so much for us to marry. I suppose I was caught at a low point. You were content for things to stay as they were, interested it seemed only in making more and more money. Sometimes it was as if you didn't care about me any more, other than us being partners and making a success of the business. We hardly made love at all as time went on and sometimes I felt love didn't matter to you any more.'

As if he'd hardly been listening, he broke in sharply. 'Who is he?'

Crushed, she could only reply, 'I knew him a long time ago – before I ever met you. We were to be engaged. But his people saw my family's downfall as complete humiliation and put a stop to the engagement.'

She started to relate the story of how she'd had to keep her family going, though Simon already knew all that, didn't he? She realized it immediately as he interrupted her with a curt, 'How long?'

'How long?' she echoed, not understanding the question.

'How long have you been seeing each other?'

She told him how she and Chester had met again by chance at the London Fashion Exhibition in March, and how she had accepted his invitation to have coffee with him and talk over old times. 'I saw no harm in it then,' she said.

Simon listened without a word as she went on to tell him how she had intended only to let Chester see how contemptible she thought his

326

behaviour had been towards her and to show him how well she had done for herself without him.

'But it was all a long time ago,' she said. 'And we became more like old friends having coffee together. He told me he was in the middle of a nasty divorce. He was miserable and I felt sorry for him and in a way it made me feel superior. Then, somehow, I don't know what really happened but...'

She let the rest trail off. It was in danger of becoming a sordid story and she wasn't prepared to subject Simon to painful details. It was then she realized he was behaving strangely, every now and again clearing his throat like a person bored.

Defeated by this apparent indifference to what she was trying to say, she repeated bleakly, 'If only you and I had been married.'

'Then we'll get married,' he said, taking her by surprise. But there was no love in his tone. She reacted immediately.

'No. I want you to *want* to marry me, not just as an arrangement but because you love me.'

'I do love you.'

She couldn't believe that, not after what she'd been telling him. 'In spite of what happened?' she burst out in disbelief.

'In spite of what you say happened.' He turned his face towards her. He was looking at her, studying her levelly, and suddenly she broke down.

She felt his arm go about her, drawing her close. Now crying into his shoulder she felt his arm tightening even more as her words came tumbling out, drowned in sobs and practically inaudible.

'I'm so sorry, I'm so sorry,' she kept saying. 'I've been such a fool. Nothing I can say will put it right. But I want only you, only you, darling...' She was becoming more and more incoherent as he held her to him. How could he forgive? But that was just what he was doing and she didn't deserve him.

The memory of how coolly Chester had informed her that he was going back to his wife, betraying her for a second time, almost made her want to rage against him again. But even as she wept against Simon's shoulder, sense told her that it would be disastrous to say any more about Chester. It was over. And she must stop punishing herself, too, for her foolishness and weakness. So long as Simon still loved her and consented to marry her, she was prepared to forget the past and spend the rest of her life loving only him.

# Twenty-Seven

The wedding was short and simple, by special licence at a registry office on the third Friday in August. There were few guests: Ginny and Robert as witnesses, James and his wife, Betty who'd been with her and Simon all these years. Stephanie and her family were in Italy on holiday, their first ever trip abroad, but sent their love on a postcard with a view of Rome.

The little party had a quiet meal in a nearby restaurant, no one else was invited, not even friends, for as far as others were concerned they'd been married for years and there was no point in letting the cat out of the bag now.

The whole thing had taken a couple of hours, with Simon and Julia returning to their place of business as if nothing had happened. Business still came first. They were coming towards the end of a decade of rapidly changing fashion, from the voluminous fashions of 1921 to the skimpy ones of 1928 and 1929. Julia foresaw a settling down next year to sleeker, more flowing garments, already beginning to make an appearance. She couldn't afford to be caught out, as had happened once before. At times she worked herself to near exhaustion to get the finished samples off to the factory for making up and dispatching to the shops.

She missed Ginny's lively presence about the place as she draped her toiles, the muslin cloth from which she would cut her copies, on the plaster model she'd used for years or on one of her live models, altering a hemline, a bodice, a sleeve. Dear Ginny would endure these long, boring hours without complaint, allowing herself to be pulled this way and that so as to get a new idea just right, a trim added to the waist, a strap to the shoulder, a bit taken out of a bodice, a little more draping to a skirt – always with a smile as a garment slowly, laboriously took shape.

The girls Julia now used seldom smiled, behaving more like statues, straight-faced, eyes fixed, suffering what they were being paid to do as she fitted the material on them, pinning, cutting, redesigning as she went until finally she was satisfied, the finished garment ready to be completed and hung from the racks for dispatch to the factory to be made up and sent out.

Before Ginny had married she had proved herself to be almost as gifted as her sister at sketching. With an eye for colour she had even begun to work from just an idea in her head, often improving on Julia's own ideas. She might even have become a designer in her own right. Instead she had become a wife.

They were living near Robert's parents and would often drive over to see Julia, unlike James and Stephanie, neither of whom she saw very often now their mother was gone.

'It wouldn't hurt either of them to come over

and see you and Simon now and again,' Ginny said. 'After all, considering the situation we were all left in after Father died, we've all done pretty well for ourselves and it's all thanks to you, Julia. They should show some appreciation.'

It was a shame the others didn't see it that way, but Julia was finding life too busy again to care about them. The order books were always full. They were even planning to enter for a fashion competition and had also arranged to go over to France before Christmas to attend the Paris Exhibition.

Married life, as for most newly-weds, held a certain wonder for Julia. She had always imagined that after all their years together marriage to Simon would feel no different. But she was wrong. Loving Simon all but overwhelmed her, as if that business with Chester Morrison had never been. All that remained of that episode was an occasional disturbing dream in which Simon appeared to be running away from her, with Chester holding her back as he faded into the distance. In the dream she searched frantically for Simon, asking people if they knew where he was and meeting blank faces – her penitence perhaps. Simon never referred to her affair.

At other times she would dream that Simon had gambled away everything they had, reducing them to living in some horrible hovel, its walls falling in so that everyone could see her striving to pretend to be rich. Perhaps this was inspired by the memory of the earlier trauma that had befallen her family.

Yet she felt it had some substance to it. Simon did play the stock market far too rashly. Time and again she would warn him to think about what he was doing but he always laughed at her when she tried to recount her dream to him.

'While the market's this buoyant, I intend to make the most of it. Everyone else is doing it. No reason to worry, darling. Shares in all the big corporations are rising to unimaginable heights and I don't want to be the one to miss out.'

Perhaps he was right. Their business was thriving and dreams were, well, just dreams. And she had her own private hope about which she had so far said nothing to him: her period was now more than a week overdue. She was sure she felt different too, an odd yet indefinable change in her body. Maybe it was only her imagination – it was best to let another month go before raising his hopes.

But what if he didn't want children? He hadn't been too eager for marriage, so maybe he would not be eager for children either. She knew he hadn't seen his own parents for years. She had sent them an invitation to their wedding but there had been no reply. In the past he'd told her of the rift his refusal to take up his father's business had caused. It seemed that, having spent a great deal on sending his son to public school and then to university, his father had been angered to a point of blind fury when Simon had disappointed him. His parents had never forgiven him and he in turn had determined never to forgive them. But would that jeopardize his wish for a family of his own? Perhaps he wasn't cut out to be a family man. She had never asked.

This evening she and Simon were lounging quietly together on the sofa in front of a dying fire. They were glad to have the evening to themselves and were enjoying coffee and brandy after a good dinner and listening to soft music being played on the wireless. Beyond the drawn curtains an October downpour was battering at the window panes but she felt cosy and warm and looking forward to him making love to her when they got to bed.

'Have you ever thought of having a family?' she asked tentatively.

Coming out of the blue, the question obviously startled Simon. He sat bolt upright, his gaze instantly full of concern. 'You aren't, are you?' he exclaimed.

She'd have loved to have said yes but merely replied, 'It's just, how would you feel if I were?'

She had never expected to see a glow of joy spring to his eyes but what really took her aback was the dull gleam of suspicion that she saw there. She almost cried out: 'It's not like that! We took precautions.' But what would that say of her, heaping degradation upon degradation?

Powerless to say anything, she could only pretend she hadn't noticed the look as he got up off the sofa, a little too abruptly she thought, muttering something about it having been a long day and that he needed to go to bed.

Seated at the breakfast table Simon scanned the financial pages of *The Times* with his usual quiet expectancy.

'Quite a good few of the shares I've been buying have already gone up several points these last couple of weeks,' he murmured as though talking to himself. 'Good as investing in bricks and mortar, you can't go wrong.'

'Shouldn't you sell some?' Julia queried. 'Reap some of the profit, just in case.'

She still couldn't get those dreams out of her head.

Simon grimaced. 'Not when they're still on their way up.' There was no gentleness in his reply. He might as well have been addressing a colleague, having not once this morning called her darling. To Julia it felt almost as if a knife were being turned in her flesh.

'In fact I might take a look at a few more before they go up too,' he went on, still as if to himself. 'At this rate I can make a real killing!'

Julia sipped steadily at her cup of tea to allay the misery in her stomach. In front of her a plate of cornflakes remained untouched. She never ate a cooked breakfast though Simon always did. Mrs Allan, who cooked and cleaned for them, always made sure that his plate was full to the brim with fried breakfast food. Julia had often chided him that he ate like a navvy rather than someone educated at Oxford.

She put down her teacup. 'You invest far too much, darling, far too rashly. Be careful.'

But he merely went on scanning his paper, muttering, 'I do know what I'm doing.'

'Are you sure?' she ventured. 'What if it all went wrong?'

He looked sharply at her. 'It all depends on what *you* think could go wrong.' Then, as if he had become aware of the connotation and was already regretting his words, his tone mellowed.

'I can completely rely on my bank to look after my interests and I've always been given good advice by them. I've been a damned good customer of theirs all these years and they've never let me down.'

As he went back to studying the market Julia trickled some milk on to her cornflakes and took a small spoonful. But the cereal tasted like chaff in her mouth. From the time he'd found out about her foolish, if brief, affair, he'd not been the same man. Though he'd said little about it and – as the dramatists would have put it – *taken her back*, seldom did any term of endearment pass his lips.

Love making too had fallen by the wayside. Since she had mentioned two weeks ago the possibility of being pregnant, which now appeared to be a certainty, any move to cuddle up to him would reap a small kiss and be told it could be dangerous to make love in her condition. But was he thinking of the baby itself or whether in fact it was his? How did one ask such a question as that? She'd even found herself hoping the pregnancy was a false alarm, so that everything could slowly be forgotten. But it had not been forgotten and there seemed nothing to be done.

She needed to pour her heart out to someone. Stephanie would not care and it was unfair to worry Ginny just now. She telephoned James at his bank and he agreed to meet her for lunch at Lyons Corner House.

'We're not happy,' she told him bleakly. 'I'd be better leaving him. I can't take much more of the tension that's come between us.'

James, solid and serious-minded, stirred his coffee at length while all around came the busy chatter of others at lunch. 'Why should there be any tension?' he asked finally. 'You've been together for years and now you're married, you should be ecstatic, so what's the problem?'

'I don't quite know,' she said, stopping abruptly as a Lyon's nippy came with the ham sandwiches James had ordered.

'Yes you do,' he prompted severely as the waitress departed and Julia realized he'd detected the lie in her tone.

She let the minutes tick by, helping herself to a sandwich merely for something to do while debating whether or not to tell him the truth. But she had to say something, had to own up. After all, she needed help. 'I suppose it is my fault.'

She broke off, waiting for him to prompt her. When he didn't, she knew there was no going back.

'A few months ago,' she began, 'I met a face from the past, someone we all knew.' She was going to have to say it: 'Chester Morrison.'

She heard James draw in an annoyed breath but hurried on before he could say anything, running quickly through the story of having coffee, meaning to humiliate him, but then forgiving him and beginning to think of him as an old friend. But sooner or later the truth was going to have to come out if she needed his advice.

She continued, telling James how she had begun to meet Chester regularly and how she had begun to find herself becoming a little infatuated with him. Telling her brother how their relationship had begun slowly to develop was the hardest thing she had ever done.

'I became completed carried away. I think I fell in love all over again – at least I thought I had. Then out of the blue he told me he was going back to his wife. I was shocked. I felt so betrayed that I created a scene there in the street.'

'*You* felt betrayed!' James broke in cruelly. 'What about Simon?'

Julia fell silent, abashed by the truth. Tears sprang to her eyes. She bit at her lip, trying to stem them. When she finally made herself reply, her voice trembled so that she could hardly say the words that came pouring from her.

'I know I'm to blame. But Chester and I, we didn't do anything, I was just drawn to him because Simon and I weren't married at the time, with no sign of us ever getting married, and I'd got tired of waiting. I just think I was caught on the rebound. I was very low.'

It didn't matter whether or not there was truth in all she said, only that she needed to say it. 'I've been a fool, I know. But honestly, nothing went on between us, but Simon only sees that I've been unfaithful.'

'But he married you.'

'I know. I think he only did it because he wanted to make things right. He's that kind of person.

337

He says he still loves me, but it's only what he says.'

'Have you thought that he does truly love you, in spite of what you did?'

'But it's not just that, James. I think I might be carrying. If I am it's Simon's baby because Chester and I made sure to take...' She broke off, then finished, 'We did nothing.'

She saw James compress his lips. 'It's the truth!' she burst out. 'But Simon's behaving as if it isn't; as if it's not his child, and that's why I can't stay with him.'

Her voice fell away and she lowered her head in shame. 'It's best I leave,' she said. 'But it's not what I want,' she added miserably in the same shaky voice, tears now pouring down her cheeks, making fellow customers at lunch glance at her curiously.

James was leaning towards her, his voice low. 'Then don't.'

She looked up to see that he was offering her a handkerchief, which she took to dab furiously at her eyes.

'Don't leave him, Sis,' he was saying, using his old pet name for her in the way he'd done when he was a young lad. This time it wasn't spoken teasingly. 'Don't cut off your nose to spite your face, Julia. If you do you'll ruin two lives. Promise you'll hang on to him. He needs you, Sis. He might need you more as time goes on. Say you won't let him down.'

It was so earnestly said, almost prophetic, that she stared at him before again bowing her head, this time in compliance.

338

By the time they said goodbye to each other, he had convinced her of the stupidity of letting emotion run away with her. She'd stick to the promise she had made. She even found herself waiting in great anticipation for the beginning of next month when her next period would be due, if it came at all.

Meanwhile there was always work. Whatever her differences with Simon, as partners they still continued their business compatibly enough side by side.

# Twenty-Eight

It was all very well for James to counsel her to stick it out. She was trying but how did one stick it out, when there was never any response?

Six weeks now and it was destroying her. To make it worse she had missed her second menstrual period which should have been around the beginning of this month, October. It confirmed her condition. James's advice was right. How could she leave Simon now?

She sat tense and uneasy in an armchair. Dinner had been cleared away and Simon was lolling on the sofa. There was a time when he would have patted the cushion next to him for her to come and cuddle up to him. It was so obvious that he saw this child she carried as not his. How could she prove to him that it was?

Knowing how foolish she had been tortured her constantly. She yearned to be able to go back and change everything. She started to think that for both their sakes it might after all be best if she did leave. Desperately she tried to will Simon to glance up from his catalogues, but he continued reading, deliberately it seemed cutting himself off from her. Her insides felt as if they were being tied in knots; she had to find a way to bring up the subject of the baby.

340

She'd tried several times in the past but at the slightest reference to her condition he would change the topic so abruptly that she had no heart to repeat herself. She could read his thoughts almost as if he'd put them into words: 'I don't want to know!'

She knew Simon was the father of her baby; she just had to make him believe it. But how? There was only one way to resolve the doubt and that was to have their doctor examine her and hope that he would be able to confirm when she had conceived. The following morning she made an appointment to see him the same day.

'I've made an appointment to see Benjamin Marwood at the surgery,' she told Simon as soon as they had opened up for the day. Dr Benjamin Marwood was a friend as well as their doctor. 'It's at nine thirty. I'll be gone half an hour.'

She said it in such a brisk tone that he looked up, startled.

'Why? Aren't you well?' he asked anxiously. She was hardly ever ill.

'I merely need to consult him, that's all,' she said and went out leaving him to think what he liked.

In his surgery Marwood washed his hands, dried them carefully, his head half turned towards the screen behind which Julia had gone to tidy herself.

'Well, Julia, I can confidently say you are going to be a mother come May. I'd like to be the first to congratulate you.'

As she emerged from behind the screen to

gather up her hat and handbag, he came and planted a peck on her cheek. Having now discarded his doctor's white coat, he was again the family friend.

'I am sure Simon will be over the moon, if he isn't already. Perhaps we can all go out for dinner to celebrate on Saturday evening, what do you think?'

Julia's smile was happy and full of relief. 'That would be nice. I'll tell him,' she said, trying to control her emotions. Here was the proof she needed.

She could hardly wait to get back and tell Simon, to take him aside, banish his doubts and fill his heart with joy.

'Simon, can you spare me a moment?' she said to him as she came into the boutique. 'I've something important to tell you.'

He'd been talking to someone. Politely excusing himself, he came over to her. 'Not now, Julia. I'm in the middle of some important business.'

'This is important too – very important,' she said. 'I've some good news and I need to talk to you now.'

'Just one minute then,' he replied and moved away, leaving her to chafe. She knew it was the wrong time to talk of family affairs but there were some things that took precedence over all else, even business.

It was ten minutes before Simon finally shook hands with the man and courteously showed him out. By this time Julia's exhilaration had fallen away to be replaced by seething indignation at

Simon's casualness. When he finally turned his attention to her she was in no mood for joy or anything else as he asked how she'd got on at the doctor's and if she was all right.

'I'm fine,' she answered tersely. 'There's nothing wrong with me. But this is a private matter and I need to talk to you upstairs.'

'We can't both leave the shop. A buyer telephoned while you were out. I made an appointment for you to see her at eleven thirty. I hope that's OK.'

'I can't think about that now,' Julia hissed in low, imperious tones. 'This won't take long.' Turning, she made for the door that connected the shop to their apartments above.

Mystified, he followed her, having told their staff to carry on, that they wouldn't be long. This presumption annoyed her further.

In the hallway of their apartment, she stopped and turned to him, aware of the anxious pumping of her heart. Most of her joy and spontaneity had disappeared after the delay Simon had caused.

Quickly she related to him what Marwood had told her and waited for his reaction. It was so long coming that for a moment she really thought he still didn't believed her. She was starting to become angry but managed to contain herself.

'Did you hear what I said?' she asked. 'Benjamin confirmed that I conceived after we were married. The baby's yours, Simon.'

It was humiliating to have to spell it out like this, and to have him looking at her as if he still didn't believe her. Yes, she'd been a fool, she who had once condemned Stephanie for the self-same behaviour. But Simon wasn't above blame. Too taken up with his business and his investments to pay real attention to her he'd pushed her away from him. How could he doubt her now, when she had irrefutable proof that this baby was his?

'Did you hear me?' she repeated, her voice beginning to break down.

She saw him blink. It was like seeing someone coming out of a coma. 'You mean...'

'Yes,' she said as he hesitated, 'I'm two months pregnant.'

In a second his arms had folded about her and she found herself being pressed against him so tightly that it was difficult to breathe.

'Oh, God, I'm sorry!' he was saying. 'So sorry, the way I've behaved. I don't know what got into me to doubt...' He was smothering her face with kisses, holding it between his two hands. 'I'll never ever forgive myself for the way I've behaved. How could I ever have...? My dearest darling!'

Happiness swept over her. And utter amazement too. The way *he* had behaved? She should be the one begging forgiveness. All her life she would regret the silly episode with Chester, even if it faded from his mind in time. One thing she was sure of though – she didn't deserve a man like Simon.

As he read his *Financial Times* at the breakfast table, Simon became suddenly alert. 'This looks

344

interesting! The Stock Exchange is showing lots of activity in the new-issues market – could be a good time with this strong sterling – dollar exchange to get in while things are buoyant.'

Julia glanced up from her cornflakes. 'Be careful, love,' she said, almost automatically now. 'You *will* think before you buy anything, won't you?'

His wild dealings as she saw them still worried her endlessly though he seemed ever blessed by the Midas touch.

He gave her a patronizing smile. 'You should know me by now, darling. I always take the advice of my more reliable sources, none of your bucket shop betting!' he ended with a laugh.

Bucket shops were more like stock market bookmakers; no shares were bought or sold, punters bet on prices only. The Tories had promised to do away with them if they were returned to power in the May General Election, but they had been pipped at the post by Labour, so the bucket shops still operated.

'I'm just worried that you might get too carried away,' Julia said. 'The unemployment rate is still so very high and no one knows when it will ever come down.'

'But that doesn't affect us,' he said, turning back to his newspaper. 'It's been high for years, but business is good, shares are good, and I'm thinking of popping into my bank to have a chat with them. I've got my eye on one or two quite good-looking investments.'

That the economy remained in a mess didn't seem to concern him so long as his shares were doing well. What if he did sometimes take too many chances for her liking, borrowing more and more heavily to finance this long-standing obsession with investments? His bank appeared happy enough, even eager to advance him whatever he needed, certain of its returns from which they benefited handsomely.

Nor had the fact that half the nation was living in poverty ever affected their business. They mixed with successful people like themselves, and what if Britain under this new Socialist government *was* still fighting for economic survival, looking to America to prop up the economy? So far it hadn't caused Simon problems so why should it worry her? Julia sighed and gave up.

On Friday morning Simon casually unfolded his *Financial Times* as usual to read while eating breakfast. Teacup in one hand, he laid the paper flat on the tablecloth to scan the headlines while he drank. But the cup never reached his lips, his eyes caught in disbelief by the bold, black wording.

'Good God!'

Julia looked up. 'What is it, darling?'

He didn't reply. Dropping the cup back on its saucer, he began sifting frantically through the pages, his brow creasing. Then, pushing the crumpled newspaper at her, he gabbled, 'New York – there's been panic selling – shares tumbled to virtually rock bottom overnight – everyone trying to offload but no one's buying. They're going crazy over there. They're saying

346

it's chaos!'

He chewed his lip as Julia read the headlines: 'BLACK THURSDAY! WALL STREET CRASHES!'

But by the time she looked up, Simon had recovered a little. He even gave a smile at her worried expression, ever the optimist. 'I must phone the bank, see what they've got to say. The market will rally, of course. Investors will jump in, buy low and prices will shoot up again. I might get hold of some good stock before they do. That's how it works. Buy low, sell high.'

He gave a laugh but Julia wasn't convinced. 'Please, darling, don't do anything rash. You never know, something could go wrong.'

'What could go wrong?' he laughed again, seeing a chance in this for himself. 'What will happen is that the big bankers will have to step in and prop up the market and everything will recover. Now's the time to jump in.'

'But there has to be a cause for such a sudden collapse,' she said but he was already making for the phone. He returned straight-faced.

'They told me to hang on for a bit to see how things proceed. I think they're being a bit too overcautious. This is the time to buy. They can be fools at times!'

He seemed to have no qualms at all, but an awful feeling had begun to develop deep in Julia's stomach. Her father had been optimistic too though he had always kept his dealings secret, hoping desperately for the luck that always seemed to evade him. Simon, however, enjoyed the exhilaration of making money. Only last week he had borrowed hugely on a good tip and was even now waiting to see that investment reap dividends.

In all these years he'd never suffered any serious setbacks. There had been a few minor ones but he'd always bounced back, usually doubling his investments, and Julia had to admit they might not have made such a success of their business if it hadn't been buoyed up by some timely selling of shares. Yet she couldn't help the fear that nothing lasts and that a day might come when things could go badly wrong. She didn't like the feeling of dread that was now churning in the pit of her stomach. Was this the day?

To her relief, despite calling his bank fools, he controlled the impulse to buy even more shares while they were low. Julia then began to wonder if she might be to blame for his caution. What if they shot up again and he'd missed out? How would she feel watching his disappointment?

The evening papers proved she'd been right to advise caution. Each one carried accounts of a continuing unprecedented wave of fear and panic-selling as almost thirteen million shares changed hands on the New York Stock Exchange. Wall Street witnessed dazed brokers having to deal with terrified investors who were ordering them to sell at any price. At the peak of the panic, buyers were simply non-existent, with reports of the market in fact having ceased to function, stocks being dumped overboard for whatever they could bring.

As Simon read, Julia could see his face blenching. 'It'll right itself,' he gasped, but she knew, and felt he did too, that it was wishful thinking.

Later edition papers continued telling of shocking collapses in value so that by eleven thirty New York time, the bottom had dropped out of the market, with police trying to control hysterical crowds in the streets. The tiniest rumour of intervention would send prices back up only to drop still further minutes later. Small investors were besieging the banks, clamouring to withdraw their money before they lost everything. Simon began thinking of his own hefty shares.

'If mine ever dropped like that we could be in deep trouble,' he kept saying. He had borrowed heavily throughout the last few years and if the banks called in their money, they would indeed be in trouble.

Then, as suddenly as it started, the panic died. Investors were told that it had been the fault of the ticker-tape system's technical inadequacy to deal with such a massive volume of trading and that the big bankers had agreed to prop up the market with their own money.

As the US market began to rise, Julia felt herself able to breathe again and Simon even recovered his composure enough to feel more than a little disgruntled.

'I said I should have bought while I had the chance. I said the bank is a fool! I should have taken no notice of their stupid warnings and bought!'

He was soon to change his mind. On Monday the first shock waves from Wall Street hit the

London Stock Exchange. Almost hysterically Simon telephoned his bank to be told the best thing would be to sell whatever he could and take whatever he could get.

'I can't!' he gasped at Julia. 'Not at the price they are now.'

'You must. You said yourself the bank knows best. If you don't...'

She let her words fail on the unthinkable. Much of their business had come more and more to depend on income from his dabbling, as she often jokingly called it, in the share market.

It was their hard work too that provided for the major part of their comfortable lifestyle, but without his shares they might never have been able to survive in the cut-throat fashion world. They might have fallen by the wayside long ago to remain just a small boutique. She recognized that fact now, despite her fears that Simon often seemed far too rash. She'd never been tempted to have a go herself despite his urging her to. She knew where her money was safest; maybe not earning dividends or making interest, but safe nevertheless. Her father's failures were still implanted in her memory after all these years. Now it seemed as if failure was about to come knocking at their own door.

The familiar saying popped into her mind: 'A fool and his money are soon parted.' She turned away from the thought. Simon was no fool; a risk-taker maybe, but he had always managed to be ahead of the game.

Their partnership had been successful and they had done well. She had to remember that as she felt for him in the worst moments of his life, watching as he sat with his ear practically glued to the wireless for news as it continued to filter through.

# Twenty-Nine

The London Stock Exchange was displaying little of the panic that had descended on New York, with every stock exchange across America having closed. The most London was saying with typical British understatement was that the market here was very unsettled!

'Even so, I'm phoning to see what my bank has to say,' said Simon.

Julia stood anxiously beside him as he spoke into the phone, watching as he grew alarmed at what he was hearing. She saw him pale, caught his horrified whisper, 'Sell'; started as his voice rose to a near shriek.

'Yes, sell! For Christ's sake, *sell*!'

When the person on the other end of the phone spoke again, apparently asking him to confirm his request, he repeated even louder, 'Sell, damn it! Sell for what you can get!'

What Julia didn't realize until later was that shares across the board were falling even as he was speaking. Even in the minute it took for them to ask for confirmation of his request and for him to repeat it, shares had fallen still further, things were moving that fast.

Several minutes later, Simon having paced the lounge continuously during that lull, waving his hand dismissively at her when she tried to say anything, the phone rang. Simon almost leaped at it, yanking the earpiece off its hook and making the stand shudder.

'Yes?'

He listened intently, his expression unreadable, every now and again saying, 'Yes' and 'I see', his tone dropping. Finally he replaced the receiver, his face chalk-white. He looked bleakly across at Julia.

'It's all gone. I'm down tens of thousands and it's still dropping.'

'Oh, Simon,' was all she could say but he seemed not to hear her.

'The bank advised me to get rid of everything while I could, but they're worthless. I've been wiped out!' His voice had dropped to a whisper.

'I've nothing left. It's like a nightmare! How could it happen?'

His voice broke. Julia had never seen him as he was now, his expression completely stark, his eyes reddening, his lips palsied. Her heart almost breaking for him, she ran to take him in her arms and hold him, her own sobs stifling any words she might have spoken, had there been any to speak.

With the market continuing on its downward slide Julia came slowly to the conclusion that it was now up to her to try and pull things together. But could she? She remembered how she had helped her family back on to its feet. She'd been at her wits' end then. Now she was going to have to go through it all again, this time with the man

353

she loved more than anyone else in this world.

But there had been more fearful news. Hardly had the bank sold him out, as he saw it, than they called him in for a talk the next day. He had hardly slept all night and looked thoroughly drained. When he returned from his interview he resembled a dead man. Julia was reminded of her mother's shocked and dazed expression when her father died.

'They said how sorry they are, and that there are thousands of others like me, but they'll no longer be able extend credit to even their most valued customers. It seems banks are in as much trouble as anyone, they're down by millions.' Despite his expression his voice was steady. 'Our only course now,' he went on, 'is to sell all we can of the business.'

'Simon, we can't. This is our life, our only livelihood. We've worked so hard. There has to be another way.'

Devastated, she wanted to tell him that this wasn't the end of the world, that somehow things would get better. In America it was being reported that some people had committed suicide because of the Crash, having lost every- thing. That was not going to happen to him. They hadn't lost everything. They still had their business. They would limp on, somehow.

But there were overheads to consider and Simon was not slow in pointing them out. 'There's rental, the cost of keeping up our stock, paying our staff, the factory, the warehouse, they all want paying. Stationery, postage, lighting, heating, that exhibition you were planning. We were off to Paris, remember?'

With that he walked away, leaving her to mull over what he'd listed. He was wrong, she thought. They would make a go of things, if only on a more modest scale. But in his present frame of mind there was no talking to him. He had lost all interest in the business, leaving her to rack her brains as to how to cope. Over the following week he seemed to sink lower and lower. He was hardly sleeping, had let his work fall away and was constantly on the telephone looking for the slightest glimmer of hope of recouping his losses. It was all useless.

The second of November saw a little of the hysteria fade from Wall Street but the damage had been done. As autumn moved forward businesses and even industry reflected how serious things had become. Workers were being laid off by the thousand, unemployment was suddenly burgeoning again. With people watching the pennies the last thing they were looking for was frivolous clothing and dress shops were going to the wall. Julia too found herself struggling, seeing fewer and fewer orders coming in, the telephone ceasing to ring, buyers seeming to disappear. Even the wealthy, on whom the fashion industry relied, were being careful with their money. Many of them had been hit hard by the Crash, seeing their investments go up in smoke. According to the newspapers the world was falling into decline. Only France it seemed was still apparently thriving, a law unto itself. But that had not helped the London fashion trade to recover.

As they moved towards Christmas Julia felt that her world was slowly falling apart. So many times she was tempted to resort to the metal box she had hidden away under the floorboards of her bedroom. But she told herself that there was still hope; there was no need yet to use those savings. Even so the Slump, as it was beginning to be called, was beginning to bite as the world fell into the grip of depression.

'It's all newspaper talk!' Ginny said when she came to visit. 'The world will recover. The countries' governments will see to that.'

'How are you both managing?' Julia asked, looking from Ginny to Robert.

He smiled and tilted his head. 'We're just about holding up. We'll be OK if we can ride this out.'

'And James still has his bank position,' Ginny cut in.

'Yes, thank goodness,' said Julia, then asked about Stephanie.

Ginny let out a wry laugh. 'You know Stephanie. She always lands on her feet somehow. I think they're all right. She should get in touch with you more after all you've done for her, for all of us. But Stephanie has only ever been interested in Stephanie.' To which Julia had to agree.

Around the end of November a tiny light was seen on the horizon as the US Government promised action to lift the world out of the decline. At home the Labour Government announced a forty-two-million-pound public works programme, hoping to lighten the situation. This initiative was seen as too little too late by

356

sceptics, but it was encouraging all the same. Simon brightened for the first time since the disaster.

'I knew something would be done,' he said to Julia. 'I think we're probably going to make it. If we can just get over the next couple of months we'll be back on track – a good start for this little one.'

He patted her midriff, which was already thickening slightly. It was the more noticeable as she had always been so slim. She laughed happily; it was good to have him acknowledging the baby. Catching his hand, she held it there and he bent to kiss her. It was so good to have him like this, to see him looking a little brighter. For his sake she hoped he was right about a better future for their child to be born into.

For all the Government's promise about its public works programme, the New Year came and went with unemployment still rising.

'We're going to have to lay off most of our people,' Julia told Simon in January. 'And that might have to include Betty.'

Simon looked shocked. 'Surely we can't do that.'

'If we want to keep afloat, we've no option.' It would be one of the most painful things she had ever had to do. 'If we don't cut back somehow, we'll be facing bankruptcy in a few months.'

Simon could only agree miserably. But it was becoming a downward spiral.

Julia had kept quiet about her own savings in case he thought to try and increase them by further investments. But even if she used them, there wouldn't be enough to keep them in business.

'How are we going to manage without machinists or cutters?' he asked

'I'll have to go back to doing much of the work myself.'

'You can't. Not in your condition.'

She gave a small laugh. 'There are months of work left in me yet.'

'Even so, where are you going to get samples made up in bulk?'

There were no factory outlets now as they had little money to pay them. She was down to using any means to induce shops to take her creations. Often she was turned away with apologies; shops too were finding it hard going. She knew she had to try or go under, but even she was losing heart. The cash she'd stowed away over the years would not be enough to keep them going for many months. Banks had long since been scared off lending money and Simon's jewellery side of the business was almost non-existent now.

'At least you can do the books,' she had joked. They had been forced to dispense with their accountant a while ago to try and save some costs.

'What books?' he had joked in return, though it no longer seemed a joke.

She kept wondering how she would manage when she grew near her time, trying to bend and stretch to cut out patterns, her stomach impeding her. What then? Would she have the will to carry on?

And when the baby was born? What a world to bring a child into. They owed the bank thousands. If in the end they couldn't pay, unable even to afford to rent out this place, they'd be forced to sell up. What would they get for a business in this financial climate? Whatever they realized, the bank would take all that was owed to them first. She and Simon would be finished. There was no place for sentiment in business.

# Thirty

The New York Stock Exchange had lost over ten billion dollars. The richest country in the world had seen its lovely bubble burst. The dreams of big spenders were gone. The poor of America could only see themselves getting poorer as big businesses tightened their belts.

It was the same in Britain. Like so many others, Layzell Creations owed the bank thousands. Despite having once been a good customer, Simon found that his bank was in no position to offer kindness. Like many other private and public companies, it was feeling the draught. Simon was left fighting a losing battle.

'If we do go bust,' he said gloomily as spring brought less and less sign of their business ever getting back on its feet, 'they'll surely call in their loans. And then we'll have had it.'

'Something might turn up,' Julia said desperately. 'All we need is one good fashion show. I could organize one.'

'And who will come to see it? Even the big fashion houses are starting to feel the pinch. What chance has a small establishment like ours?'

'Just one small show might keep us going a bit longer,' she said stubbornly but he shook his head.

'It could be years before this country recovers, not to say the world. People think we had bad unemployment in the twenties. You just wait. This new decade will make all that seem like a tea dance!'

She hoped not. She'd known sudden descent into poverty before. She didn't want to experience it again. All she prayed was that Ginny, Stephanie and James, together with their families, would all be able to weather the storm. Having come through their first downturn of fortune all those years ago, it would be cruel to be knocked down once again. And it was cruel that she and Simon had worked so hard only to lose everything.

She thought suddenly of Chester Morrison and wondered how he would cope when he tumbled into hard times – as he inevitably would, along with everyone else. Perhaps his wife would leave him all over again. She wasn't sure if that thought made her pity him or feel that it would serve him right.

But no matter what the future brought, she would be there at Simon's side, would live in a slum with him if need be. It wouldn't come to that, of course. There were still her savings, kept for when and if there proved no other way out. What she didn't want was to see this money go the way of their other finances. And so, for the time being, she held on to it.

For the first time she felt sorry for those thousands of small investors who had sunk all their hard-earned cash in so-called gilt-edge certainties, dreaming of watching it multiply to give them a better future. Now the dream was gone, all of them caught in the market and, worse, thousands losing their jobs as mass unemployment began to bite.

Were she and Simon about to join them? Not if she could help it, she thought determinedly.

'The bank's calling in the loans,' Simon whispered as he folded the letter. 'They're taking the business. We've nothing left. We've lost everything we've worked for.'

'Not everything,' Julia said, her lips tightening.

It was time to delve into her savings, money the bank had no idea she had and were not likely to know. But was it enough to rescue them from this hole into which they were being thrown? She'd never really totted it up. She was no miser, crouching in a corner counting, counting; rubbing her hands over every farthing. It was there just in case and that was all it had been to her.

With Simon looking on, Julia pulled back the corner of the heavy, luxurious carpet. Beneath lay the loose square of floorboard which, using her fingernails, she took only a moment to prise up to reveal the metal box fitted smugly in the wide space it occupied. She lifted it out by its handle; it felt lighter than she'd expected as she set it down on top of the dressing table.

She caught a glimpse of Simon's expression and immediately read his mind. It was saying that whatever she'd saved in this box would never be enough to start them on their way up again – a few hundred pounds maybe, no more than that. She looked away. A few hundred pounds! She'd been stashing it away for years, there had to be two or three thousand.

With a key from a small drawer in the dressing table she unlocked the lid and opened it to lift out the sizeable wad of notes and divide it in two for them to share the counting. The resigned look on Simon's face as he started to count began to change to one of incredulity. So did hers. She hadn't realized how much she had managed to accumulate by adding a few notes here and a few there over the years.

When they had both finished, straightening up to look at each other, Simon's face was a picture to behold.

'What have you made yours?' he queried, his voice hoarse.

'Three thousand odd,' she answered in a whisper. 'Give or take a few smaller notes, unless I counted wrong. I kept losing track. And yours?'

He took a deep breath: 'Five thousand seven hundred and ninety.' His eyes were wide and staring. 'How in God's name did you manage to accrue...?' He fell silent, unable to go on.

Julia laughed. 'Thrift!' she said.

Of course, it was nowhere near enough to clear their huge bank debts. They were still going to lose their business. Keeping it was past hope. What the money could do was give them a modest start somewhere else. Even so, in this present climate it wouldn't be easy.

'Do we have the courage to start again?' she asked, her laughter gone. She knew she had. She had done it once, she could do it again. But could she count on Simon?

All around them people were giving up, seeing no glimmer of light. But some were fighting back. In the East End battles were taking place between police and workless demonstrators over mass unemployment.

'We'll get through this,' she encouraged.

He responded with an enigmatic half-smile that conveyed neither yes nor no.

It was all gone. Standing at the door of the empty lounge while the removal men struggled down the stairs with the last of the apartment's furniture, Julia looked around the spacious hallway. The doors to the box room, the two large, sumptuous bedrooms, the kitchen and the bathroom were all closed.

Now that she was being forced to leave it all, it was as if she were seeing the place for the first time. The same thing had happened when she'd had to leave the lovely family house in Sewardstone Road all those years ago. She was reminded of it now.

Fighting her emotions, she turned away, buttoning her jacket across her growing abdomen. Three months to go to the birth of their baby – Simon's and hers.

Slowly she pulled on her hat, picked up her handbag and the small case containing a few personal items, and prepared to follow the removal men downstairs.

Simon called up, 'Are you ready, love? The taxi's waiting.'

'Coming!' she called back.

She crossed the hall and, without pausing even to glance over her shoulder, closed the door firmly behind her.

The furniture van was taking its time. Awaiting its arrival, Julia and Simon stood gazing at the empty living room of the flat they'd rented above a tiny shop.

'It's not bad, is it?' Simon said, his arm going about her shoulders. 'It can't compare with the one we had of course, but...'

'It's nice,' she cut in. 'I liked it when we viewed it. It's very nice.'

And it was. It was roomy and airy and the living room window faced east for the morning sunshine to pour through. Their bedroom was east facing too. The spare room looked south, as did the kitchen and the small bathroom. The tiny rented shop below was to become a boutique of sorts when they were ready. From the lounge window Julia could just see Haggerston Park peeping between a gap in the shops and flats opposite.

As they stood looking out, Simon's arm tightened about her shoulders. 'We're going to be all right,' he encouraged.

'Of course we are,' she said simply, 'more than all right.'

She heard him sigh and hoped he wasn't doubtful.

But instead, he said, 'I'm going to miss our old life though. We made such a lot of friends. But I don't suppose we'll ever see them again. They'll

365

have gone their different ways, forgotten us already.'

'Friends like that aren't worth a thought,' she said evenly, remembering the so-called friends who had melted away when she and her family had been near destitute. 'We don't need any of them,' she said aloud and meant it.

'And our lovely apartment,' he went on wistfully. 'I suppose if we worked hard we could have it all again, when times get better. You never know what's around the corner, do you?'

'No, you don't,' she answered. 'And maybe that's just as well. We might not like what we find.'

She smiled, still gazing across at the narrow vista of the park. At least she'd be able to breathe whenever she looked out at it. It could never compare, of course, to Victoria Park which she had once overlooked, so many years ago, in another life, it seemed. Yet, in a way, it rather felt as if she had come full circle.

'I don't think it's always wise to go trying to find out what's around the corner, darling,' she said as she leaned against him and took in a deep breath, letting it trickle out in a sigh.

'Maybe not,' he agreed, and then brightened. 'But maybe, when this country recovers, we'll be able to get back to where we were.'

Julia smiled and nestled against him.

'Don't let's start looking to aim big any more,' she said slowly, 'all that fretting and fighting and struggling. Let's just settle for being contented.'

Suddenly she did feel contented.

'You could go back to selling jewellery,' she

murmured, 'nothing too posh in this area. And I could do a bit of designing, just ordinary garments.'

Fine silks were a thing of the past. 'I'll see if I can contact Betty.' They still kept in touch and she knew Betty hadn't found another job yet. 'She might like to come back. I know my own limitations well enough. We could work together as we used to.'

Suddenly she raised her face to him, smiling up into his face.

'I've a good feeling about this place,' she stated and planted a gentle kiss upon his cheek.

As she did so she felt their baby kick, almost as if in agreement with her statement. Yes, this *was* going to be a very good place from which to start again.